PROVENANCE

PROVENANCE

ROBERT MOELLER

New York

PROVENANCE

© 2016 **ROBERT MOELLER**.

All rights reserved. No portion of this book may be reproduced, stored in a retrieval system, or transmitted in any form or by any means—electronic, mechanical, photocopy, recording, scanning, or other—except for brief quotations in critical reviews or articles, without the prior written permission of the publisher.

This is a work of fiction. Names, characters, businesses, places, events, and incidents are either the products of the author's imagination or used in a fictitious manner. Any resemblance to actual persons, living or dead, or actual events is purely coincidental.

Published in New York, New York, by Morgan James Publishing. Morgan James and The Entrepreneurial Publisher are trademarks of Morgan James, LLC. www.MorganJamesPublishing.com

The Morgan James Speakers Group can bring authors to your live event. For more information or to book an event visit The Morgan James Speakers Group at www.TheMorganJamesSpeakersGroup.com.

A free eBook edition is available with the purchase of this print book.

CLEARLY PRINT YOUR NAME ABOVE IN UPPER CASE
Instructions to claim your free eBook edition:
1. Download the BitLit app for Android or iOS
2. Write your name in **UPPER CASE** on the line
3. Use the BitLit app to submit a photo
4. Download your eBook to any device

ISBN 978-1-63047-537-6 paperback
ISBN 978-1-63047-538-3 eBook
Library of Congress Control Number: 2014959666

Cover Design by:
Rachel Lopez
www.r2cdesign.com

In an effort to support local communities and raise awareness and funds, Morgan James Publishing donates a percentage of all book sales for the life of each book to Habitat for Humanity Peninsula and Greater Williamsburg.

Get involved today, visit
www.MorganJamesBuilds.com

Habitat for Humanity®
Peninsula and
Greater Williamsburg
Building Partner

ACKNOWLEDGMENTS

Thank you to the entire Morgan James Publishing team and special thanks to David Hancock for your generosity and your belief in *Provenance*. To Margo Toulouse, for your patience as I learned the ropes. I appreciate your great spirit, your love of the West, and your guidance through the publishing process. To Jim Howard, for your bright mind and your expertise in branding (a word I barely knew before except as it relates to cattle!). To Rachel Lopez, for the most beautiful cover I have ever seen (ever ever ever!). I am impressed by and grateful for your artistic eye and amazing talent.

There are many patient and talented editors who saw *Provenance* through its various versions and growing stages and who believed in the vision as well. Thank you Lucy Flood, without you this book simply would not have happened. You guided me, coached me and prodded me when I needed prodding. Your partnership was a true blessing! Thank you Lucia Brown, for your eagle eye and kind words. Thank you to the team at Split-Seed editing, I am so very appreciative for the care and detail you showed. In particular, Angie Kriesling, you brought keen attention and a thorough and thoughtful approach which added depth and detail to the story, and Katherine Rawson, you applied the final polish and caught a critical plot issue! I am forever grateful to you both.

Tim Sandlin, thank you for being my coach, my advisor, my friend as well as a constant resource on writing. Your critiques of *Provenance* were invaluable—

and your stewardship of the Jackson Hole Writers Conference is a gift to our community and to visiting writers as well.

Thank you to my Jackson Hole support team that keeps me going, fed, happy, loved—and most importantly laughing even in the depth of winter! Carol Taylor, your friendship fuels me, your wisdom astounds me, and your sense of humor slays me! Laura and Ivy, I couldn't have asked for better housemates. Thank you for the delicious dinners, the stimulating conversation, the hang-out time and for being generally wonderful souls. Addy Hutchinson, thank you for your great company, for taking me places I never would have gone without you, for the precious horse time, and the dear friendship we have formed. Shauna Fraser, my "task rabbit", thank you for keeping me <u>organized</u> (I know it's a tall order!) and for being such a bright light in my life.

I dedicate this book to my family, the greatest gift of my life.

Rob Moeller, my beloved son, you put up with my foibles, you take care of things that I have no idea how to do, and you are always there for me through thick and thin. You are a dedicated son—and an exceptional human being. Patricia, my daughter-in-law, thank you for being Rob's teammate in life—and in his care for me. You are an excellent example of motherhood, a true inspiration of physical health and a loving soul as well. Thank you to my grandsons, Tristan and Augustus. Your spunk, intellect, sense of humor and loving nature are more than I ever hoped for in grandchildren. Getting to see you grow up has been one of the greatest joys I have experienced in my life.

My son-in-law David Cottrell, thank you for that moment where we met in Shaw's market in Tiverton which I will never forget. You are an remarkable man, with a presence and humor that I have always admired. I can't imagine a finer son-in-law. Thank you for being in this family.

And, last but absolutely not least, my daughter Kristen Moeller, you are the PRECIOUS PRESENT—you always have been and you always will be. Your own development as a writer is an inspiration to me—and many others. You are why this book was published. I am grateful for your endless efforts and energy, your extensive knowledge of the world of publishing, your deep belief in this book and support of me in <u>finishing</u> this book over the years. Without you, *Provenance* would have always remained a dream.

PROVENANCE

CHAPTER ONE

The little caravan was made up of belled packhorses and several wagons, one enclosed, the others mounded with loads covered by layers of canvas. Accompanying the convoy were four mounted men, armed and wearing the colors of Ludovico Sforza, one of the most powerful men in Milan's shifting political scene. Their mission was to deliver expeditiously and safely their single passenger and his belongings, an assorted and somewhat unusual cargo of paintings, rolls of canvas, wood panels of varying sizes, a variety of animal skulls and skeletons, a few heavily wrapped human bones—a hand, a femur, and a clavicle—several odd wooden constructions, some vellum-bound books, and a thick package of manuscripts and drawings, which the long-haired and somewhat peculiar traveler kept at his side.

The lone passenger was a thirty-year-old painter. He had decided to leave his native Florence in response to an encouraging letter from Sforza, who, aside from being an incredibly powerful man, was also an art patron. Sforza was impressed by the painter's abilities. It was late November in the year 1482. So set was the young artist on going to Milan that he abandoned—unfinished—a monumental composition for a church just outside the city of Florence. The restless, insatiably curious, and ambitious young man had also failed to complete another major painting in tempera and oil on a walnut panel, and had never even started another important commission for which he had been paid a fair sum in advance. And now here he was on the way to Milan with everything he owned, determined to attract patronage and a goodly wage in exchange for his varied and considerable talents.

The sun was setting, casting golden light and dark but luminous shadows on the rich countryside of tilled fields interspersed with long passages of dense woodland. The air was crisp, the horses nervous, jogging despite the long distance they had covered since early morning. Eight kilometers ahead lay a farming village where the party was to pass the night. Simple but adequate lodgings and stabling awaited the soldiers, drivers, and their passenger, who was to be given every consideration necessary for his safety and comfort. The four armed men, members of Sforza's special guard, were to keep vigil over the baggage while the hostlers and their helpers watered, fed, and minded the horses during the chilly evening. The travelers would be up before dawn to take the road again, leaving this last night's lodging with the prospect of arriving in Milan before nightfall the next day.

The road just ahead disappeared into thick forest, which ranged on each side of the track as far as the eye could see. As the party entered that long stretch, the density of the forest seemed to muffle the sound of the belled horses and the men's shouted conversations. Well into the darkening woodland, the chatter was interrupted by the sound of barking dogs. Suddenly, a pack of scruffy hounds streaked out of the woods, followed by three breathless hunters hurrying to keep up with the mongrels, who were in full cry as they followed the scent of their quarry.

The dogs' frantic movements made the hunters think that a fleeing animal must have recently crossed the track upon which the caravan was traveling. The caravan horses stopped and began to whinny and snort, shying and pulling at their lead ropes. The dogs milled about, still baying. The packhorses' nostrils flared, their eyes showed white. Then one of them, its packsaddle and panniers mounded with a bulky load, reared and yanked loose the lead rope tied to the horse at the head of the pack string. The terrified animal reared again, then wheeled around and set off at a gallop into the woods, disappearing into the gloom.

The hounds turned from the track and set off through the forest after the frenzied animal. Two of the hunters blew on their hammered copper horns, attempting to hail the dogs back. Moments later, the caravan emerged from the trees. The howling died down. The remaining horses settled. Still in the woods, the scent hounds circled around the hunters, drooling and panting heavily, tails wagging. Silence for a moment. The hostlers gathered reins and lead ropes. The captain yelled "Quiet!" The travelers listened for some sound of the missing horse. Nothing. No sound of an animal in the trees and brush. No rattle of the crude bell.

The horses were gathered and lined up. The head man, a burly captain responsible to Ludovico Sforza for the transport of the young painter, advanced in unmistakable anger toward the nervous hunters, who stood among the dogs. He set one hand on his hip, the other resting on the hilt of a short sword suspended from his belt. For a moment he said nothing. He just stared at the three men.

"You louts! You have disrupted the progress of this conveyance to deliver our passenger, who is expected at the court in Milan by tomorrow evening. You and your ill-trained pack of curs have delayed our progress. You have caused one of our horses, heavily packed with valuable goods, to disappear into this forest's foul darkness. You will tell me your names and you will confess the location of the sty where you live with this mangy pack." The three shaggy men did so. "You will set out from here immediately and bring the missing horse with all of his load to the village just ahead. If you fail to do so, our knives and swords will open your guts and you will be fed to your skinny mutts, and the white of your worthless bones will be left to the wolves, the boars, and the ravens, if they are so foolish as to touch your worthless hides, and your damned souls will wander in this foul land as you await your certain journey straight to hell. Understand?"

One of the men started to stammer; his companions frantically nodded their heads.

The captain held up a staying hand, "I am Captain Montorsoli of Ser Ludovico Sforza's guard. You will find me at the tavern in the village—up the road. Off with you, sons of a mule!"

The three ragged hunters gathered their dogs and hurried into the forest after the packhorse.

The pack string and wagons, one of which carried the lone passenger—who never stirred throughout the entire commotion—set off along the well-worn route toward the village. Two hours later, the travelers stopped at the small inn where mean accommodations were shown to the silent, somewhat inscrutable young artist and the captain in charge of the caravan. The party was fed at a long crude farm table furnished with rough-hewn, rickety, three-legged stools. Remains of cold roast chicken and some cold gummy rice were served to the group on greasy, stained trenchers, upon which lay wooden-handled knives. Bad red wine accompanied the meal. After supper, the hostlers tended the horses while the guards spread their well-used, rolled mats and lay down under the two wagons. The captain and his passenger were led to a room with three low wooden platforms covered by straw-stuffed mattresses. The artist spread over one of them a paint-spattered cloak.

The captain unbuckled his chest armor and collapsed. "Sleep well, artist," he muttered, and fell asleep. The captain's snoring competed with the sounds of the chickens and the donkeys on the other side of the wall. The painter, wrapped in his only cloak, stared through the dark at the ceiling and contemplated his lost belongings.

One of the panniers strapped to the runaway horse held a painting on a wooden panel, mostly finished except for passages in the drapery of the figures in the picture. The painting was in oil and tempera on a poplar panel—images of the Virgin and Child. The odd and unprecedented feature was that the adoring Virgin was portrayed holding on her lap the Infant Christ, who in turn was cradling in his chubby arms a house cat. The composition had appeared to him in a dream a few years ago in Florence where he lived in a small room lent to him by his teacher. He awoke out of the dream immediately and lit the simple candle in the tiny chamber. By that flickering light, he quickly sketched the vision. In the morning, at the *bottega*, he made more sketches, which finally led him to lay out the strange composition on a gesso panel. It was an extraordinary departure from the traditional iconography to which many of his contemporaries in Florence's burgeoning art world faithfully adhered.

More and more often, he dared to break from accepted artistic traditions and draw inspiration from his imagination, heeding his unique response to nature and his surrounding world. When he set these visions down on paper, transferring them to a prepared painting surface, these formal ideas and images both pleased and challenged his teacher and a few of Florence's open-minded, intelligent ecclesiastical patrons and donors.

The artist felt the public wasn't ready for a strange representation of the Virgin and Child with a cat, so he hadn't revealed the painting during its slow progress. Hence, he packed the unfinished composition with the rest of his belongings, thinking that Milan, even richer than Florence, might offer the prospect of finishing the picture and finding a place for it in a church or private chapel.

At last the artist fell asleep, praying that the runaway horse, the panel, and his other precious belongings would be found and returned by early morning. A cock crowed at daybreak, and the captain roused the sleepy young man lying bundled up in his cloak. He sat up on the board-hard bed and took in the early morning chill. The captain buckled his breastplate, short sword, and dagger and hurriedly left the room.

Outside the lodgings, he found the hostlers readying the horses for the last leg of the journey to Milan, some four hours down the road. The guards were swallowing down bread soaked in milk and butterfat.

"Any sign of those ragged scoundrels?" the captain asked.

"No, sir," one of the men muttered.

"Nothing?" The captain stared in the direction they had come the previous night.

"Sons of Judas." He pointed to one of the soldiers. "Get our good host out here."

In a few moments, the soldier brought forward the hostel owner, still dressed in a rag of a nightshirt.

"You," the captain barked. "Lead these three men to the shack where the three peasants whose names we gave you live with their mutts. When you find them, drag the buggers here. And be quick about it." The three soldiers led the hostel keeper away on a packhorse. Hugging the horse's mane, he gave the soldiers' directions as he shivered as much out of fear as cold.

"The rest of you hitch the horses. We will leave as soon as my men come back with or without that crazy nag." They entered the hostel and then came back out.

The proprietor's ruddy-cheeked wife soon brought warm milk and butterfat and a half loaf of day-old bread. The young artist left the warm hearth to sit at the table beside the captain and the others.

"If my guards don't return here dragging that horse and the imbeciles who caused this mess, we have to proceed directly to Milan no matter," the captain said. "Ser Ludovico's fussy. If we leave without the horse and your load, I'll make it clear to our host that he must send word to Milan when and if the horse and its pack show up. A little silver will ensure that we will be informed as soon as possible."

"Thank you." The reticent artist nodded slowly.

In a few moments, the three soldiers returned with the hostel owner in tow. The poor man, still shivering in his ragged nightshirt, slid painfully off the draft horse.

"Nothing," said the sergeant, next in rank to Captain Montorsoli. "Only an old woman who stuttered that the hunters were out looking for the runaway. But no sign of them."

"Damn it to hell," fumed the captain.

The young artist looked crestfallen.

"There's nothing to do then but to get on the road. Our boss will have our heads if we don't get back soon with our young passenger." Montorsoli turned to the silent painter. "I'll wager that Ser Ludovico will send a man back to go after those peasants and find your missing baggage." Montorsoli enjoyed frequent use of the word "peasant" because he felt his true station to be well above the lowest class, though his own parents, Milan natives, came from humble origins.

The party soon prepared and rigged the horses and wagons, tying down the loads especially securely to avoid any further mishaps. By midmorning, they set off again, moving more swiftly than the day before, mindful of the short afternoon as fall daylight diminished in the face of oncoming winter days.

Somewhere in the middle of the dense forest a ways from the pack string bound for Milan, a lone horse grazed. A rectangular package containing the painting of the Virgin and the cat and a thin stack of sketches and drawings rested in the grass nearby.

CHAPTER TWO

Sam Driscoll sips a cup of lapsang souchong tea as he sits on the sundeck overlooking an inlet that flows into Long Island Sound less than a mile away. It is a crystal clear morning, and he shifts his gaze to her, she whose photographed image he holds in his hand. She herself rests in the Met, and a copy of her resides in Sam's library on a pedestal. She is an exquisitely carved piece of Egyptian sculpture, made of polished yellow jasper to which an unknown sculptor gave life. It is a fragmentary carving—a bit of neck that supports a broken, life-size head, of which survive the cheek, a delicate chin, and sensuous lips. To kiss or speak, perhaps to sing.

Fifteen years into his extensive art-buying career, Sam has fallen in love with more than one piece of art, but this particular object has had, for quite a long time, a profound hold on him. Perhaps she was an Egyptian queen of the Eighteenth Dynasty. Holding the photograph, he gazes at every detail that brings her forth out of the jasper. His client, Tom Baxter, had a copy of the sculpture made for Sam to mark their fifteen years of working together. Sam is embarrassed to think about the way Tom controls him with such gifts. And yet he loves the sculpture.

Sam's deerhounds stir. The male, Dundee, rises, nails clacking over the wooden deck. He nudges Sam's arm, and Sam guides the dog's head close to his, scratching down the bridge of the dog's nose. The phone on the other side of the porch door rings. Sam rises and enters the house as the message starts recording. It is his Cassie.

"On my way there. I'll be there in an hour. Soon, love." She hangs up.

"Soon." Sam walks back to the deck. "We have an hour before our lady arrives." The dogs get to their feet. Off the porch, fairly jumping over the three steps to the ground, the hounds race off, down the long field, leaping over the stone wall into the high grass bordering the rock-strewn beach. Sam whistles them in when they move out of sight, and they return, tongues lolling, slowing to a walk.

Sam walks over to a weathered shingle shed. He opens the double doors. His beloved thirty-two-foot Friendship sloop rests on a cradle on a trailer, filling the shed. The boat is an older plank-hulled beauty, Maine built, which Sam has had for years. To him, in its category, the sloop is as beautiful and stirring as a superb painting or other precious work of art. With her varnished mast, gaff, and trim and elegant cutter bow, she is among boats exquisitely graceful. She rides so close to the water that on her, he feels every movement of the water, hears the sound of the ropes moving through the pulleys, and he comes back to a primal, younger part of himself that is deeply in his body, deeply aware of the movements of life itself. Knowing that the sloop exists makes his daily life meaningful.

Sam never fails to look at her hull appreciatively with a practiced eye—trained and critical—a result of the many years he has sought and assessed paintings and works of art for his wealthy clients. Even to his experienced eye, she is stunning in her perfection.

Sam has been craving this weekend, in which he will again lovingly prepare his sloop for the water. *Silkie* she is called. The letters are carved into the stern board and gilded. It is a special joy—and damn good luck for Sam—that Cassie enjoys this preparatory work also. Sam runs his hand over the boat. He doesn't have to do this, but he likes to feel every aspect of her, observing anything he missed when he put on the first coat of paint the previous week. He notices spots where he applied excess paint that need to be sanded down, or where slight divots need to be filled. He takes his time, going over every section of the boat.

Sam has nearly finished his inspection when the dogs lift their heads. They bound toward the kitchen at a graceful trot. Sam follows his hounds and finds Cassie in the kitchen, unpacking delicacies not available in Stonington or Westerly. She is dressed in one of the many suits she wears for her work as an event coordinator.

"These weeks get awfully damn long," Sam whispers, pulling her in to him.

"I know," Cassie answers. She nods toward the asparagus on the granite countertop. "Dinner is shad roe, asparagus, one of my salads, a bottle of Toasted Head chardonnay, and outrageously rich chocolate and peanut butter ice cream."

"Remember how we celebrated spring last year with shad roe and asparagus?" Sam says, smiling, touched by one of many rituals they have invented to give shape and meaning to days and seasons they spend together.

"Is that new?" Cassie asks, pointing at Sam's most recent purchase, a Homer watercolor of the Maine coast. They stand close together admiring the painting in silence and relaxing into their reunion after several days apart. The past weekend, they spent four hours in the Homer exhibition at the Museum of Fine Arts marveling at the man's energy and his uncanny, unerring draughtsmanship. "It's a Homer, isn't it?"

"God, Cass. You're always dead-on. You're a natural."

Cassie turns away. She has never been able to take a compliment. "Got to put on my painting clothes," she says as she retires to the bedroom to change. It is eleven o'clock and the sun is high; the day is warming. Sam smiles as Cassie reemerges, grabs his hand, and pulls him outside. "I kind of think I love this boat as much as you do," she says as they walk into the shed.

A week ago they finished painting the white hull and putting on a coat of bottom paint. Today's task is to buff and smooth that first coat before applying a final skin of the traditional red anti-fouling paint. Sam grew up with this ritual, which dates back to the days when he and his sister prepared and raced twelve-foot, five-inch gaff-rigged sailboats with their father on the Sakonnet River in Rhode Island—and at fifty-four, he still hasn't tired of it. Though *Silkie* will never be raced, he and Cassie care that her beautiful hull glides, slipping like silk on silk through the water on a reach, or surfing with the swell, full sail out, planing before the wind.

The delight of working over the form of the boat, the smoothing and refreshing of the surface, make them sensitive to the shape of that classic hull, while allowing them an intimate knowledge of the boat as an exquisitely designed work of art. For Sam, the experience is no different from enjoying the form, surface, and texture of a fine piece of sculpture, only with this one he helps to create the sculpture every year, and in the process he prepares himself for the gift of sailing her. It's one of the few places in his life where he is the artist, and there is something more pure in his relationship to this piece than to any other. He can never fully control this work of art; the water is constantly changing her.

"Cass, I can't wait until we can live here full-time."

She looks up, her face betraying a hint of shock.

"What?" Sam asks, noticing her surprise.

"Full-time?" She looks at him skeptically. "Please, me here full-time?" She points the paintbrush at herself and then waves it around. "I'm a city girl. I love being in the center of things. You know that. I'd never make it here."

His face falls.

"You aren't serious, are you?"

"Entirely serious."

Cassie stares at him.

"You know my heart has always been out here on the water or in Wyoming, but this is so much more practical than Wyoming." Sam notices that while she was waving around the paintbrush, she accidentally flung a dab of paint onto the tiller hanging from a hook nearby. He picks up a rag and stoops to remove it. His movements are agitated, and he senses that Cassie feels his annoyance.

She doesn't say anything more, and Sam hesitates to tell her what this place means for him. He hates big pauses like that—so full of uncomfortable distance. There's no use pressing it. "Tell me about the Samuel Hazard Brown School benefit," he says.

Cassie visibly relaxes, her brush hanging loosely at her side. "Huge success. The event was packed. The auction produced megabucks and more. A bunch of people just flat out wrote checks. One guy even tried to tuck a check down my front."

"Horrors, fair damsel. The perils."

"The check was for . . . guess!"

"Two thousand."

"No."

"Five thousand."

"No sir."

"Umm . . . ten?

"No, turkey. Fifteen. Fifteen thousand dollars."

While they work, Sam and Cassie share news and outcomes about their working week. That's one thing they both do beautifully—work.

After three hours of steady effort, they finish their task. Relieved and satisfied, they return to the house for a cup of tea and a snack before washing up. Cassie wanders over to the refrigerator. She scans the random arrangement of images and quotations attached to the fridge door's white surface. Her eyes catch on a photo of Sam held in place by small magnets. Cassie carefully removes it. "The African adventure," she says to herself, removing the photo from the refrigerator. In the photo, he is standing with six African children outside of their school. He went there to help evaluate where the nonprofit group One Water should put their first two hundred wells. Not that he knows a thing about digging wells, but he does donate a fair amount to them each year and enjoyed helping them scope for new wells.

Cassie wanders across the kitchen to where Sam is standing, holding a kitchen towel, one end in each hand. She raises her arms to Sam's shoulders. He looks at her intensely, silently for a few moments then gazes toward the bay window.

Cassie stares at him. "Would you go back to Africa?"

"Yes," Sam says, pulling the picture out of her hands and putting it back up on the refrigerator. He looks at her. "I love how it's so free from the big egos in Manhattan."

"They're not all jerks," she says.

"I know. But you know the ones I'm talking about, the ones like Ricci who only care about using art to inflate their staggering self-images."

"You're getting upset, Sam. Let's move outside where we can catch the breeze off the water."

Sam follows her outside, still feeling his own distaste for that part of the art world. It bothers him that Cassie doesn't have the same disdain for ego. They settle in the screened porch on a soft, cushioned wicker sofa, the deerhounds lolling at their feet. They sit close to one another, saying little, gazing over the marsh grass on either side of the inlet and beyond to where the flat horizon and the beach begin. This landscape is punctuated only by a few modest houses set up above the dune grass, looking like little boxes in the distance ready to jump up or down the shoreline if given the right reason or signal. For Sam, this place represents his past, where he comes from. Right now he feels like he has lost the thread of who he was.

Sam thinks of the Wordsworth poem that goes:

The world is too much with us; late and soon,
Getting and spending, we lay waste our powers:
Little we see in Nature that is ours;
We have given our hearts away, a sordid boon!

Cassie dozes, her head on Sam's lap, while he contemplates the poem. After a while, he gently puts his hand to Cassie's temple, lets his fingers run lightly through her hair. Her eyes flutter, then open. She smiles and slowly sits up.

Sam stretches, rises from the couch, reaches for Cassie's hand to pull her up to stand close to him.

"Let's take a shower. Want to walk a bit later?" Sam suggests.

"Ye-e-es." Cassie yawns and stretches.

The dogs stir and shift a little, and lay their heads down again.

Sam and Cassie kiss gently before she starts toward the bedroom.

CHAPTER THREE

Tom Baxter sits at home in New York on a bright Saturday morning in May. For him, home is thirty-nine rooms layered on four floors including a surrounding, lavishly planted terrace at the top of the city's most sought after prewar apartment building a few blocks from the Metropolitan Museum of Art—views of Central Park, a south-facing side, an entrance off Fifth Avenue, an address for those at the pinnacle of wealth and power high above America's most affluent thoroughfare. The apartment is home and symbol to Tom Baxter and his cool and shockingly beautiful fourth wife, Sylvie. *The apartment.* It is simply called *the apartment* by Tom and Sylvie, by the staff of seven, by Tom's business partners, indeed by all who see it, whether they are summoned there for service or invited to one of the Baxters' frequent and predictably splendid social events.

Of course there are more spacious lodgings in New York, but none grander. Some have noted that art, architecture, and design imitate life. Is the reverse equally true? Here immense scale and volume amplify the intended message to all who are admitted: this home is an emblem to the wealthy, the worldly, and the powerful.

The apartment defines its residents, a mute yet eloquent witness to the couple's priorities and values. Indeed, these rooms in former days have housed European nobility, Old Money, as well as titans of the American business world. Five or six times the spaces have been gutted, stripped to raw walls, conduit, and pipe, like the dreary bones of a premier opera house that has been periodically refitted to project a defining image of wealth and power—immediate, elegant, unmistakable.

Tom Baxter's meteoric rise in the business world had reached its apogee just when he met Sylvie. A year before their marriage, Tom and Sylvie retained the interior designer Lawrence Waters to completely redo the vast space, which they found tired, mute, dreary even. At that moment, Waters was the star of the New York social elite. His signature designs invariably reflected an accessible yet elegant international look—aristocratic and eclectic, invoking no particular historical style.

For Tom and Sylvie, Waters's creation for their first apartment together was supposedly a projected medley of the Baxters' self-image. There was an English table here, a French piece there, touches of things Italian, varied styles, all of it lush, a chatter of status. The new couple moved into a swirl of eighteenth- and nineteenth-century architectural elements framing a mix of colors, faux finishes, sumptuous fabrics, appropriate furniture, and decorative objects made to order and plucked by Waters and staff from the European and American trade.

Floor-to-ceiling shelves held books exquisitely bound but not chosen for content or the pleasure of reading. Upon delivery to the apartment, the volumes were placed here on a desk, there on a table. An open book was placed as if the reader had been interrupted and would soon return to the waiting pages. The result was the unmistakable evocation of taste and culture meant to define the new owners and impress their guests. Added to the mix were a few pieces acquired over the course of Tom's first three marriages, relics of earlier decorative schemes undertaken with a similar agenda, all of it declaring that the residents were paragons of taste. And of course there were paintings, mostly large decorative pieces of the eighteenth and nineteenth centuries, chosen for their compatibility with Waters's design.

That major project was completed two months before Tom and Sylvie's wedding. It became the setting for engagement parties and elaborate soirées that marked the Baxters' ascendancy into the elevated inner circle of New York social life. More and more social columns featured the couple, not to mention *S* magazine's cover piece on them. The magazine's editors supposed themselves to be arbiters of taste and were assumed to be so by the readers of *S*. Among the subscribers were those who were "in" and a large following who were still "out" but increasingly hopeful, in addition to many fans who would never make it over the high social threshold. Some regular readers were content to shake their heads in disbelief as they turned the pages. Society as spectator sport.

Scarcely six months after their wedding, Tom and Sylvie decided the apartment—all thirty-nine rooms—was just not right, not what they wanted after all. They took their pair of purebred miniature French poodles, "Heloise" and "Abelard"—one black, one white—and moved to the nearby Savoy Manhattan, which just happened to have available two huge penthouse suites, which the hotel owners speedily adapted for the Baxters' needs. There they lived, despite feeling somewhat cramped, while the apartment was redone—again.

This time the vision was entirely French. Sylvie, though born and raised in Morocco, is French, after all. Their travels to France, their fascination with eighteenth-century French furniture and decorative arts, their growing familiarity with the best of French eighteenth-century architecture and installed rooms in American museums and several in Paris, gave them direction as their personal tastes developed. Further, their cultivation of wealthy French business associates and titled Parisians, many of them members of their social circle, excited their commitment to "*le goût dix-huitième Français.*" Things French would provide exceptional opportunity to learn about an extraordinarily rich and complex cultural moment while inhabiting it. Tom and Sylvie became true amateurs in the best sense, and Sylvie became a serious student. Tom, though he would have liked to, could not devote the time to such immersion in the subject of "French taste."

So there, at the summit of a prewar tower rising above Fifth Avenue, entered Daniel Méserve, a man with an aura of a Svengali, ambitious though benign. Justifiably considered brilliant, he had a fathomless knowledge and understanding of eighteenth-century European art and architecture, particularly that of France. He and Sylvie conversed in French, no matter that the language left Tom completely out. Méserve conjured a plan based on French eighteenth-century rooms and elements that incorporated authentic French *boiserie* as well as copied suites of stunningly painted and gilded wall panels. The ceilings in many cases were painted in *trompe l'oeil* fashion, blue sky, clouds, and *putti*, to give height and interest to the surface above the furnishings. Over time, the initial furniture would be replaced by the most exquisite period French furniture.

In the sprawling, multilevel residence high above Fifth Avenue, Tom's sanctuary was equipped with all the latest high-tech devices and decorated with a massive mahogany nineteenth-century English desk, a leather-covered mahogany swivel chair said to have belonged to Winston Churchill, two matching leather armchairs, a three-cushion sofa in the same leather, and massive built-in bookcases containing leather-bound volumes chosen for scale and appearance. Sylvie and Méserve convinced Tom to accept an immense, opulent Aubusson carpet that once decorated Napoleon III's office.

Well along into the realization of Méserve's eighteenth-century French fantasy, Tom and Sylvie met Sam Driscoll at a gala held at the Frick collection. Chance brought them together in front of the controversial Rembrandt *Polish Rider*. Sam was telling the notable museum director Nigel Brooke about what he knew of the picture's attribution, explaining that the differences in the brush strokes could mean that two different people had actually painted the masterpiece, when the Baxters stopped just behind Driscoll.

Several minutes later, as Sam turned away from the painting toward Nigel, Sylvie said to him, "I'm moved by your understanding of the picture."

When they heard that Sam had been a museum curator and director, and that now he was an art advisor, they asked for his card and followed up later to hire him. Sam's first role for the Baxters was in the final planning for *the apartment*. Sam counseled Tom and Sylvie to outfit the apartment's windows with the latest ultraviolet mediation and glare-control glazes and helped them acquire a Cézanne, Renoir, Sargent, Winslow Homer, and Childe Hassam for Tom's office. Sam selected them because of their exceptional quality as well as their compatibility with the smaller scale French and American Impressionist paintings that hung between the bookcases facing the window wall. But Sam chose the paintings too because, unlike Napoleon's rug, he sensed that Tom actually had an interest in Impressionist painting.

Tom sits facing the paintings when the intercom beeps. "Tom darling, François would like to know your taste for lunch. I told him that we would like to be served at twelve-thirty so you can make your afternoon appointment."

Tom settles back in his office chair, closing a corporate report. "What would you think about those pancetta, onion, and arugula sandwiches with pesto on French bread? You know, the ones that François made last week?" The invisible voice-recognition device transmits the message down the hall to where she sits in another room.

"That's fine with me, *chéri*, but it *is* very fattening, you know."

"But my dearest, you don't show it. 'La ver-ri-tee.' Nothing but the truth."

"You're very sweet. *Mais non*, my poor American. It's 'ver-ee-tay', darling. Say it."

"Please. I'm far from being a poor American."

"Oh, phoof."

Tom rises from his chair and starts along the bookcase down the length of his office to the far wall upon which hangs a full three-by-five section of a painting by Édouard Manet of the *Execution of Maximilian*, which Sam discovered in a little-known private collection in Mexico City. As Tom walks down the hall, he looks at the photographs by Stieglitz, Brassaï, Karsh, and other master photographers that line the hallway down to another set of double doors, the entrance to the second library where Sylvie sits in an embroidered silk Louis XVI *bergère* commissioned for a private apartment in the Louvre. She is immersed in the *New York Post*. A small Chinese lacquer-topped table with graceful legs sits between Sylvie's chair and its twin. On the tabletop lies the Saturday *New York Times*, joined with the Arts section of the Friday paper.

"What have you found, Sylvie?" Tom looks from his chair over to his wife. Her head is hidden behind the open newspaper. Sylvie does not reply.

"Let me see . . . hmm, you would be reading . . . uh, the city news. No, the sports page. No. Got it! The *society page*!"

"Tom, you are not funny." Sylvie blows air through her slightly pursed lips, a comment of sorts as only the French can do.

"Sorry, my dearest. I didn't mean to . . ."

"And you read the *Post* too when you are quite through with your boring *Wall Street Journal* or your *Barron's* . . ."

"Guilty. I glance at the *Post*. Just when that bloodthirsty shrew of a gossip writer is after Alfred and Liz Schroeder or Bunny what's-her-name. What *is* her name?"

"Bunny Blandford. Do you really forget her name? You are always looking at her *décolletage* whenever she appears." Sylvie still has not lowered her newspaper wall.

"Sylvie, I do and I don't. In that order. I only have eyes for you. Dear."

She slowly lowers the pages to her lap. "Perhaps you should match the name with the *décolletage*, my sweet. That might help your memory, yes?"

Tom settles into the plush of his French chair. He adjusts the readers on the bridge of his nose so that he can read the Friday Arts section. Sylvie returns to the comings and goings of the New York elite.

Several minutes later, Tom says, "Great God, Sylvie, look at these photos and this superb Degas!" Tom gets up and hands the *Times* Art pages to Sylvie. He stands behind her chair, studying the pictures and the text as she does. The painting to which he refers is an unusual wide-angle view of the Tuileries Garden in Paris depicting casual strollers, one with a dog on a leash, enjoying the Paris day in the 1870s. The painting is composed in a way that clearly shows the influence of Japanese prints and perhaps early photography upon Degas's sense of artful perspective and arrangement of his subjects.

"It looks lovely, Tom." Sylvie studies the photo. What an . . . unorthodox composition. And the light."

During the past four years that Sam Driscoll has been the Baxters' art advisor, Tom and Sylvie have seen and considered for acquisition many paintings, pieces of sculpture, and works of art that Sam has located for them. He has counseled and educated them well. Sylvie would be considered the star student by any standard. She has a naturally fine eye. Sam knows this; Tom does as well. Modest as she is in many ways, Sylvie is confident in her judgment. Though Tom would never admit it, he first watches for her reactions to the art before making his own judgments.

"The Degas illustrated below is to be included in an exhibition planned for an opening in St. Petersburg next year in the spring," Tom reads aloud over Sylvie's shoulder. She hates this, but she reins in her impatience. "The show is comprised of twenty French Impressionist paintings which have been 'discovered' in the depths of the Hermitage Museum in that great city. The official Russian press has described the collection as that of an unknown Russian collector."

The author of the article goes on to comment that the prevailing informed outside opinion is that the collection is, simply stated, "'spoils of war'" seized by the Russians in Germany, in 1944, from sites where the paintings had been hidden by the Nazis and private owners. Tom continues to read:

"Further, it is widely believed that this collection is only a small gathering of the art and treasure confiscated on orders of the highest command, Goering and Hitler himself, requisitioned—looted—from Jewish collectors, art dealers, museums, and other sources. Over the many years since the war it has become quite clear that the twice-pillaged art is housed in St. Petersburg, the scarred but renascent Leningrad, and Moscow. Despite this universal knowledge and repeated requests and pressure, the Russians have steadfastly refused all suggestions that they return the paintings to the original owners. And now it is presumed that the Russians are considering the sale of some of these masterpieces by the greatest names in Impressionist, Post Impressionist and early twentieth-century Modern Art. A sensational prospect with profoundly troubling ethical consequences."

"We could go to that exhibition, take Sam, fly to Paris, spend a few days, go on to St. Petersburg, come back to Paris for the night, and fly home," Tom says.

Sylvie tastes shock on the back of her tongue. To her, buying the spoils of war somehow perpetuates the original atrocities. She knows that Tom thinks of art in business terms, and that sometimes she should also think about the investment aspect, but the fact that he wants to make his next killing off of art looted in warfare nauseates her. With him galloping ahead to his next plan, she feels she hardly has energy or space for her reply. She stares at the newspaper.

"Sylvie?"

"Yes, Tom," she replies rather flatly.

"What's the matter? Isn't that a good plan? Wouldn't you like to see the exhibition, go to St. Petersburg?"

"Yes, I know we haven't been there."

"So . . ."

"*Tout à coup*. I mean, suddenly, when you say a plan like that so quickly it seems that it is all a fact, already decided, *fait accompli*. Like a train went by and I missed it. Can you understand that?"

"No, I can't, Sylvie, no."

"I'm sorry, then. It is that I . . . lose my breath. I do not want to buy art stolen by Nazis and then have to spend the rest of my life wondering who it really belongs to. How can I explain that?"

"*You have.*"

Sylvie lets the newspaper settle into her lap like a rumpled accordion.

"Should we talk about this?" Tom asks.

"Your plan? The way that *you* say it?"

Tom shrugs and returns to his chair.

"Here, your paper, Tom." Sylvie reaches across the table that separates them, then stands up and takes the painting that Tom gave her for their last anniversary from where it is hanging on the wall.

"May I help you?" Tom asks.

"I've got it."

"Where are you taking it?"

"I think it would work better in the bathroom."

"The bathroom?"

"Yes, the WC."

"You no longer like it?"

"I think it would look better there."

"You're trying to hide it?"

She keeps walking.

A year or so after their wedding minor scrapes like these, more serious bumps, and periodic collisions seemed to punctuate the Baxters' life together. Their hyperactive lives have kept them oblivious to the fact that testy interaction more and more colors their behavior together in their impossibly full social schedule.

For lunch, they move to the breakfast room, a circular planned recreation of a *petit salon* twenty-five feet across, walled by floor-to-ceiling mirrors alternating with painted and gilded panels by Claude-Nicolas Ledoux of *bacchantes,* some bearing garlands, the others holding elaborately carved urns.

Tom breaks the silence. "Sam's coming to the office tomorrow before we view the sales. I'll ask him what he knows about this Russian collection, whether any of it might actually come on the market."

"Fine, Tom. Remember, art is more than a deal for me. I want to feel like I am choosing the finest art collection in the world, not that I am being rushed into your next big acquisition. I don't want war spoils hanging on our walls either."

"Sure," Tom says. "I want you totally on board. And only paintings that are exportable. Clear title, that kind of thing."

"Sam certainly should be able to help us with that part," Sylvie says, almost whispering.

Tom finishes the last bit of his sandwich. Relaxing into his chair, he interlaces his hands behind his head and stares at the crystal chandelier hanging from the ceiling. "There has been more and more news of ownership disputes affecting museums and dealers. You know, like that great Monet exhibition in Boston. Remember how during the show one picture was identified as stolen by the Nazis? I read the other day that the painting has been seized and legal action is pending."

"That's why we're fortunate to have Sam. We can be reasonably sure that *we* won't have to face a mess like that."

"God forbid."

"Plus, he knows my taste," Sylvie says.

Tom and Sylvie return to the small library and their reading until it is time for Tom to leave for his regularly scheduled two-hour grooming—hair to nails—with hot facial towels impregnated with aromatic herbs. The staff at the exclusive gentleman's club are masters, not only considered the best but also the most expensive in the city, offering renewal, enhancement, and pampering to their steady clientele of notables and celebrities.

Tom kisses Sylvie on the top of her head, which she acknowledges with a weak smile. "Don't forget, Tom, we have the event for the Harlem kids tonight, the fundraiser for their camps."

"I won't," he says, turning toward Sylvie, who has her newspaper raised. "And I'll ask Sam right away about the Russia sales," he adds, not even seeing her face flush.

CHAPTER FOUR

Crossing 72nd Street at Madison, Sam glimpses Harry Gordon walking in his usual mode of total absorption in some image he has just seen. Harry is a "runner," a kind of independent operative in the art trade, not exactly a dealer, more of an agent, usually for a seller who is unwilling to canvass the pool of potential buyers. Occasionally, Harry takes on consignment paintings that are languishing in a dealer's storage racks. He covers sales in smaller, outlying auction houses, always looking for the unnoticed lot, and now and then he markets more important pictures that have failed in the New York auction network. Sam has done some business with Harry Gordon—several good second-tier Impressionists, a Le Sidaner, an excellent early-1878 Guillaumin, among others.

"Harry!" Sam calls as he approaches on the crosswalk. Harry looks up, scanning the oncoming pedestrians, and locks in on Sam.

"This stretch of Madison Avenue is like a village. It's alive with art types," Harry says.

Sam is fond of Harry, a Brit with apparently infinite energy and a knack for locating good things in unlikely places. Harry puts his hand on Sam's shoulder, picks up Sam's pace and direction.

They walk into Kostas, a Greek-owned restaurant situated smack in the middle of a kind of gallery row, a cluster of dealers stretching along Madison Avenue from the 60s uptown to 86th Street. This stretch is Sam's beat.

They greet the owner, who smiles as he shows them to a booth table. The place is upbeat with waiters yelling across the counter to the kitchen. The waiters can make a coffee milkshake so thick that the spoon stands straight up in the glass.

"So what are you looking for?" Harry Gordon says as they sit down.

"Very good to superior Impressionist pictures," Sam answers. "Hudson River School, luminist pictures, Church, Kensett, Whittredge, American Impressionists—the usual suspects."

"Did you buy that fabulous 1865 Inness at Christie's?" Harry asks eagerly.

"No comment. My clients can speak about their acquisitions. After all, it's their collection." Sam is known in the trade and by the circle of major collectors as the model of discretion, but still people quiz him. He holds his cards close in the competitive world of high-net-worth buyers and dealers. "C'mon, Harry, what are you hiding in your briefcase?"

"Well, let's see here." Harry reaches in his bulging briefcase and withdraws two file folders. Then he turns to reach for something else, changing his mind with no comment. "These might touch the heart of one of your high-flying collectors." Harry smiles and hands the folders to Sam. One folder contains a transparency of a pastel-and-graphite image of a clown walking behind a horse entering a circus ring by Lautrec, one of his "Cirque d'hiver" pictures.

"Amazing quality, don't you think?" Harry asks.

"Superb, really nice." Sam admires the transparency, which he holds up to the light of the window on Madison Avenue. He first saw a Lautrec during a summer visit to Paris after his junior year of college. Seeing a Lautrec always takes him back to that time.

"Immaculate, fresh to the market. In a private collection in Paris," Harry adds.

Sam continues to look at the transparency with obvious pleasure. "What's the price?"

"The owner is asking one-point-five million. I'm in it for 5 percent."

"Is there any room in the price?"

"We can always ask," Harry says.

Sam has never placed a Lautrec with any of his clients. Yet he loves the artist. He feels strongly about this one. He can only dream of taking it home for himself, funds permitting, which they don't. Always, that tug, a yearning to own a picture with which he could live constantly, regard it frequently, look to it for pleasure, seek its essential meaning, the heart of the matter crystallized when it was made by the artist. To his regret, Sam has to detach himself from the kind of intense consideration of the object that first drew him to this work. Too often, in advising collectors, he is required to assess works of art as things for sale, high-priced goods—as potential prizes detached from their aesthetic and historical origins, status symbols, enormously expensive commodities even, for which the competition is fierce. Here, now, in Kostas, sitting across from Harry with a transparency of a fine Lautrec in his hand, Sam has to remind himself to be on the alert, to direct his attention as a shrewd critic and negotiator.

"I'd like to hold onto the transparency, Harry. Okay?"

"Fine with me; the picture is at Day & Meyer. We can go have a look if you want to. Take a peek at the Sisley," Harry urges. Sam holds the other transparency up to the light. The image is a view of Marly, dated 1875. Good lively brushwork, a resolved, clear image, a balance of vigorous paint handling and keen observation of the scene before the artist. Nice fresh, cool palette. Sam favors Impressionist pictures of the '70s.

"You know, Harry, I lust for these '70s pictures! Can you imagine Monet, Pissarro, Renoir, Sisley, side-by-side in the great outdoors, talking and painting with one another. I love how they were exploring all kinds of new possibilities. These guys were keenly mindful of nature's underlying structure."

Sam pauses. "I don't want to be grabby, Harry, but I'd like to take this transparency, look up the picture in Daulte's catalogue raisonné, and give the picture some thought. I've got a couple of ideas for it." Sam is thinking, possibly about Tom Baxter's collection and also another collector who just happens to have an active interest in Sisley.

"Take it," Harry answers, "as long as you need it, Sam. I'm glad you like it."

Harry Gordon sips his coffee while Sam sucks the rich coffee mix with obvious relish. The waiter delivers a BLT to Harry and a shrimp salad sandwich to Sam.

"Sam," Harry begins hesitantly, "I want you to take a look at something else. It's way out of my realm, something of a puzzle. I don't know what to make of it." He slides a large manila envelope across the table. Sam opens the flap and pulls out an eight-by-ten-inch color photograph and holds it in both hands. Harry steals a furtive glance around Kostas to make sure no one is watching.

"Keep it close to you and out of sight, Sam. I had to beg for the photo, and I promised that I wouldn't show it around."

Sam stares at the image as he starts in on his sandwich.

Harry goes on. "The owner had it stashed away in his storage racks. I found it when he left me in the storage to answer a phone call."

Sam doesn't respond or look up from the photo.

"When I asked him what it was, he got flustered and wanted to put it back in the racks." Harry looks expectantly at Sam. "I know it's not the kind of thing you're usually looking for, but I didn't know who to discuss it with. I wondered if you might have an idea."

Sam looks up from the photo, says nothing, and looks again at the picture. He shifts in his seat, pushes his unfinished shake to the center of the table. "Well, Harry," he says, eyes locked on the photo, "it has something to do with Leonardo."

"Leonardo?" Harry says a little loudly, and then whispers, "Leonardo da Vinci?"

"The same. Someone in the circle of . . . or a copy, maybe a variation . . ." He does not repeat the artist's name.

"Is it old? Nineteenth century? What?" Harry questions.

"I don't know," Sam answers. "First I would call it 'Leonardesque.'"

"The guy who owns it deals in nineteenth century to early Modern—pictures like this are not his thing either."

"Did he tell you where he got it?"

"No," Harry answers. "He didn't want to talk about it. He was kind of perturbed that I had seen it. I asked him what he knew about the picture. All he said was nineteenth-century copy of a Renaissance picture. The end."

Sam studies the photo again.

"Well, obviously it's hard to make a definitive judgment about a picture from a photograph. This seems somewhat related to a Leonardo composition. It's a variation on a theme so far known only through some Leonardo sketches in the British Museum, the queen's collection at Windsor, one in France, and another in the Uffizi in Florence. The sketches are generally called *The Madonna and Child with the Cat*."

"So it could be right, yes?" Harry asks eagerly.

"I have my doubts. That's my first reaction. The known drawings are only very quick sketches. We don't know of any finished drawings, or what could be considered a preparatory drawing."

"It's an odd idea, the cat, I mean." Harry Gordon is not educated in art history, but he has a keen eye. And unlike others in the trade, he does not try to appear more knowledgeable than he is.

Sam is aware that the motif of the Virgin and Child with a cat is a singular, original, iconographic twist associated as far as he knows only with the mysterious, quirky painter, architect, engineer, and anatomist whose bearded otherworldly visage may have survived in a possible self-portrait and whose universal learning is thought to have given rise to the term "Renaissance man."

"There is no known version of the Virgin and Child with a cat painted by Leonardo or his many followers." Sam speaks softly, almost as if he is talking to himself. "To find a sizeable painted version of the theme might suggest a lost original painting of the subject by the master," he continues, "or there could have been a lost version of the theme by a student or follower. But the appearance of that theme or subject leads back to that group of drawings in the British Museum. I've seen some of those drawings. I'm fascinated by them."

"So do you think it has any value? It's on panel, and much of the surface looks to me to be in sort of rough shape," Harry says.

"Is the panel fixed to a cradle?" Sam looks again at the transparency. "I don't see any serious evidence of cracking."

"Yes," Harry answers, "there is a cradle on the back of the picture. Compared to others that I've seen—and I haven't seen that many—this cradle seemed rather amateurish."

"Well," Sam says, "cradles have been used ever since the early days of painting on wood to prevent torsion and damage caused by expansion and contracting of wood in varying climactic conditions. In this case, the cradle itself might give us a clue, if it isn't a comparatively recent one."

"I think I could arrange for you to have a look at the picture, Sam, if that would interest you." Harry very much wants Sam's opinion of the picture.

"I'd like to see it. May I take this photograph too?"

"Absolutely," Harry replies. "How about the Sisley and the Lautrec? Do you have anyone for those pictures?"

"Perhaps," Sam answers, placing the two transparencies and the photo back in the envelope and putting that in his briefcase. "I've got to be off, Harry. I've got a one-thirty. Will you let me know when we can view these pictures together?"

"I'll arrange it in the next couple of days. I'll get them moved to Day & Meyer. Not an ideal setting, but it's discreet," Gordon says with a wink.

After leaving Harry Gordon, Sam walks briskly to 71st Street where he enters the Frick Art Reference Library, fixated on the haunting image of the mysterious picture. He presents his reader's card and takes the elevator to the third-floor reference room. The library is an unparalleled resource of art books, archived photos, and documents. At the reading desks sit scholars engaged in research, Columbia and NYU graduate students, dealers investigating new acquisitions, and the occasional collector determined to discover every reference about a prospective purchase.

At the card catalogue under "Leonardo da Vinci," Sam finds scores of references. He notes the call numbers of the latest monographs on the artist—there are two new ones: Kenneth Clark's masterful survey and the volumes reproducing the published drawings. Sam takes from his briefcase a spiral notebook in which to record his thoughts and observations about the "Leonardesque panel."

Settling into the books before him, he scans the material, looking for clues and relevant images. As he knew would be the case, there are no paintings in the volumes at hand that appear to have direct relevance to the subject, which he carefully keeps out of sight in his briefcase. It seems to Sam, and it is a sheer guess, that the composition, subject matter, and general composition predated Leonardo's move from Florence to Milan, perhaps around 1482. There are several variations on the Virgin and Child theme generally accepted as dating from this time. Scholars speculate that Leonardo's reference in an existing autograph-manuscript to his commencement of two pictures of the Virgin and Child could refer to one or another lost painting, one of them possibly a *Virgin and Child with a Cat*, a composition known only through the British Museum and Uffizi drawings that Sam has mentioned to Harry Gordon.

Sam is sitting at the end of one of the reading tables with his back to the wall. Slowly and carefully, he withdraws from his briefcase the photo that Harry gave him and studies it closely. Sam writes in his notebook, "The Virgin and Child are composed in an arch-shaped panel, the Virgin to the left of the Infant Christ, who is shown facing right embracing a cat. Similarly, in this cat picture the artist has rendered the Virgin as a young woman, hair in a similar braid as in the Benois Madonna in the Hermitage in St. Petersburg, eyes led to a window on right. Cusp-shaped design as in Benois? Arch to the right as in sketch of Virgin and Child in the British Museum."

He continues writing: "Mary's attitude is loving, passive as she gently holds her son. His attention is directed at the cat, whose head stretches toward the right-hand side of the arch-shaped panel. Her drapery consists of layered silken garments of green, with the undergarment draped over her legs a light blue. Her hair is braided in the style of the time. She wears a brooch encircled with pearls. Both figures are shown with a thin nimbus. The painting resembles one of the pen sketches in the British Museum, while it shares certain similarities with the Benois Madonna, securely attributed to Leonardo and usually dated around 1478–1480." To Sam, it is the handling of the paint, somewhat inconsistent—the apparent flatness of form in several areas of the painting—that suggests the work of a copyist rather than Leonardo's hand.

Of course, Sam's observations are based on a photograph. Any further conclusions, partial or definite, will depend on careful study of the painting itself. Sam decides to contact Harry Gordon to reiterate his desire to see the panel, as well as the Lautrec and the Sisley. Sam is much more focused on the mysterious painting of the Virgin and Child than the more straightforward Impressionist pictures. He has been introduced to an art historical puzzle. Could the panel be a nineteenth-century copy? If so, the late copy could well reflect an earlier painted version of the *Virgin and Child with a Cat*. How much earlier? Does the model for the copy still exist somewhere? Could the panel be an earlier copy, perhaps a fifteenth- or sixteenth-century replica of a lost original Leonardo, thereby developing further the unusual subject, known by the sketches thought to have been an unprecedented Leonardo invention?

One other remote possibility occurs to Sam. Could it be that the inconsistencies in the rendering and the uneven quality of execution, the unsuccessful modeling of form in certain passages—could these aspects possibly indicate that later overpainting masks a partially hidden painting beneath the surface? Would ultraviolet examination, X-ray, carbon-14 dating, and other laboratory analyses of pigment and the wood upon which the painting was applied reveal anything substantial as to the age and attribution of the picture? Could the painting, with its obvious thematic ties to Leonardo da Vinci, bear the hand of the master himself? Probably too much to hope for, Sam thinks, but still a seductive riddle, the kind of engagement with a work of art that doesn't often present itself in his profession.

The outcome will be of intense interest to Tom Baxter, who, from the beginning of their long association, has urged Sam to find the very best for his growing collection. A bit crude perhaps, but he has nevertheless expressed dedication to a high standard of acquisition. Sam has helped to form an inarguably fine collection, but in prizing the reputation of the art above the art itself, he feels untethered from what he loves at the heart of this work. His pulse quickens at the thought of this picture proving to be the rarest of the rare.

Sam leaves the books on the cart, packs up his briefcase, and departs the Frick.

CHAPTER FIVE

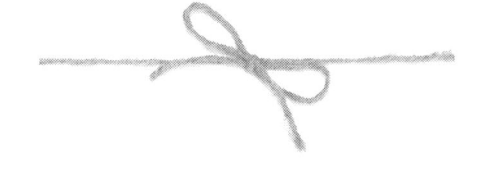

"I'll start the bidding at ten million dollars. I have ten million. To begin, ten million."

Timothy Gilbert, the impeccable British chairman and charming chief auctioneer of Blackburn's North America, stands at the rostrum in full-dress black tie holding the small ivory "hammer" slightly elevated as he scans the room, seeking eye contact, nods, opening bids.

It is Tuesday evening, May 7. Sam and Tom are seated in the main auction room at Blackburn's where four lots have been sold in the spring sale of Impressionist and Modern Art. The evening sales in all three of the major New York salerooms are the premier events of the season where the most important and valuable properties are offered to crowds of wealthy collectors and their agents. Sam and Tom are seated in the third row center, a privilege extended to important collectors with high bidding records. Discreetly scanning the auction room, Sam notes the usual crowd of potential buyers and "wannabes." He sees many familiar faces, a mix of the nameless well-appointed international set who attend all the major sales because they just *have* to be here clutching catalogues and never-used numbered paddles. They are driven by an insistent need to belong or appear to do so.

Also sitting up front are powerful dealers and potential "heavy hitters" who are being cultivated as buyers, the mission of the Impressionist and Modern staff and Blackburn's client development group. Routinely, Tom directs Sam's attention to friends and business associates whom he greets with a mouthed hello and a subtle hand gesture. Sam notices that Tom acknowledges many who are placed behind them—to Tom's obvious delight.

"Where's Ricci?" Tom asks.

"Heard he's in Sicily."

"Everything that man touches turns to gold."

Sam cringes. Even though he has to work with him, Sam detests Ricci. Hearing Tom praise him annoys Sam.

"That's a nice Cézanne, don't you think? But not as nice as ours," Tom adds in a low voice.

"I agree," Sam whispers.

"I'll start the bidding at twelve million dollars. That's twelve million with me. Now thirteen million. I have thirteen million dollars; thirteen million here."

Sam never tires of watching Gilbert, who at the moment seems to be easy, engaging, and delighted to acknowledge bids however they come—from the floor, over the phone, or from the Impressionist department staff, posted on either side of the rostrum, who are there to execute bids from absentee clients and instantly transmit them to Gilbert.

Tom turns to Sam. "He moves like a maestro before a symphony orchestra."

"Yes, or like one of those old-time magicians who produce fluttering doves out of a top hat."

Tom nods with a smile.

Though these occasions are basically obligatory sales events, Sam's reward is his fascination, his perception of the bidding process as a weave of distinct gestures, movements, and utterances both visible and audible, all generated and woven into a unique process—even an upscale ritual. That ritual moves valuable and important art, shifts immense sums of money, while the performance develops status among the players and attracts worldwide attention. It is a riveting display of human nature. Sam is captivated by the predominantly silent competition and its dramas, its moments of gestured signals, the rustle of turning catalogue pages, an occasional call of "sir!" as a house bid taker catches the auctioneer's attention.

Sam turns around to scan the seated rows as Gilbert takes a bid from the back of the room. Tom does the same. Instantly, seated attendees look again at the photograph of the Cézanne; some look to the catalogue, others to the projected image near the rostrum to see the object that draws bids from the room as well as the phone. Tom fidgets as he grows impatient with the slowing pace of bidding on the Cézanne. He wants to get on with Lot 19, which he hopes to buy. His lot is what he calls the "target picture."

"Sir?" A house bid taker catches Gilbert's attention.

"Fourteen million, I have in a new place now. Will you say fifteen million?"

Tom and Sam both turn again, as do others in the main room, to see if they can spot the new bidder.

Sam notices how some faces in the auction room assume an expression of serious concern and concentration as if to indicate to anyone watching that somehow *they* are directly, importantly affected by the course of the bidding, or that they are contemplating entering into the competition. A question of appearance, Sam has concluded over the years.

Sam and his key client turn and face front. The bidding is up to nineteen and a half million dollars. The steps are now five hundred thousand increments.

They watch Gilbert as he repeats the last bid: "Nineteen-point-five million, I have now; nineteen-point-five million. Any more?" Palpable silence runs a current of expectation through the room.

"There are two bidders on the Cézanne," Sam whispers to Tom. "They're considering their next move, gauging each other's energy and determination."

Tom nods in understanding.

"Twenty million dollars in a new place." Gilbert is radiant as he leans toward the location of the bidders.

"Twenty million." Tom points to the tote board showing the figure in six currencies.

"Bidding has slowed," Sam whispers.

"It's kind of like a tennis match. Volley, return, volley, return," Tom says. "Where's the bidder in the room, against the telephone?"

"See that guy eight over to the left in our row?" Sam nods in that direction. "Savile Row suit, tinted wraparound glasses, stocky, tanned, gray hair?"

"Yeah. That's the bidder against the phone?"

"Watch Gilbert," Sam says.

They watch Gilbert. The auctioneer smiles, looks down at the rather tough-looking bidder directly below him.

"The guy looks like the Godfather," Tom whispers.

The Godfather sits staring impassively at the Cézanne on the easel.

"The bid is with me now," Gilbert calls out as he shifts his attention to the middle of the room.

Sam and Tom watch the Godfather eyeball the Cézanne, his chin resting on his thumb and index finger. Sam can see a massive gold ring on his little finger.

"Will you give me four hundred thousand more? Twenty-point-four million?"

Sam leans over to whisper. "Watch how Gilbert teases out a bid."

Sam is always impressed by Gilbert's knack of tempting, then extracting a bid from a hesitant buyer. He leans toward Tom. "Gilbert knows just how to coax an uncertain or cagey bidder at the last moment. He kind of persuades the client that it will be in his best interest to go up another notch. Watch."

A moment later the Godfather nods to Gilbert and mouths a figure.

"Yes, I'll take twenty million, four hundred thousand."

"Twenty million, four hundred thousand. I have twenty million, four hundred thousand. I have twenty million, four hundred thousand. Twenty million, four hundred thousand. Any more?" Silence but for catalogues opening, including Sam's and Tom's. Many of those in the room think they are surely ready to write the hammer price for future reference as useful information on the appropriate page of their catalogues.

"Twenty million, four hundred thousand," Gilbert calls out again. "Twenty million . . . four hundred . . . thousand."

Tom watches Gilbert sway forward and backward, raising his hand in which he holds the ivory hammer.

"Any more?" Gilbert asks into space as casually as offering to refill a client's wineglass at a presale reception. "No more?" Behind the bank of telephones on the stage, Sam sees the special client services agent trying to get Gilbert's attention. He's met and talked to her at Christie's social functions, discovering how bright she is. She has wit, a fine New York family name, excellent contacts.

There are quite a few people spread around the room watching to see who will bid and making sure the auctioneer becomes aware of the bidders interest in the present lot.

"Sir?"

Gilbert directs his attention to the raised hand gesture of the elegantly dressed young woman holding a telephone to her ear.

"Sir? Twenty-one million," she says, her expression concentrated.

Sam and Tom and just about everyone else in the room are surprised.

Gilbert looks over at the young woman then addresses the audience. "I have a new bid on the telephone, now twenty-one million. Twenty-one million dollars." Hardly a pause. "Do I have any more?"

"You, sir?" Gilbert bends forward like a ship's figurehead toward the wraparound glasses and the massive glinting gold ring. Sam and Tom watch the man press his chin into his hand, looking first at Gilbert, then at the picture, then at his very buxom companion. The Godfather scowls; the room is absolutely still. Then he shakes his head curtly, just once.

"Another bid?" No reply.

"One more?" Again the auctioneer raises his hand which holds the gavel.

The packed room is eerily still.

"I'm about to sell . . . at tw-en-ty-one million dollars. Sure?" Gilbert teases. "All through? One more? Just another step. No? All done then." Gilbert slowly raises his arm holding the hammer. "I'm selling now at twenty-one million dollars. Tw-en-ty-one million dollars, I have now. Last chance . . . sold at twenty-one million. Thank you."

Gilbert brings his hand down smartly on the rostrum top; the ivory makes a satisfying clack. Tom and Sam watch the heavyset man in the second row sit still for a moment then look sourly at his blonde companion in exasperation. She sits stony-faced. The crowd applauds, chatters in relief.

The revolving easel turns to reveal Lot 18, a mediocre Sisley of 1882.

"Twenty-one million dollars," someone says in wonder.

"And now Lot 18, *Paysage à Moret-sur Loing* by Alfred Sisley, signed and dated 1882."

And on it goes.

Sam turns the page of his catalogue to the Sisley.

"This one has been in the trade bounding around, looking for a buyer," he says to Tom. "It came up at Blackburn's two years ago. Bought in." Sam points to the lower left portion of the catalogue illustration. "It's got one little tear just here."

"It's no beauty," Tom answers, looking to Sam, needing to confirm that he too can recognize a good and desirable picture or a dull and wounded bird.

Gilbert begins to offer the Sisley, which draws little interest and is brought in well below the low estimate. Then he turns to the rotating easel that has whisked away and delivered the sorry Sisley, and addresses the audience.

"And now, Lot 19, the superb *Bords de la Seine à Argenteuil*, dated 1872, signed Claude Monet in the lower right. I have five million to start."

This is the picture that Sam has encouraged Tom to buy this evening. Sam will do the bidding.

"Let's hold our bid," Sam whispers. He has counseled Tom to hold his bid until the early and widespread bids have tapered off, leaving several determined buyers to test the eagerness of one another until the contest settles into a rhythmic challenge back and forth between the fewer and fewer remaining bidders. Two minutes later, there are only two bidders, both on the phone. The pace slows. One of the Blackburn's staff speaks into the phone. He then shakes his head when Gilbert asks, "No more?" Gilbert raises his hand, preparing to strike his hammer. He holds his arm above the rostrum.

"Sam!" Tom whispers sharply, turning to his art advisor with some alarm.

Sam raises his paddle to chin level. Gilbert looks toward Sam and Tom.

"New bidder. I have seven million in the room. Seven million."

The telephone bid taker is the Impressionist department head. He raises his hand; Gilbert catches the signal.

"Seven million, five hundred thousand now. On the telephone. Will you say eight million?" Gilbert asks, leaning in and addressing Sam. Sam immediately raises his right hand to his chin, acknowledging Gilbert's invitation. This move is intended to quickly fend off the competing bidder by a demonstration of abundant funds and unequivocal intention to win the picture. The Blackburn's agent speaks softly into the phone to his client, then stops. No response. Gilbert waits, eyes fixed on the man on the telephone. Sam waits; Tom shifts a bit nervously in his chair. Silence.

"Any more?" Again the hammer is in the air; the Blackburn's Impressionist expert stops talking to his client and shakes his head, clearly out of the bidding.

"I'm selling now for eight million dollars. Last chance . . . eight million dollars." *Thwack!* goes the hammer on the rostrum top. "Sold for eight million dollars." Sam raises his paddle at lapel level so that Gilbert can see the number.

"Number 158, thank you very much. And now we have Lot 20, the Modigliani portrait."

"Christ, Sam." Tom gives Sam a long, slightly stunned look; then, shaking his head, he briskly pats Sam's arm. After a hanging moment, he has won the fine picture at the best possible price. Sam's cool strategy has paid off. Tom looks to his left, then his right, smiling, acknowledging, and enjoying the stares and envious glances.

After the sale, the two join the crowd leaving Blackburn's, Tom relishing the attention and several congratulations on his purchase as he heads out the door into the street. Tom Baxter loves winning.

Tom asks Sam to head next door to Gallagher's Art Gallery to look for a present for Sylvie. As they turn left toward Gallagher's, Tom strides out ahead of Sam.

"What needs to be done with the painting before we hang it?" Tom asks.

"There's not much to do," Sam says. "The varnish is too bright. The picture needs a drier finish, and the stretcher could stand to be keyed to take the slack out of the canvas."

"How long will that take?" Tom frowns slightly. He invariably expects to have his way and anticipates it.

"I'll call Alain first thing in the morning. I'm sure he can take care of the picture by end of day Friday."

Tom nods. "Sylvie put the painting I gave her for our anniversary in the bathroom. But she will surely love this one," he says, opening Gallagher's door for Sam.

"Yes, I am quite certain of that."

"In the meantime, I need a present to prime her."

Sam enters and finds himself standing in front of a piece of stained glass so exquisite it takes him back to the first time he entered Chartres Cathedral. As he stares at the glass, he feels that same ache.

"Beautiful piece," Tom says.

"Yes, extraordinary."

Sam is about to make a guess about the origins of the glass when Tom says, "Sam, I asked you a long while ago when we started to bring me masterpieces, and you've done it. You've really done it." Baxter glances at the piece of glass, but Sam can tell Tom does not really let himself experience it the way he does.

"I keep thinking about the art we've seen in museums together. Last year at the Louvre, the Uffizi, the National Gallery, the Getty. The Getty. Now that's a collecting story. We lost one to the Getty. Remember, Sam?"

"I do remember, clearly. A close one, a great Renaissance picture," Sam replies. "There aren't many opportunities like that. But then, you never know."

"Let's head back to the jewelry," Tom says.

Sam has a hard time pulling himself away from the glass. Sometimes he feels envious that Tom can buy everything he wants without really being attached to any of it. He is also ashamed of feeling jealous of someone who thinks about art in the way Tom does.

"Who's to say that we couldn't find a world-class picture that any of the great museums would envy?" Tom says, approaching one of the jewelry cases.

Sam begins scanning the jewelry. In the last two years, he has gotten to study Sylvie as she has taken an increasingly active role in the decision-making around their art collection. Sylvie has subtly and purposely opened Tom's eyes to images, styles, art historical currents, absolute masterpieces of which her husband was until fairly recently completely unaware. Sylvie loves art, but she is also passionate about making her house one of the best collections of art in the world. The prestige that comes with that distinction fuels her drive. The Baxters' collecting is a marriage of many things, among them love, friendship, social activity, and not least, ambition. In Sam's view, Sylvie's ambition precipitated the marriage in the first place.

Sam looks at a stunning necklace with a sapphire pendant. At that moment, a sales representative approaches him. "May I help you?" the man asks.

Tom steps forward. "Thank you, I have all the help I need," he says, gesturing to Sam.

"I may need you to pull something out of the case in a minute, but in the meantime, I'll keep browsing," Sam says. The man nods and walks off a ways.

"The Frick, Sam," Tom says, watching Sam scan the jewelry case. "The Rembrandt self-portrait, what might such a picture, *that* picture, cost today? *If* it were available on the open market?"

"If it were available?" Sam reflects, shaking his head slightly. "Lord. It's a superb example. What? Eighty-five, one hundred, one hundred twenty-five million? Just a guess. There are no precedents. Tough question."

"Okay." Tom has started on what is plainly a serious inquiry and a tantalizing exercise for his imagination. "What about the Met's Brueghel?"

"Well, it's one of a series. Vienna has other related pictures. I'd say the same, way up there; ninety million. A hundred million at any rate."

Sam is starting to feel discomfort. He has a limited capacity or desire to discuss theoretical values of art with genuine interest. But his professional obligation to Tom requires that he serve and advise his clients in every aspect of collecting.

"In the saleroom, where the only published records are available, I think the top figure was $88,533,000 for a Van Gogh portrait of Dr. Gachet. Japanese buyer. An early Rubens fetched more than $78 million. Then the $104 million Picasso. There may have been private sales that we don't know about. There have been rumors of sales over $150 million." Briefest pause.

"I've had this idea," Tom says, glancing absentmindedly at a different jewelry case. "I would consider setting aside—presuming business continues as it has—a certain sum. I haven't decided yet what that figure would be."

Sam listens intently, even as he notes a pearl necklace Sylvie might like for informal occasions.

"That sum of money would be reserved for the purchase of one truly great masterpiece. Universally recognized as such. It would be the centerpiece of our collection." Tom is choosing his words carefully.

"That would be an extraordinary approach to making a stupendous acquisition, Tom. But," Sam adds, "how to locate and acquire such an object or painting?"

"Luck, alertness, and money."

"We can try, my friend. It would be an exciting challenge. Depending upon where the work of art in question is found, we may have to work with export regulations and controls, for one thing. Many countries have strictly enforced laws governing the export of works of art across their borders. England and France require licenses, given begrudgingly only by government appointees, cultural authorities, review committees, and such. For instance, moving listed cultural property out of Italy is nearly impossible. International attention and activity in regard to provenance, of what are considered cultural treasures and artifacts, is rising."

"There's always Switzerland," Tom says, smiling. He is well aware of the supposed ambiguities and irregularities that periodically surface in accounts of sales and movement of important works of art through Switzerland. Frequently unsubstantiated rumors in Tom's view. "So we've just got to find something exceptionally rare with an impeccable provenance as you might put it."

"And is exportable. That would be the bottom line," Sam replies.

Tom taps on the glass above a sapphire ring.

"No. Too big for her hand," Sam says. Nothing grabs Sam. Most of it is too gaudy for Sylvie's taste.

"Let's look at scarves," Sam suggests, turning to the Hermès scarves.

"Perfect. Sylvie loves scarves."

As Sam sorts through a shelf of folded scarves, Tom says, "Our collection consists mostly of paintings. Wouldn't it make sense to limit this search to paintings, particularly to European paintings? Perhaps to one masterpiece of exceptional quality, rarity, and importance?"

Sam pauses to look at the intricate design woven on a lavender scarf.

"Sam, you could start immediately to put the feelers out. It will have to be done quietly and selectively though. I'll be identified by every dealer in the world as a sitting, check-writing target," Tom adds with a wry smile.

Sam nods and holds up the scarf.

Tom looks at the scarf. "It's terrific, Sam."

"Yes, she loves lavender."

"Sometimes it feels like you know us better than we do." Tom bites his lip, picks up the stunning piece of silk, and summons the shop clerk with a nod.

CHAPTER SIX

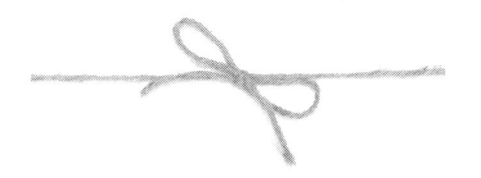

At two-fifteen sharp, Sam sits down in Day & Meyer's waiting room, hoping that Alain Bovin will arrive a little before Harry Gordon so that he can brief the conservator on what they are about to see.

Sam leafs through *Art World Digest*, the most reliable publication devoted to the art market. Looking up from a dense article about charges of collusion brought against two major auction houses, Sam sees Alain stride through the main door and into the lobby. The elegant marble-walled space resembles an important bank interior more than an art storage warehouse. Day & Meyer has courted and served many wealthy clients, collectors, and dealers who, during visits, are strategically screened from one another, thereby guaranteeing anonymity—this, in addition to the strict security protocols required for high-value storage facilities. Discretion is the firm's watchword.

"Alain, I'm glad you're here." Sam means that. He has worked with the Frenchman often to examine prospective purchases for clients and to do routine maintenance of clients' collections.

Sam leads Alain into one of the smaller rooms used for examination of small works of art and paintings brought to the client upon request by a trained porter. "Glad to do it." Alain glances around the soundproofed, private room. "What are we looking at today? You sounded a bit mysterious on the phone."

Sam hands the photograph of *Virgin and Child with a Cat* to Alain. "What I can tell you is very little," Sam explains. "The composition relates in some way to a Leonardo idea that only survives in four ink sketches—two in the Uffizi, two in the British Museum. I've seen the two in London. The idea of the Virgin and Child with a cat is unique. I find it fascinating, haunting even."

"The style is somewhat reminiscent of Leonardo," Alain says, not lifting his eyes from the photo. "But, judging by the quality of the painting over much of the surface, I'm not even sure it's a painting of the period. It's odd, though. You say that no other painted version of the theme exists?"

"Nothing appears in the literature," Sam replies. "No new discoveries in the latest Leonardo catalogue raisonné published two years ago."

"What do we know of the provenance?"

"At this moment, nothing. Harry Gordon showed me the photograph yesterday at lunch. I sensed a bit of hesitation before he took it out of his briefcase. It's not really his kind of thing."

"The panel looks quite sound, no major cracks. Is it cradled on the back?" Alain looks up from the photo.

"Harry said it was, and that it looked a bit rough."

"Maybe the reverse of the panel, the cradle, even the type of wood will give us an idea," Alain says.

One of the receptionists knocks on the door and announces that Mr. Gordon has arrived to see Mr. Driscoll. Sam and Alain get up to meet Harry near the elevator, which will take them to another viewing room two floors above where the paintings that Sam has asked to see will be set up on easels. On the third floor, Harry leaves Sam and Alain in the viewing room while he goes with two porters to bring in the Lautrec, the Sisley, and the mystery panel.

Shortly, Harry and the porters arrive in the viewing room.

"What do you want to see first?" Harry asks.

"Let's start with the Lautrec," Sam suggests, wanting to allow some time to warm up for the Madonna and the cat.

The three men turn toward the picture and stand before it, saying nothing until Sam speaks.

"Amazing draughtsman," Sam says. "What an unerring sense of line the fellow had. He never missed . . . look at the horse in the ring, the expression on the face of the clown, the different reactions of the people in the crowd—the detail that characterizes and distinguishes the figures. Aye-yi-yi." The other two men smile slightly. Most dealers with whom Sam does business understand that his excitement before a picture does not necessarily forecast a sale. He is deliberate and careful in his consideration of a piece of art.

"Harry, do you think the paper has darkened a bit and maybe the colors have faded somewhat?" Sam asks.

"I see what you mean. We can take the back off and look at the paper under the matte."

When Harry opens the hinged matte, revealing the full size of the sheet, the men see that underneath the matte the paper is indeed somewhat brighter. Alain adds that he thinks some of the pastel passages have gone a little dull, another effect of too much steady light in settings where former owners were not aware of the slow damage that overexposure to natural and artificial light can cause works on paper. Harry puts the drawing back in the frame. Sam and Alain sit down before the easel upon which Harry Gordon places the Sisley.

"Good '70s picture," Sam says from his chair. He and Alain get up and go to the easel to examine the painting more closely. Sam gently touches then lightly taps the painting's surface. Alain does the same.

"Heavy, tough relining," Alain says, picking up the picture to look at the reverse side. Then he replaces the painting on the easel and moves the tips of his fingers once again over areas of the painting's surface where vigorous brushwork and heavy impasto have been laid on the canvas in the spontaneous fashion adopted by the French Impressionists beginning in the early 1870s.

"The paint surface has been somewhat flattened because of the relining, which I think was done not so long ago," Alain says, stepping back from the picture.

"You're right, Alain. Absolutely," Sam says. "A heavy hand and a needless relining. I don't see any signs of cracking or cupping. Let's look at it under UV."

Harry turns out the lights, and, as Sam crisscrosses the handheld ultraviolet light over the painted canvas, the three men examine the surface for the characteristic purple blotches and flecks—telltale indicators of in-painting and retouching.

"Not much repair," Alain says. "The picture is intact. Makes you wonder why they relined the canvas in the first place. It was kind of a common preemptive process some years ago. Unnecessary fear of paint loss compromised too many pictures."

"A shame," Sam says. "A fine image has lost a fair amount of its power because of a heavy hand and a dumb decision."

Harry's mouth turns down. O for two.

"For my next and last presentation . . ." Harry turns on the lights, takes the Sisley off the easel, and replaces it with the *Virgin and Child with a Cat*. "I shudder to think what this tough and learned jury will say about this picture."

"Sorry, Harry. We call them as we see them." Sam gives Harry a consoling pat on the back while stealing his first look at the panel painting.

Sam is unprepared for what he sees. Silence. Nobody moves. Of course, Harry has seen the picture before at a gallery. He stares at the picture of the exquisite, youthful Madonna and the infant Child reaching across her lap, beneath the mother's adoring gaze, holding in his arms a cat stretching toward the right side of the picture, either just caught or about to squirm out of the baby's embrace.

Alain, the first to move, steps closer to the picture and drops to one knee to peer closely at it where it rests on the easel. He looks steadily at the painting, several times using his magnifying glass. He shakes his head, puzzled. "I've never seen anything like it."

He steps back from the painting. Turning to Sam, who is standing with arms folded, Alain says, "It's an incredibly beautiful image. It is quite Leonardesque, as you put it earlier. But not consistently. There is something going on in the picture that I don't yet understand."

"Let's look at it under UV," Alain continues. He switches on the ultraviolet lighting trained on the easel. The painted images assume a hazy, gauzy appearance with some thumb-size and smaller purplish passages distributed over the surface, indicating overpainting and retouching, predictable repairs on a painting of considerable age. He examines a series of darker patches, several near the lighter purple patches on the surface of the panel.

Alain pushes the yellow button on the UV lamp that illuminates a fluorescent tube designed to throw a slightly cold light, approximating daylight, over the picture's surface. He holds the lamp still on an area around the Virgin's neck and chin. He switches the UV back on. Two different shades of purple leap to the eye under the UV light.

"Curious," Alain says, almost inaudibly. He switches on the fluorescent bulb and takes out a magnifying glass, focusing his attention on the same color that he has been inspecting with both modes of the dual-purpose lamp. Using the magnifying glass, he touches the different-hued areas on the Virgin's neck, pressing his attention on those same areas. All the while, Sam stands quietly next to Alain, giving the gifted restorer the time to discover what he can about the painting. Finally, Alain steps back from the easel and asks Harry to turn on the incandescent lights above the painting.

"I don't know what to tell you about the painted surface," Alain says. "Let's look at the back of the picture." Harry carefully lifts the picture from the lip of the easel, turns it, and applies a foam strip to the top of the panel where it tilts into the top support of the easel.

Alain and Sam move in closer to the picture. In a crisscross arrangement over the back surface of the panel, a darkened grid of roughly one-by-two-inch-thick pieces of wood—equivalent to the length and width of the panel—are laid and notched into one another. They are fitted and glued to the back to prevent warping or deformation of the panel, a hazard caused by changing moisture content of the surrounding air or, possibly, temperature shifts. Cradling has been a precautionary technique of preservation applied to panel paintings since well before the widespread introduction and popularity of canvas as support for paintings.

"It looks like the cradle is old, not of this century certainly, and it definitely appears to have been repaired once, possibly several times," Alain says, his attention never leaving the panel reversed on the easel. "It's hard to tell, but my guess is, from what I can see of the panel surface on the back—here at the edge and here," Alain pauses, "the panel may very well turn out to be poplar." Sam thinks he notices a fleck of paint on the panel, possibly from a wall where it was once displayed.

"That may be helpful in answering the grand questions of what, who, and when," Sam says dryly. Then, seriously, "Enter dendrochronology and hard science. Harry, did the guy who owns this picture give you any useful information that you can recall? Anything at all?" Sam frowns slightly, staring at the mute back of the panel with his arms folded across his chest.

"Not a useful word, Sam. Just 'get it out of here if you have someone to show it to. But have it back by the end of the afternoon.' He has an odd attitude, and he seems uncomfortable, no, impatient. Maybe the picture's hot, as you Americans say."

"God forbid," Sam replies. "One more look at the image?"

"Fine, Sam. I'll get it back in its crate and return it to its grouchy owner." Harry holds back from telling them that he also gave a copy of the photo of the painting to Mark Ricci's people. He knows he should tell them this important fact, but he knows how much Sam dislikes Ricci, and he's afraid that if Sam hears Ricci has a copy, Sam will lose interest. Harry plans to come clean in the next few days, though. Sam and Alain step up to the easel to look at the picture one last time.

"What do you think, Sam? Alain? Any ideas?" Harry looks expectantly at one, then the other. He is used to presentations and possible deals not working out, but three passes on three pictures in an hour's time, meaning three lost commissions—that's disappointing.

"Harry, how much is the owner asking?" Sam inquires, not taking his eyes off the picture on the easel.

"He was a bit peculiar when I asked him that," Harry says. "He stared at me for a few seconds and then said, 'Two hundred fifty thousand, no more, no less, that's it.'"

"So . . . that's it." Sam steps back from the picture and turns to Alain. He has hardly enough information to know whether he should bring the painting to Tom's attention. While two hundred fifty thousand might be chump change to Tom Baxter, Tom certainly doesn't like spending that kind of money on a problematic painting. Besides, Sam wouldn't want to risk his own reputation on a picture that most likely isn't a Leonardo. Even so, Sam looks to Alain for a clue. If Alain really thinks it is a potential Leonardo, Sam will call Tom on the spot to see if he can put the painting on hold and buy himself more time. "What do you think?"

"Seen enough for right now," Alain says.

"Harry, thanks for arranging all this on such short notice. I'm very grateful. I'll be in touch, okay?"

"Righto, Sam," Harry says with a rueful smile.

Sam and Alain take the elevator to the ground floor and then outside onto Second Avenue. They start uptown and across to Third Avenue toward Alain's next appointment. "Well?" Sam begins.

"Fascinating." Alain pauses. "Tough, at least as much as the naked eye can tell."

"Say more," Sam urges.

"Well, I could imagine that there is possibly an image or partial image beneath the top surface," Alain replies. "The way the picture looks under UV is quite strange. Different shades of purple in spots oddly overlapping. And then there are very small areas of dark fluorescence different from the rest which have very sharp outlines."

"I follow you," Sam says. Alain often produces a diagnosis or a perspective that results in a discovery or an occasionally startlingly brilliant restoration strategy.

"When I looked at some of those small, sharp-edge patches in full light and with my high-powered loupe, I saw an edge all the way around that looks like a surface spot. There are tiny holes in the visible surface. I'm guessing there is a painting beneath the one that we see. I didn't want to mention this in front of Harry Gordon."

Sam turns toward Alain on the busy sidewalk. "If there is another picture underneath, it could be relieved of the painting on the top surface. Right?"

"That depends. It's a slow mechanical process. Pick, pick, pick with a scalpel. Solvents are too risky. Softening the top layer of paint could affect the layer below. The first step would be X-ray, and infrared examination and photography."

"Holy smoke. What a project, what an odyssey. The reward could be extraordinary. Do you think I should have put it on hold?"

"We don't have much to go on as of yet. Besides, Gordon would tell you if he was showing it to anyone else, right?"

"That's true. He's never simultaneously shown anything to anyone else. Until Tom Baxter sees it, he's not to show it to anyone else. That's our implicit agreement."

"Sam, not long ago I worked on a painting, of less potential importance, brought to me completely overpainted. Beneath it was the original composition, the original color, the original masterful work. The owner had called it a copy after Fra Bartolomeo."

"I remember seeing that picture last year in your studio."

"Yes, it was maddeningly slow and fussy work; but in the end, we uncovered an exquisite picture," Alain says. "This may turn out to be a similar case." The two men reach the little café where Alain is meeting his next client.

"I want to talk to Tom about this picture. He's back at the end of the week."

"It's not really his kind of thing, is it?" Alain says. "A Renaissance picture, a religious subject and all, don't add up to Baxter's taste, as far as I understand it."

"True. But he wants a prize that will immediately identify him worldwide as a great collector. The greatest."

"But this painting," Alain points out, "is a question mark. Yes, if it turns out to be an unknown Leonardo or Leonardo follower, it could be the greatest discovery in recent memory. At the same time, it could be a mess or a workshop picture, painted over."

"Yes, but what if? If the picture *is* Leonardo, Tom Baxter is recognized—if it's right—as a financial genius in the business world, the husband of one of the most beautiful and intelligent women in the world, and the greatest collector of the moment. King. Entrée anywhere."

"Yes, I know how he is," Alain says dryly. Alain, who works on pictures for major collectors and great museums, is not easily impressed by status or pretense.

"He's back in New York in two days. I'll see if Harry can arrange another viewing. Would you be willing to go through the exercise again?"

"Sure, glad to."

"Done," Sam says. "I'll track down Baxter. Then I'll call Harry for another viewing. For now I'm off to the Met."

"See the tapestry exhibition, Sam. It's fabulous, and it will never happen again."

Sam nods his head as he begins walking toward the Met.

CHAPTER SEVEN

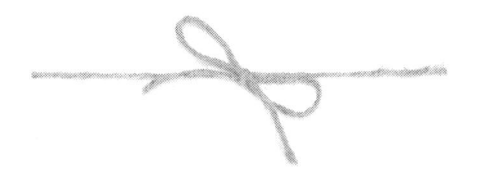

The elegantly dressed Mark Ricci faces a thick stack of neatly arranged files, memos, and bulletins that have accumulated during his ten-day vacation to Italy, now carefully sorted for his attention. He is standing in the middle of his office, the size of a medium-sized ballroom facing 65th Street. He feels especially grumpy. Life in New York can't compare to his villa in Ischia and the days he spent trolling around in *Espresso*, his huge, rakish, state-of-the-art motorboat, equipped with a high-speed runabout hung from enormous stern davits, and a four-place helicopter tied down to its pad on the topmost level of the hyper-yacht.

Mark sits down at a massive Georgian mahogany partner's desk, its timber displaying marvelous rich color. Toward the top of the pile of material is a file marked "Leonardo (?) Panel" with a covering note from Dennis Nicholson, the twenty-six-year-old sales-minded art historian whom Ricci has taken on as a research assistant.

Mark opens the file to find a neatly typed account that Dennis has written after seeing a painting described as *Virgin and Child with a Cat*, of which a photograph is paper-clipped to the information sheet, which Mark now reads:

"Harry Gordon called for you on May 4, saying that he had a couple of pictures to show you. I told him that you were away and would return on the ninth. Gordon insisted on bringing photos, one of which was a just okay Pissarro, a late one. The other photo he left is attached. It is, to me, a remarkably unusual image; but it is a puzzle. As you can see, the picture seems to be stylistically connected—somewhat—to Leonardo, but the quality and handling are uneven. It would be interesting to see the picture, which Gordon says is in New York."

Mark looks again at the photo and telephones Dennis. "Dennis, I'm looking at the questionable Leonardesque panel. What's the story regarding price? And where is the picture at this moment?" He holds the phone in one hand, his other hand absentmindedly running up and down the lapel of his custom-made, Italian, double-breasted suit. Today, after his return from Italy, his suit feels more close-fitting, particularly in the taper at waist level. He spared nothing for pleasure while in Sicily and then Ischia, running around in his private boat.

"Harry Gordon said the guy who has the panel quoted a price of two hundred fifty thousand, no more, no less."

"Well, have Gordon arrange for us to see it. Get him to tell his contact that we'll only consider the picture here. Tell him we'll give the guy receipts and any paperwork that will keep him calm."

"Okay," Dennis says. "I'll track Gordon down and see what I can arrange."

"Get it over here."

"Will do."

Mark Ricci hangs up the phone. He likes abrupt closure with staff or fellow dealers. Then he returns his attention to his accumulated business correspondence and catalogues. He thumbs through the sales catalogues for the upcoming Old Master Paintings and Drawings sales scheduled for the second week of May. He folds the corners of five pages illustrating lots to be sold between the three major auction houses. These are pictures he wishes to see, one or two for inventory, others as speculative possibilities for clients. Sometimes Ricci will strongly encourage a collector to consider an auction picture, for which he occasionally will offer to bid on the client's behalf. From time to time, he will grow impatient with a hesitant collector; in those cases, he will buy the picture and offer it to the timid client at a price that includes a significant markup to a retail-level price, comparable to established prices of similar pictures in Ricci's stock.

With the next client, Ricci might relent and pass an auction picture along at his cost, especially if he has another more important, more expensive picture in mind for that customer. Few of the buyers Ricci supplies understand that they've been regularly manipulated by his persuasive sales techniques. The bottom line is that they are acquiring very good to superb pictures from and through Mark Ricci at inflated prices. And Ricci is banking huge sums for his business.

Dennis calls as Ricci is getting deep into his accumulated mail. "What is it?" Ricci's customary clipped greeting for an internal call.

"Harry Gordon says he can have the picture here day after tomorrow, Thursday afternoon."

"Why not sooner?"

"That's the best he can do."

"Dennis, bring me Ranger and an espresso."

A few moments later Dennis knocks on the door, opens it, and releases the dog, who heads straight for Mark Ricci and the couch. Dennis sets the espresso down on a side table. Mark sits near the champion-stock brown pug on the couch and pets him. The dog curls up on the end of the couch on a red cashmere shawl. His dark brown ears are surgically arranged to droop precisely evenly on each side of his head. As Mark continues to pet Ranger, he considers his lot.

Returning to New York and his art business means no more lounging in the sun, no dawn-to-dawn pampering by phalanxes of staff, no real Italian food, no soft, sybaritic nights and fawning Italian women. Just a five-story gallery in a prewar building on the Upper East Side and his 86th Street and Fifth Avenue penthouse apartment. Mark sips the double espresso and picks up the *Art Newspaper* and then *Art and Auction*, both required reading in the art world. "Idiots. Damn idiots." The dealer folds both of the papers in half and stuffs them in the ormolu-and-mahogany wastebasket at the end of the couch.

Ricci calls the head of Impressionist Paintings at Blackburn's auction house. To persuade the Blackburn's man to divulge some sensitive information about a painting, he dangles the prospect of consignments for the fall sale of paintings both from his stock as well as from the collections of two of his clients. Ricci ceaselessly tries to persuade his collectors to "upgrade" and purchase from his gallery or focus on pictures from upcoming auctions—always designated by Ricci.

Only very occasionally will Ricci or one of his research assistants discover an overlooked or misattributed picture, a "find" that might return a large profit on a small investment. There are ever more people wanting to get in on the act: dealers, advisors, collectors, and all sorts of "wannabes." Ricci thinks frequently of the old days when there were far fewer egos wanting the momentary rush of power and notice that come along with real or perceived connection with important works of art. Those "important" paintings have become extravagantly priced because of the upward spiraling market and diminishing supply.

What Ricci never will understand or admit to himself—not to mention anyone else—is that he embodies that very equation of power with possession of art: the rarer, the larger; the more costly, the better. For Ricci, art is the subject of the deal, and his cleverness and power to persuade have made him rich.

Thursday morning at ten, a truck belonging to "Grogan & Sons, Art Handlers and Shippers" arrives in front of the Ricci Gallery. Two men carry a sizeable, carefully wrapped package up the steps from the street and into the elegant foyer. Dennis Nicholson accompanies them in the large elevator that takes them to the fourth floor where Mark Ricci waits impatiently in his office. The Leonardesque panel, unwrapped, is placed on the velvet-covered easel in Mark's office. Mark stands next to Dennis, saying nothing, just looking. He walks up to the painting, stands a moment, and barks an order. "Bring me a chair. And the UV."

Dennis places a chair just before the picture; he plugs in the handheld ultraviolet light.

"Turn off the lights," Ricci says into the air. He kneels down in front of the picture and slowly scans the surface with the UV bulb, every now and then pressing the button on the lamp that turns on the fluorescent bulb providing normal viewing light. The dealer clicks back and forth between UV and fluorescent, moving the lamp from side to side, from top to bottom. Finished after a few moments, he sits back in his chair. The office lights are turned back on. Ricci sits before the picture, leaning forward, hands on his knees. Dennis stands to the side and a step behind Ricci's chair.

Ricci, without turning around toward Dennis, says, "It just might be. Maybe. What do you think, Dennis?"

More and more frequently, Ricci includes the young assistant in presale viewings and initial visits to collectors who are thinking of selling or trading pictures.

"I think we ought to get the painting X-rayed and have George Wilson go over it," Dennis replies.

"I agree with you," Ricci says. "I don't want to let this picture out of my sight. Get Harry Gordon on the phone. Right now." Ricci sits before the panel, attention fixed on the image of the Madonna and Child with a cat.

Dennis hands him the phone.

"Gordon, Mark Ricci. I have this painting of the Virgin with a cat in front of me. Who's the owner?" He pauses, waiting for a response. "Why can't you tell me? Do you know *who* the real owner is?"

"Okay, a dealer," Harry Gordon responds.

"I hear he's asking two hundred thousand?" He pauses again. "Three hundred thousand? That's crazy. The picture is kind of strange and beat up. I want to keep it overnight. Can you arrange that? Okay, call me back." Ricci hands the phone to Dennis. Moments later, the phone rings again. Dennis hands it to Ricci, who smirks before he speaks to Gordon on the other end.

"Tomorrow, late in the afternoon. Tell the guy okay. We'll return it or make him an offer before five tomorrow. Are you included in the price? Okay, fine. Call me at four tomorrow," Ricci says.

Ricci hangs up, gripping the phone, lost in thought. The hint of a wicked smile plays on his face—he's not sure what exactly the painting is yet, but he can smell money.

CHAPTER EIGHT

Sam's taxi pulls up at the west wing entrance to the Boston Institute of Art. He's been on the phone much of the afternoon, arranging for Tom's return from a work trip to Dubai so that he can see the panel of the Virgin and Cat. Harry Gordon normally gives Sam a grace period of three days to get Tom in to see a picture, and he's open to Tom viewing the Madonna and Cat first thing on Saturday morning. Sam has been lucky to track Tom down by phone to Dubai, set the appointment with Harry, and still make an early shuttle from New York to Boston, allowing him to meet Cassie at six-thirty for the Thursday night opening of the John Singer Sargent exhibition. But he'll have to forego his Friday plans with Cassie and instead return to Manhattan to prepare Tom for the viewing. Tom likes to have at least twelve hours to absorb Sam's preparatory information before standing at the bargaining table for a potential piece of artwork.

Sam looks around the museum. Cassie is a member in the museum's higher donor category, and Sam became a life member because of his ten-year curatorship and periodic help in furthering the institute's acquisition program.

The evening promises to be splendid; buffets, bars, elegantly decorated tables, and musicians are arrayed throughout the surrounding galleries, the impressive new rotunda space, and the Renaissance and Baroque painting gallery with its lofty coffered ceiling and walls of travertine.

For Sam, there is the chance to connect with collectors and curators, and every now and then he meets a potential client or perhaps a collector planning to sell a fine picture that might interest one of Sam's clients. He leaves his overnight luggage at the coat checkroom and heads for the bottom of the escalator where Cassie is waiting with a broad, welcoming smile. They hug for a moment—this is part of their ritual after the steady weeklong separation, required by their professional demands.

After two years, a certain heaviness has seeped into their time together, particularly during the last weekend at Stonington. When they spoke of these shifts in their emotional weather, they decided to let the matter alone, hoping that it might dissipate. Sam has been looking forward to this weekend on Cassie's turf. A part of him is sorry that he will have to return early for Tom.

Tenderness rises up in Sam as he looks at Cassie. "Cass, my love, I'm so glad to be here with you."

Cassie puts her arms around Sam. "I wish it were bedtime," she says, squeezing him.

Sam is surprised by how good it feels simply to have her arms wrapped around him. "So do I. But they said over and over in graduate school, 'Art is life.' So here we are."

"How narrow-minded." Cassie smiles and links arms with Sam, and they step onto the escalator that will take them under the huge skylight to the exhibition entrance. At the top of the escalator the grand space outside the exhibition galleries is decorated with large urns filled with lavish flower arrangements. Flanking the entrance are huge reproductions of a Sargent Venice picture and a grand portrait of Sir Frank Swettenham, British governor of the Malay straits, dressed in white uniform emblazoned with a medal, posed at ease by a gilt chair over which falls a cascade of Malaysian silk brocade.

Sam sees his former clients Ben and Sandra Wolfe, who have become very good friends, standing beside Mark Ricci. Imagining what Ricci might be saying makes Sam cringe. Fifteen years ago, Sam's former curatorial department in the Boston Institute referred the Wolfes to him. The Wolfes needed assurance that an English refectory table they were considering acquiring was authentic. They had learned that fake and over restored furniture, European and American, abounds in the trade at all levels.

Sam very much liked the Wolfes and agreed to visit the North Shore dealer to examine the table, after which he became convinced that it was largely remade, incorporating old timber, some original parts—the top was honest with some obvious repairs—and some distressed pieces, probably salvaged from old wrecks.

Though they didn't buy the table, they asked Sam to work with them on finding Japanese paintings. Sam had studied and become adept at Japanese calligraphy and was himself fascinated with fine Japanese paintings, hanging scrolls, hand scrolls, and Zen calligraphy of the Edo period and earlier, but he had never offered advice in that field. For six years the project was a joy for Sam, an adventure for the three of them, and an exciting course of study that took Sam and the Wolfes to major museums, private collections, and eventually to Tokyo and Kyoto.

"Sandra! Ben! Great to see you. Are you leaving? We're just about to plunge in."

"We just finished," Ben says. "It's amazing to see so many of the great pictures all together. This exhibition is an absolute stunner. Never seen anything like it."

"Wait till you see the Boit children," Sandra says, referring to the unprecedented portrait of four children in a darkened interior, an adventure in its daring composition, painted in 1882 clearly reminiscent of *Las Meninas* by Velázquez, who was so influential upon the young Sargent. "It's like seeing it for the first time right next to the Burckhardt portrait."

"And the little portrait of Vernon Lee from the Tate with that amazing shorthand Sargent uses to show the reflected light on the sitter's glasses." Ben Wolfe seems almost giddy.

"We've got a seven o'clock dinner reservation at Fresco," Sandra says, guiding Ben by the arm away from Ricci. "Ben's heard great things about the wine list."

"I'll call you," Ben says to Sam. Sam and Cassie smile, waving goodbye.

There's Ricci. Sam must speak to him now.

"Hello, Mark. I didn't realize you went to art museums. Thought it was only your gig if it involved money."

"No, like you, I'm out here trawling for the next client." Ricci looks away from Sam and Cassie toward the Wolfes.

Even by Ricci's standards, that is an aggressive comment, especially since he knows how close Sam is to those particular clients. Sam remembers how in the middle of the Wolfes' love affair with Japanese art, they bought with Sam's help a superb Monet painting of chrysanthemums painted in 1897. Watching the Wolfes become fascinated by how nineteenth-century Japanese prints depicting flowers were notably influential upon Monet's work touched Sam deeply.

Sam looks back up at Ricci. "Very unlikely that anyone as schooled as they are would want to work with you, Ricci," he says, unable to contain himself.

"Listen, Sam. I just got back into town. Are you and your Mr. Big coming over midweek to see my new Degas?" Tom Baxter is known by a few nicknames: TB, Mr. B among them. Mr. Big is a handle that Ricci uses when talking about Baxter. The nickname bothers Sam.

"Tom's in Dubai. We'll be there, Mark, Monday, eleven-thirty sharp," Sam replies. "Give me a bit of background so I can prepare Tom on our way over."

"Pastel over monotype, two dancers on stage, good size, fabulous condition, out of a private collection, done probably, oh, 1878." Mark Ricci rattles off the particulars of the Degas like someone describing the features of a car or a computer.

"And the price?" Sam always likes to get to the point of Ricci's prices because they are invariably inflated—outrageous—and Sam can be preparing for the negotiation after doing his backup checking of comps, prior auction prices, reports of dealers or private sales.

"We'll discuss that Monday."

Sam doesn't particularly want to be seen with Mark Ricci in that venue, and he puts his hand on Cassie's lower back and pivots away from Ricci. Cassie and Sam pass the audio-guide rental booth and hand their tickets to the attendant. The first gallery displays documentation of Sargent's early life and examples of his first efforts. There are sketchbooks and loose drawings, presented in flat-topped cases, which demonstrate the young boy's precocious abilities.

"Cassie, look at this watercolor that 'Johnnie'—his mother called him that—painted in 1870 . . . fourteen years old. Just about the time when Thomas Moran did those amazing watercolors of Yellowstone." Cassie, with one hand on Sam's shoulder, bends forward to see the small sheet showing the Eiger peak in Switzerland. Sam turns his full attention to the young artist's take on the rugged Swiss alpine scene.

The exhibition is vast. Sam and Cassie walk slowly through the galleries, sometimes together, sometimes separately as each is drawn to an image that attracts them. Cassie finds Sam standing before Sargent's large painting of the Boit children—four daughters unusually posed in a spacious room in the wealthy family's Paris apartment.

"It's beautiful," Cassie says, "very beautiful, but somewhat disturbing. It's the way two of the daughters are shown in the fore and middle ground and two are kind of lost in the shadows behind."

Sam nods. "This picture has always been a puzzle to me too. Is it Sargent just being innovative, or is he responding to some personal impressions from his time with the sisters?"

"I wonder how the parents felt about the portrait," Cassie asks.

Sam feels the excitement rising in his throat at getting to share this moment with Cassie. He feels most intimate with her when they are discussing art. "We don't know the answer to that, but when it was exhibited in the Paris Salon the reaction of the critics was mixed, though Henry James did write an enthusiastic article about the picture in *Harper's*."

"Just no animation, nothing childlike—even the little one posed with a doll."

"Yeah, the mood of the picture is definitely subdued. Even gloomy," Sam says. "I get no sense of youthful energy, none of the lightness of childhood."

"I wonder what became of the beautiful little girls," Cassie murmurs. She receives a text message and starts to fish her phone out of her pocket. Sam hates that the message will break up her absorption in the art because he loves when she lets herself be absorbed totally by anything other than work, but especially by art.

When Cassie finishes typing on her phone, Sam says, "All I can tell you is that family records indicate that none of the girls ever married."

"I guess you'd say there is more to this picture than meets the eye."

"I don't know that I would say that, but some people would," Sam says, teasing Cassie. "Let's have a look at Madame Gautreau."

Sam and Cassie approach the startling full-length portrait popularly known as *Madame X*, which is dramatically installed. It is set apart in the gallery on a specially constructed full-length wall, which is painted in a lighter shade of gray than the walls of the accompanying exhibition spaces.

"Look at *her*," Cassie says. "Now that's attitude."

"This was a woman who was socially ambitious and totally aware of her allure. Interestingly, Sargent approached *her* two years before he finished the portrait in 1884."

"And this is the picture that caused such an uproar when it was first exhibited. Right?"

"That's the one." Sam explains, "It was originally presented to the salon and titled *Portrait de Madame X*. It produced a storm of criticism and derision."

"She looks a bit uncomfortable," Cassie says. "Look how her hand is posed on the tabletop. Yet she looks like a *Vogue* model of the 1950s. But she sure carries it off. Or Sargent did."

"Her story is like a page six piece in the *New York Post* set in late nineteenth-century Paris. Gossip, infidelity, ruthless no-holds-barred social climbing, conspicuous consumerism, rampant vanity."

"Plus *ça change*, plus *c'est la même chose*."

"*Exactement*," Sam says. "Let's head over to see the Broadway pictures. You'll quickly see living proof of Sargent's encounter with Monet. Okay?"

Sam and Cassie make their way through the exhibition, spending a good deal of time before the watercolors and the late landscapes, evidence of Sargent's joy before mostly undeveloped nature in America and abroad. Sam cannot think of anything more romantic than being there with a woman who gets lost in art.

Two hours after entering, Sam and Cassie agree that they are full of Sargent and in need of a change of scene and a glass of wine. They leave the institute and step into the comfortable air of a spring evening. Along the streets the trees are showing new leaves.

CHAPTER NINE

At nine in the morning, Ricci's receptionist announces the arrival of George Wilson, the painting conservator. Receptionists for the gallery, always beautiful, are expected to provide special favors for the dealer, and their tenure depends as much upon Ricci's personal satisfaction as their performance as initial greeters and message managers seated decorously in the Ricci Gallery's grand foyer.

"George, how are you doing?" Ricci gets up as Dennis Nicholson appears with Wilson at the door of Ricci's office-viewing room. The dealer steps forward to greet the restorer. Wilson is a good-looking, gray-haired professorial type, about sixty, well dressed in tailored clothes looking like Savile Row but purchased at Marks & Spencer.

The panel of the *Virgin and Child with a Cat* remains on the easel where it has been frequently and closely examined that morning. Wilson stands away from the picture for a few moments.

"A variation on a Leonardo composition," Wilson says softly to himself. One finger pressed pensively to his bottom lip, the restorer then walks slowly toward the panel, stopping a few paces away from it. He clasps his hands behind his back, silent.

Dennis brings in the UV lamp. Wilson takes it, smiles, and walks to the picture, first looking at the painting in full light through the large magnifying glass. He steps back from the easel, studies the panel a moment, and then approaches the easel again.

"Could you turn off the lights, please?" Wilson asks in his soft, precise tone. He turns on the UV lamp and sweeps the light slowly up and down, back and forth. Then the fluorescent bulb washes the surface as Wilson studies the areas over which he has paused with the UV. Again, the UV. Then once more the fluorescent.

"Fine," Wilson says, straightening up and stepping back from the picture. The gallery lights are turned back on.

"Well, what do you think?" Ricci asks.

"There may be a painting beneath the image that we see now. I can't be sure. There are small losses visible on the surface that reveal paint of almost identical hue below."

Wilson walks back to the easel.

"May I look at the reverse, Mark?"

"Dennis, turn the panel around," Ricci orders. Wilson examines the reverse of the panel and its cradle.

"Cradle looks old to me. Quite old. And there's a monogram of some sort incised, just here. Do you see?" Wilson points to the lower right-hand corner. Ricci nods without comment.

"Let's see the front again," Ricci says. Wilson remains close to the picture. Ricci stands beside him.

"Not that great. Do you agree?" Ricci turns to Wilson.

"Yes, possibly—probably—a later hand. A workshop piece. Hard to tell what's under there."

"So what do you think?" urges Ricci. He often forces conjecture into absolutes.

"I think you or the owner ought to look into X-ray, paint analysis, and perhaps carbon-14 testing as far as the panel and cradle are concerned," Wilson replies flatly.

"If there is a painting under there, could the later surface be removed?"

"Yes, a fair chance. Painstaking work. A scalpel probably. Bit by bit by tiny bit." Wilson turns to Ricci. "That's all I can tell you now." The restorer does not want to elaborate or indicate his own rising excitement about what such a process—if successful—might reveal.

"Well, thanks, Wilson. I'll talk to the owner," Ricci says. "Would you work on the picture if the owner wants to go ahead?"

"I'd give it a go. In my time, I've handled a few paintings that were heavily, almost entirely overpainted." Wilson does not wish to appear too enthusiastic. He will give the matter a little time. Ricci will probably ask him to estimate the project, and Wilson will ask a seriously high fee on a scale with Ricci's selling prices.

"Okay, thanks again, Wilson." Ricci accompanies Wilson to the elevator. The dealer rarely accompanies colleagues in the trade or in related professions down to the ground floor. He saves that courtesy for situations that require his brand of heavy charm and particular persuasion.

After Wilson has taken the elevator down to the foyer, Ricci beckons Dennis into his office. "Dennis, send Emily to the Frick Library with the photo. Tell her to keep it out of sight. I want her to dig up anything that relates to this picture. She needs to go through all the Leonardo photographs on file there." Emily Tompkins is one of Ricci's research assistants, a bright NYU PhD student. Ricci goes on. "I want you to go through our library here. Check the new monograph on Leonardo. And check through the catalogues of drawings, Berenson, Clark's catalogue of the drawings at Windsor Castle. Don't forget Popham's book, which I know we have." Ricci's purpose is to set two bright minds on the same course to maximize the possibility of throwing light on the mysterious picture.

"You and Emily have until three o'clock tomorrow afternoon to give me some answers on this picture." Ricci turns and goes into his office. He sits alone in front of the panel nibbling on his lower lip, drumming his fingertips on the arm of the chair. Thinking what an incredible deal might be staring back at him. Maybe the biggest art deal of all time . . . just maybe. At two hundred fifty thousand dollars, it's worth the risk to Ricci.

Later in the day, he calls Harry Gordon.

"Gordon, Mark Ricci. Call the owner of this tired Leonardo copy. He's asking three hundred thousand. He's nuts."

Ricci waits for Harry to stop blustering. "Just listen, will you? Look, if I get my restorer to work on it, clean it lightly, fill in some of the losses, put a new varnish on it, maybe. Maybe I can put it into an Old Master sale in London. Or offer it to some college museum as a late copy of a lost picture. You know?"

"No, I don't think that picture is worth three hundred thousand dollars—no way. Tell him . . . tell the guy"—Ricci is talking over a frustrated Harry Gordon—"tell him two hundred thousand max and that's it. No more. Got it?"

Harry is protesting on the other end of the line.

"Look, you get two hundred thousand for a beat-up picture which I've got to put some work into for a measly profit."

Harry tries to rally with his last pitch.

"Harry. Two hundred thousand. Finito. Call me back." Ricci hangs up.

Twenty minutes later, Harry Gordon is on the line to Mark Ricci.

"Great. Fax me an invoice," Ricci says. "I'll have a check messengered to you before you close your door for the day. Made out to you. You deal with the owner." Mark Ricci has a feeling, a kind of buzz. He can't be sure why. All he can think is, maybe. Just maybe. And for a song too.

CHAPTER TEN

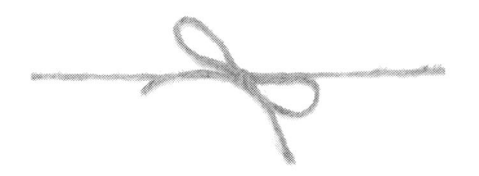

The taxi pulls over to the curb at the corner of 56th and Park Avenue at two o'clock on Friday afternoon. Sam pays the driver and heads for the door of the tall office building skinned with glass from the ground up. Sam is ready to prep Tom for their meeting with Harry Gordon the following morning. Sam looks around, noticing that he finds little pleasure amidst New York's grids of buildings walling the traffic-clogged streets. Despite his ambivalence about the city, he is engaged by some aspects of the hard-edged metropolis, such as the reflective quality of the curtains of glass that mirror the clouds and blue sky above the neighboring buildings. These somewhat surrealist vignettes remind him of certain paintings by Magritte in which the artist includes robin's-egg-blue skies and puffy clouds in idiosyncratic, cryptic compositions.

As Sam is about to enter the revolving door of the building, his phone rings.

"Sam, it's too late; it's gone!" Harry Gordon is blustering, not wanting to have this conversation.

"What do you mean gone?"

"I'm sorry. What can I say? Ricci grabbed it."

"You didn't tell me you were showing it to anyone else," Sam says, staring into an ashtray outside the office building. The picture has slipped away. And Tom Baxter doesn't take unpleasant surprises at all well. He always assumes that he will come out on top.

"Harry, you didn't mention that Ricci knew about the panel. I called after Alain and I saw the picture with you at Day & Meyer. I told you that I thought Baxter would definitely be interested. What's going on?" Sam is disappointed and angry.

"Sam, I don't always tell you about other potential buyers." Harry is trying damage control. He knows that losing Sam and Baxter as clients will be disastrous.

"You knew immediately that I was going to work on that picture. We've done lots of business together, and you know the way I work. I'm always straight with you. I told you that Baxter left town for two days and that I'd guarantee a viewing for him immediately when he got back tomorrow morning. I'm on my way to brief him. He definitely wants to see the panel. I left messages for you, Harry, and again last night. You understood all that, didn't you?"

"I did, Sam. But I can't predict what Mark Ricci is going to do. You know how he is."

"When did Ricci see the picture, Harry?"

"Yesterday afternoon. He was in Italy until day before yesterday. I'd left a photo with Dennis Nicholson, his assistant, three days ago. The day you and I had lunch. Nicholson called me yesterday. He said Ricci wanted the picture in his gallery immediately. I had no reason to say no, Sam."

"I wish you had called me, Harry." Sam looks at himself in one of the mirror windows of the office building. He looks angry. "I'm not trying to tell you your business, but I wish you had let me know what was going on. I brought Tom back from Dubai to view this."

"Sam, I said that I'm sorry. I had no idea you thought it was of enough value to bring Tom back from overseas. And Mark Ricci can be difficult when he doesn't get his way. He never forgets. I'm sorry."

"You said that," Sam replies crisply. "I suppose it would be unscrupulous or nosey to ask what the picture sold for."

"Under five hundred thousand. That's all I can say, Sam."

"Jesus."

"What?"

"Jesus. I would have advised Baxter to pay more than that, Harry. I'm not kidding."

"Why, Sam? The guy who owned it was glad to sell it at that level. He seemed relieved, in fact."

"All I can say is that that picture may turn out to be worth much, much more than the figure Ricci paid."

"How much more?" Harry asks, obviously uncomfortable.

"We'll just leave it at that," Sam says. "And you were willing to risk Tom as a client for a painting that sold for less than 500K. Shocking. Keep in touch, Harry."

"What do you mean?" Harry is alarmed.

"Goodbye, Harry." Sam hits the phone's off button, disgusted. "What a train wreck," he mutters aloud. There is a knot developing in the pit of his stomach.

Sam takes a moment to collect himself, then goes inside, signs the security register, and takes the elevator to the fifty-first floor where Tom Baxter's company, Advantage Enterprises generally referred to as AE, occupies the entire space as well as the floor below. Sam, a little shaky, leans against a wall before entering the office. He greets the receptionist, who promptly types in an internal message that brings Tom's executive secretary to escort Sam to the small conference room where the collector and his advisor routinely meet. The receptionist—her name is Emerald Robinson—is dressed simply in a black pantsuit and a purple blouse. She speaks with a West Indian intonation.

Even bantering with Emerald doesn't take Sam's mind off the scene he predicts is about to unfold in Tom's office.

Angela Hopkins, Tom's executive secretary, comes through the double doorway, which opens automatically from the offices beyond the reception area.

"Hello, Sam." Angela cocks her head. "Tom's on a call. I'll take you to the library, and I'll come after you when he's finished. It shouldn't be too long." Angela is high-energy British. "How are you?"

"Fine, Angela."

Angela motions Sam into the library adjoining Tom's office. "He'll just be a moment or two. Would you like something to drink?"

"A tall glass of bubbly water would be great. With a slice of lemon if possible."

"What, no single malt?" Sam has a taste for the peaty, smoky single malt whiskeys from Islay off the west coast of Scotland.

In a few moments the Irish woman in charge of the company kitchen and dining room knocks on the door and places Sam's water before him. "Thank you," Sam says, taking a drink.

A few moments later, Tom strides into the room.

"Mr. Driscoll! How are ya?" This is Tom's trademark greeting.

"Good morning, Tom." Sam starts to stand, his legs weak.

"No, stay where you are. So what's tucked into your briefcase? Anything wonderful to look at?"

"Well, a few things to tempt you."

Sam has brought a transparency of a superb and rare Matisse drawing of 1919, one of a series of paintings and drawings done in Nice of Antoinette, the artist's model of the moment, wearing a sumptuous straw hat festooned with feathers and cascades of black ribbons. He hands the transparency to Tom. "For openers," Sam says, aware that he is avoiding telling Tom about the fate of the possible Leonardo.

Tom looks at the transparency in the light of the north-facing window. It is a highly finished and refined pencil drawing of a subject that fascinated Matisse, who produced a considerable series of quick sketches as well as detailed drawings and paintings of the model and the fantastic hat.

"I like this," Tom says, turning to Sam as he holds the transparency in front of him. Tom faces the window again and studies the image quietly for a few moments. "What do you think of the drawing? Is it good enough for our collection?" Tom asks, still examining the transparency.

Sam brings his attention back from the possible Leonardo to the transparency. "My first impression is that it looks very, very good; but I'll reserve judgment until I see the drawing itself." He is prepared for Tom's hesitant first response. Though Sam and Tom have worked together for years,

Tom is not always expressively self-confident in the first stages of evaluating a potential acquisition, and his first response can be tentative.

"It compares very well with the best of the series," Sam explains. "Here's a photo of a related drawing in Baltimore." He places on the table a photocopy of the model facing front, wearing a costume of Moroccan design. "Look, see how Matisse seems as interested in the arabesque shapes and details of the costume as he is in the hat." Sam points out the comparisons to Tom. "The painter was obsessed with riotous pattern and sensuous line. It's as if he became intoxicated by his inventions of designs splashed in his paintings with his beloved lavish bright color. Do you get how the shapes and linear passages work on two levels at once—description and sheer abstract inventive design?"

"Right," Tom says softly as he looks at one image, then the other.

"We even have Matisse's description of how he made the hat, kind of composing the feathers and ribbons on the hat while the model was wearing it." Sam has brought for Tom a transcript of a conversation in which Matisse recalls his creating that very hat in 1919. Such discoveries generally enliven Sam. His joys are in the discovery of the object, the adventure in seeking every last bit of information about it, and the effort to get to the heart of the matter, the essential meaning and context of the work. But in this moment it all feels like a tiresome sideshow.

"This is an adventure for you in close study and analysis, isn't it?" Tom asks.

"I love it," Sam says flatly. It is strange, but Sam finds himself, more and more, slipping a bit into Tom's mode of reaching for the work of art as a prize to be seized, bringing notice and status to the player (or advisor) with the biggest pile of cash. The idea that he may have just lost an incalculably valuable deal, a shot at the Leonardo, makes his throat constrict.

"So who's got this drawing?" Tom asks, pulling Sam back to the transparency.

"Philip Jameson. Howard Inglis, who runs the New York office, called me last week. He sent me the transparency, and I told him that the drawing might be something for you."

"What's he asking?"

"Eight hundred fifty thousand. I think it's worth about six hundred thousand," Sam says.

Tom frowns. He is known—and feared by some—as a tireless, must-win negotiator, with sharp intuition and killer instincts.

"Do you think he'll come down?" Tom, elbows on the table, rests his chin on his clasped hands.

"Would you like to see it?" Sam often tries to keep Tom's primary attention on the work of art itself rather than on the deal without sounding instructional.

"Yeah, the real thing. I think Sylvie would like to see it too."

"Done. I'll call Inglis, and he'll have the drawing sent. It will probably arrive—let's see, today's Friday—we might be able to get it here on Thursday."

"Great, we'll have a look at it over the weekend."

The initial consideration in regard to the Matisse completed, Sam can no longer avoid the topic he's dreading. He reaches into his briefcase and withdraws a large unmarked manila envelope, placing it on the table.

"Tom, as you know, we discussed looking at something tomorrow that is extraordinary—what shall I say . . . unprecedented. Truly so." He knows he's stepping onto dangerous ground.

"Of course, Sam. That's why I flew home early, which was tough with twenty-five men coming from all directions—government, business, journalism, international relations, you name it, for the think tank. No phones except in case of an emergency. I'm thinking of this as an emergency meeting on behalf of our art collection."

"I've got some disappointing news on that front."

Tom cocks an eyebrow.

"Let me start by saying that I've got something here that is quite fascinating, a puzzle. It could be one of the greatest finds imaginable. Or it could be nothing. Forgive me if I sound like some of our friends in the trade."

"Who's the artist?" Tom asks.

"Possibly Leonardo da Vinci," Sam says quietly.

Tom whistles, sets his mouth in a thin smile. "Go on."

"Well, it's certainly too early to know if it actually is a Leonardo. I'd say it's a long shot for sure. I ran into Harry Gordon a few days ago. We had lunch, and during our lunch he showed me two transparencies and a color print."

"What were the transparencies?" Tom hates being out of the loop.

"A Lautrec colored drawing, a circus picture. Nice, but a bit shabby and faded. And a Sisley, a pretty good image, 1825, a view of the Seine."

Tom nods. He already owns three excellent Sisleys, all '70s pictures.

Sam hands the Sisley transparency to Tom. "The problem with that picture," Sam says, "is that it is heavily relined despite the fact that the surface shows no cracking or evidence of cupping of the painted surface. In short, relining was not needed."

"Go on," Tom says.

"Well, the impasto is quite mashed because of the relining process. The sense of quick, juicy brushwork, the brush loaded with paint—it's gone. A nice image has survived, yes, but it's . . . deadened. So I can't recommend that picture. But Sisley," Sam points to the transparency that Tom holds, "may be insignificant beside what I'm about to show you." He points to the manila envelope on the English mahogany table. "Have a look at that."

Tom picks up the envelope and withdraws the color photo inside. He holds the photo in his hands, saying nothing. In a moment, he looks up. "So what is this?"

"Harry Gordon had this picture from a dealer. Harry said the dealer was hesitant about offering the painting. He mentioned a figure of two hundred fifty thousand. He gave no information to Harry, only that his father who started the gallery bought the picture after the war from a European couple. Period. All we know about the painting. Harry would not name the gallery in question. Unfortunately, Ricci stole it out from under us this morning."

"What do you mean stole it out from under us?"

"Simply put, Tom, Harry gave a photo to Ricci's assistant on the same day that he gave one to me. Ricci just got back from one of his frequent holidays, saw the photo, called for the picture to be brought to his gallery. He bought it. The end."

"Sam, you brought me back from Dubai for a painting that you didn't have covered?"

"There's a slight chance it may be a very significant painting. I wouldn't have brought you back if I didn't think it was urgent, and apparently it was even more urgent than I thought. I probably should have put a hold on it when I first saw the photo, but in truth, I didn't know that Ricci was also looking at it. Even at that, it is a question mark, a speculative picture."

"I understand, but if it turns out to be a genuine Leonardo da Vinci, Ricci's going to ask the earth and the sun for it. You agree?"

"You're right," Sam says.

"And if it's genuine," Tom continues, "that picture could be the prize of my collection, of any collection. What do you think about the painting, Sam?"

"It's on a panel with a cradle applied to the back. The panel itself seems old and sound. No splits, no patches. Burnt into one of the cradle battens is a monogram which I make out to be 'PM.' I haven't a clue what the initials signify."

"What about the front?" Tom asks a bit impatiently.

"As you can see," Sam says, pointing at the picture, "the image is one of the Virgin holding the Child, who seeks to embrace or hold onto a cat."

"That I can see."

"Here, look at these photos. They're Leonardo ink sketches. The four of them are unquestionably accepted as Leonardo—by his hand. There are eight known sketches of the same subject. Two are in London; two are in Florence. I've seen the pair in London," Sam adds. "As you will note, the subject of all four drawings is the Madonna and Child with a cat. They are variations on a theme, attempts to work out a composition. The painting in that photo is somewhat reminiscent of the fifteenth century. Roughly. But not exactly. So the Leonardo drawings and the painting here in New York seem to stand in some relationship to one another."

Sam pauses. "Here, I've brought the latest catalogue raisonné of Leonardo's accepted paintings." He reaches into his briefcase and withdraws a heavy book, placing it on the conference table next to the reproduction of the Leonardo drawings. He opens the book to a marked page. "These three paintings represent

Leonardo's work and style of the late fifteenth century—particularly this one . . ." Sam turns over a page to the illustration of a picture known as the Benois Madonna, in the Hermitage in St. Petersburg

"What an image," Tom says with apparent genuine appreciation.

"I agree. Now see the similarities in the treatment of the format, the drapery, the pose, the placement of the hands? But the execution of the image which you hold in your hand is rough by comparison with the autographed original here in the catalogue," Sam explains.

"So, is the painting by Leonardo?"

"The obvious and pressing question," Sam replies. "My answer is, not the one that we see in the photo. But wait."

Tom frowns. Sam points to the photo Harry Gordon had given him. "Look at the photo. Do you see these small spots that look like areas of paint loss? And this larger one? They are just that. Alain is convinced there is a strong possibility that a painting lies under the present surface. Under magnification, the color on the present surface appears to be the same as the color which you can see through the hole in the surface of the picture." Sam waits a moment, letting Tom take in what he has just been told.

"Well, Sam, it either is or it isn't. Do you really think there is a painting under there that might be by Leonardo da Vinci?"

"There is a very slight chance. It may be a painting by a lesser hand. It's at least in the style of the master with slight indications of a painting beneath the surface. The panel which looks to be old, possibly late fifteenth century, and the known autograph Leonardo sketches of the composition related to this painted image all add up to the possibility of an important painting masked by the visible image in the photograph. Possibly a lost Leonardo."

"Fascinating," Tom says as he stares at the photo. "How much would a genuine Leonardo be worth now, one of this size and subject?"

"I couldn't even begin to calculate."

"Take a guess," Tom urges.

"A few Old Master pictures have fetched in the high eight figures. Possibly some have been traded privately at even higher figures. My hunch is that one hundred fifty million is where you start. An original, newly discovered Leonardo . . ." Sam says, thinking out loud.

"A guess," Tom insists.

Sam shrugs. "Two hundred, two hundred twenty-five million depending on subject and condition and a positive scholarly opinion and convincing study."

"A painting by Leonardo da Vinci in an American private collection would be a first. Wouldn't it?" Tom asks, now engaged by the vision of owning such a masterpiece.

"Yes, as far as I know."

"I'd like to see the painting, Sam. Soon. Monday before lunch. You know how I like to get out before my lunch meetings with my dealmakers and clients. But also I want to see it before anyone gets their hands on it. Can you arrange it?"

"I'll call Ricci right now." Sam reaches for his phone. "Ricci might see us now."

"I'm leaving for Dallas in an hour. I've got to be at the heliport, then to Teterboro and Dallas."

"Okay. Monday it is then," Sam says, starting to dial the number. "Mark, Sam Driscoll."

"Sam!" As many times as Sam has heard the false tone in Ricci's voice, it still grates.

"We're still on for Monday for the Degas pastel."

"You still want to come at eleven-thirty?" Ricci asks.

"Yes."

"Fantastic. And I have a new piece in from Harry Gordon, a Madonna and Child with a Cat in the Leonardo school. I'd like you to see it."

"We'd very much like to see it."

"I think it may turn out to be something really quite remarkable."

"Okay, till Monday." Sam hangs up and turns away from the window back to Tom.

"And Sam . . ."

Sam tenses.

"Sam, we've come a long way together, haven't we?" Tom does not expect an answer. "We have a beautiful arrangement. We're assembling an outstanding collection. We can match any museum, any private collector. Are you with me? Let's not miss any more great opportunities. Okay?"

"Got it, Tom," Sam says.

CHAPTER ELEVEN

Sam rounds the corner at 75th and walks toward 850 Fifth Avenue's awning. Stretch limos and luxury cars deliver Tom and Sylvie's black-tuxed and designer-dressed guests into a soft May evening for a gala dinner and a *musicale*. Sam wishes he could be at home in Stonington tucking into some pasta, a good Barolo, and still another art novel. Had it not been Tom and Sylvie's invitation, he would have declined. Allowing them to show off their private curator is part of the job. But Sam also is excited by the prospect of witnessing a gifted and renowned young viola player and his accompanist who promise brilliance and a challenging program: Enesco, Rachmaninoff, Gershwin.

Sam enters the marble foyer, waits his turn in the Art Deco elevator. The French butler, his assistant, and a small team of supplemental greeters and waiters usher the evening's guests into the Baxters' entryway. Sam watches the hosts smiling radiantly but ritually as royalty does. They welcome those on this evening's list—business associates, occasionally business competitors, board members, former statesmen, a miscellany of notables, some media celebrities, a fashion name or two, and a film star. Sam recognizes collectors among the elite, some major, some lesser, anxious to see what masterpieces Tom and Sylvie have acquired and hung. Art is everywhere in the apartment overlooking Central Park.

Sam waits in a short line filing toward Tom and Sylvie, who stand posted just inside the foyer entrance to the drawing room. After plucking a glass of Perrier-Jouet from a silver tray held by a waiter, the invitees flow into the drawing room, exclaiming in astonishment at the walls clad in eighteenth-century *boiseries*, every panel enclosing a picture by one of the greatest names in French Impressionist painting—Monet, Pissarro, Sisley, Degas, Manet—a virtual pantheon of those who rebelled against the French Salon. The effect is stunning with the superb French eighteenth-century furniture, *commodes* by Riesner, Weisweiler, Joubert, small writing desks by Macret, candle stands and side tables by Martin Carlin, enhanced by exquisite Sèvres porcelain tops, sets of gilt wood chairs, all the furniture by the most renowned *ébénistes*. Here, high above the deep sheer canyons of New York, is a setting not so different from the most elegant Parisian *hotel particulier*, a look which might be termed "neo-Rothschild"—in the density and range of masterpieces—and no accident at that.

Tom beckons to him. "Our famous curator!" Sam's abdomen tightens. A part of him wants to flee. "Great to see you, my friend."

Tom pats Sylvie, who is engaged with a venerable grande dame, Sophie Ellsworth Hammersmith, bejeweled and crowned with an opulent tiara. She is considered a social icon. Garrulous, she is going on about a recent Caribbean cruise aboard a huge yacht owned by Basil Pantilis, a Greek shipping magnate.

Sylvie blows a kiss to the grand dame, who melds into the exuberant gathering. Sylvie, ever cool but always smiling, inclines toward Sam with a reserved, loose, very French embrace, turning each cheek according to custom.

"You look radiant," Sam says to her. "Absolutely radiant." He means it.

Sylvie is an exceptionally beautiful woman who, though stunning, projects a slight distance, not quite *froideur*, which somehow is at the same time maddeningly attractive.

"Sam, we love the *Odalisque*," she says, referring to a fine drawing dating from Matisse's early Nice period—all curve, sensuous line, brilliant play of form and pattern, which Sam has just two days ago found for the Baxters.

"We want to keep it," Tom says, chiming in quickly, needing to keep abreast of Sylvie's enthusiasm. In the last year with Sam's guidance, she has taken more initiative in the brisk pace of collecting.

"I just found out that it has been requested for the show in Paris," Sam says.

"So much the better, right?" Tom replies. He takes Sam's arm. "Sam, I want you to meet Arthur MacLeod. Arthur runs AMZ Networks."

"Arthur!" Tom calls out to MacLeod amid the din of the crowd in the drawing room. "Arthur, you haven't met my curator, Sam Driscoll. Sam, Arthur MacLeod. Art, Sam Driscoll."

"It's a pleasure to meet you, Mr. Driscoll. Tom has told me a lot of good things about you. The proof of it is all around us. Fabulous, Sam," MacLeod says. "My wife and I have been thinking of upgrading our English furniture collection, and we want to add some English silver. There were some fabulous things at Christie's last month, but we just don't know the field."

Tom breaks in. "One of Sam's specialties in his museum days was English silver, and he's helped us find a few nice pieces for the house in Southampton and the ranch."

"Can we meet sometime to discuss how you might help us?" MacLeod asks.

"I'd love to," Sam answers. "It would be a pleasure."

"Give me a call, Sam. Soon. We'll do lunch at the Four Seasons." MacLeod hands Sam a card before he wanders into the gathering crowd of guests.

"I'm so glad you're *our* curator," Tom says, slapping Sam on the back.

At seven-thirty, a three-note chime sounds, signaling those gathered in the drawing room to proceed to the great dining room. Standing by the grand double doorway are footmen in starched shirts with ruffled fronts, brocaded waistcoats, black knee breeches, and white silk stockings, their feet fitted into elegant patent leather shoes with gilt buckles. The footmen direct the guests to an echelon of handsome young men dressed like the footmen who remind Sam of matched pairs of Russian wolfhounds. These vaporous youths exhibit bone structure and strange, otherworldly demeanor, faces ever so slightly gaunt. Sam guesses that the androgynous wraiths are models from the couturier houses, which seem these days drawn to blur the distinction between male and female. They guide Sam and the other guests to their places at the long banquet table where each of the invited find their names hand printed on vellum enclosed by a lovely silver-gilt frame.

There are perhaps thirty places set at the immense banquet table. Tom presides at one end beneath a full-length portrait by John Singer Sargent of an English gentleman sitting upon his fine bay hunter, Sylvie at the other end backed by the portrait of the English gentleman's wife standing by the head of her stunning thoroughbred. Sam found the pair of grand manner Sargents early on in his work with the Baxters. The paintings were created at a time when the artist did grandiose portraits primarily to attract additional clients. Despite Sylvie's reluctance, Tom insisted that these baronial images should be focal points in the grand dining room to evoke impressions of status and grandeur.

The guests take their seats. Immediately, a corps of waiters and waitresses files out of the kitchen, stopping behind each place around the dinner table. After a moment's pause, as if one, they reach in unison, pluck napkins folded like lush iris blossoms out of the dazzling crystal goblets set at each place. The help unfurl the large damask linen squares and settle them toward the lap of each guest. The servers then turn and proceed in two files into the kitchen, shortly to reenter the dining room, each bearing Sèvres, painted and gilded soup dishes on stands. The first course is a light lobster broth, in which rests a small morsel of claw meat surrounded by shaved black truffle. Wineglasses are filled with perfectly aged, carefully chilled Puligny-Montrachet. Conversation flutters like butterflies, replacing the hush of the napkin ballet. The massive chandeliers and the ormolu wall lights cast a soft, rich, ambient light in a room of flickering candles and dramatically lit eighteenth-century French paintings by Boucher, Fragonard, Watteau, and other stars of the Rococo period.

Sam is seated between Mariette de la Fosse, volatile principal soprano of the New York Opera Company, and Rachel Hunter, a much published, widely read critic of modern and contemporary art. A diva as a dinner companion on one side, and on the other an aggressive, outspoken arbiter of taste capable of fostering career celebrity or disaster. Sam has met Rachel Hunter on a number of occasions. He likes and respects her.

"Rachel, who have you discovered, and whose star is setting? How's life on the edge?" Rachel is always witty and direct, generous in exposing Sam to current emerging and influential artists.

"Sam, you make me sound like the Queen of Hearts. Off with his head and all that," Rachel says. "How've you been? Is our host keeping you breathless and busy?"

"Absolutely. We've come up with a few really good things. We're working on a great Matisse drawing that I think you'd love. I'll tell you more about it when it's done. There's a lot going on."

"There is if you have deep pockets. Scary prices out there."

"I was utterly amazed at the prices in the last **twentieth-century sales**. What's driving that market?"

"New money; lots of new collectors have struck it rich in the stock market, IPOs, and startups of all kinds. Some of these Wall Street players are having trouble inventing new ways to spend all that cash."

"How do they decide what to buy?"

"They read *Art News*, follow the sales, prowl around the big contemporary galleries, wander through the trade uptown, in Soho and Chelsea. They buy on impulse. They wing it. Often a new collector will buy a picture because a friend has just acquired a big splashy painting by the same artist."

"You know, I think some of that same urge accounts for a rising market in other fields as well. Old Master pictures, the French Impressionists, for instance."

"I'm sure you're right," Rachel says, lifting her wineglass. "Before dinner, I noticed a few keen, beady eyes looking longingly at the pictures in this humble dwelling."

"Ah, human nature," Sam says. Finishing his broth, Sam is suddenly distracted by thought of the Leonardo and its enormous significance, its tangle of puzzles. He stares at his bowl, his attention drifting from the present for a moment, the guests on either side engaged in the waves of chatter that fill the room, meaningless, unintelligible to him.

A parade of servers whisks away the broth bowls, replacing them with Sèvres plates, each bearing a tiny roasted quail set in a Madeira sauce skim laced with shaved morels.

"Oh. Now for some microsurgery." Sam turns to Rachel as he addresses the tiny bird. "Rachel, tell me, who is Judd Barnard? I read a review in *Gotham Magazine* which was, well, almost beyond comprehension. What is he about?"

"Elegy, the ancient past, mythologies, evocations, civilizations, graffitied walls . . . glimmering Mediterranean light."

"That's all?" Sam chuckles with mock dismay.

"Sam, there *is* something to his paintings, in his paintings. There is subtlety. Mood. I'll repeat: it is evocative."

"Provocative?"

"Perhaps, in a way. If you are not surprised or, yes, provoked, the artist has failed to get your attention."

"But what is there in Barnard's work? What essential quality or statement do I become aware of following my switched-on attention? What matters to the viewer after, let's call it engagement, with a Barnard picture?"

Rachel is silent for a moment, carving minute slivers from her tiny quail.

"And what does Barnard have to say, want to say, to the average viewer?" Sam adds.

"Go on," Rachel says. "I'm following you."

"Well, maybe Barnard is just putting out bits of notes and confidences."

"Yes . . . go on," Rachel nods.

"My problem then is that the bits of messages are not that interesting."

"To some people," Rachel replies, "those pictures, or some of them, are very moving. And Barnard has a large following. Big prices too."

"Can I enter the word 'promotion' in this debate?"

"Yes, you're right, Sam. That *is* often a big factor . . . in contemporary art."

"Maybe it's just me and my retrospective take on the history of art. I don't mean to sound ponderous and narrow-minded."

"I hear you. I guess it's hard to approach and open up to a Barnard picture, theoretically, without a picture before you to refer to."

"A picture, Rachel, to me is a piece of common ground, in a way a meeting place where an artist hopefully wishes to engage another person, a viewer, an empathetic and a sympathetic sensibility. Maybe that's naïve, I don't know."

"Some contemporary painters, perhaps even some historical artists, don't *care* about the viewer and his reaction. It's enough just to make the picture."

"Soliloquy or solipsism; that is the question."

"I like your notion of an artist's work as a meeting place, Sam. Perhaps the picture eventually gets seen even though that may not have been the artist's prime motive, and one must suppose some reaction as a result of its very existence."

"Yeah, you wouldn't close your eyes. *Something* happens or is felt, and you critics try to tell us the 'what' of it. Even if nothing happens, no reaction. That's . . . something."

Rachel nods. "The bottom line is that Barnard leaves messages, clues about his reactions, observations, recollections, and so on."

"I guess I'm stuck on this one. I fail to derive much more from a Barnard than my experience of a roughly painted surface, beige on white, some apparently rapidly applied, random scribbling, some vaguely phallic or erotic shapes, a line or two of Latin or another reference to classical antiquity, and a quickly scrawled signature, and maybe a date to aid future critics and art historians. Like, uh, Twombly. Oh, and the name of the place to which it refers or where the picture was painted."

"Don't look now, Sam, but I'm going to see an installation at the Whitney which is a wall covered with handwritten notes, memos, letters, and other jottings applied edge to edge over the entire surface of the piece."

"And? Is it titled?" Sam asks.

"No. And the artist, known only to the museum, wishes to remain anonymous."

"He doesn't even sign it 'Me' or 'Mine'? Could be middle European . . ."

"Easy, Sam."

"I don't want you to think that I'm a total Philistine. Seriously, I'm trying to engage with contemporary art and keep an open mind, but sometimes it's a stretch. A whole different world, breaking news instead of history to examine."

"Speaking of breaking news, what do you know about the new collector that Mark Ricci has bagged?"

"I only know that he is amazingly rich, that he buys everything from Old Masters to the art of yesterday, and he seems entirely mesmerized and dependent on Ricci."

"I find it astonishing," Rachel says, "that the bright lights of Wall Street, the big wheelers and dealers, the whiz kids, are too often willing to let an *art dealer* advise them exclusively in the consideration of exceptional and outrageously expensive art. Can you picture one of the high-profile dealers with pricey inventory taking the client to the competition, telling the prospective buyer that the guy across the street has a better Monet? Not in this life." Rachel grimaces. "That's why God invented art advisors. Right?"

"What can I say, Rachel?" Sam says. "In my mind, I often put myself in the place of a new collector unaware of the art market's complexities, and I imagine what it would be like to deal with legal issues without a lawyer or medical considerations without the benefit of a doctor. I imagine that would-be collectors, on their own, simply conclude that if they like the work of art it must be good and just fine and fairly valued. Done."

"Until the paint flakes off, the attribution is challenged, or the buyer gets the bad news at some point when he wants to sell: 'Sorry, the value is a fraction of the price you paid.' Out go the fires of interest and the desire to collect. They need you, Sam."

"I try," Sam says.

After the quail course, the Baxters' guests are treated to dill-crusted filet of wild salmon, tiny new potatoes, and crisp French string beans sautéed in butter and shallots, accompanied by a substantial California Chardonnay, followed by mesclun, fresh young leaves with a simple, well-aged balsamic vinaigrette with toasted pignoli nuts and a dusting of parmesan cheese.

By the time dessert, a chocolate fallen soufflé, is served, Sam has engaged the diva on his right as Rachel has been pulled into defending herself from a petulant but currently fashionable decorator who has done a good deal of work for the Baxters and their East Side, midtown circle. Mariette de la Fosse, the diva, is not, as far as Sam can tell, engaging. She is a bit hoarse, quite tired, and annoyed because of scheduling conflicts involving a recording contract, the soon-to-be staged *Turandot* in New York, and a concert in Berlin all happening in a month's time. Mariette's monologue lasts until the end of coffee when Tom stands, rings a silver-gilt bell, welcomes his many guests, and invites them to make their way into the music room where chairs are set up facing a piano and a music stand.

Tom then introduces the handsome young viola player who at twenty-five years old has distinguished himself with major symphony orchestras worldwide. The audience is delighted at the varied program, Enesco's *Concertstück*, Rachmaninoff's *Vocalise*, and finally a lovely rendition of Gershwin's *Summertime*. The last piece ends, leaving utter silence until the audience showers the young musician with warm applause.

Sam makes his way toward the foyer where Tom and Sylvie stand bidding their guests goodnight and acknowledging the praise and well-deserved accolades for the magnificent evening that is just now ending. Not a few of the guests, Sam thinks, are probably musing that the evening in *the apartment*—the art, décor, exceptional dinner, unmatchable guest list, and superb concert—will be damned hard to beat. Style and expense have hit dizzying levels.

"Dinner at home next to the stereo will never be the same." Sam shakes Tom's hand.

"It wasn't a bad evening, was it?" Tom says. He puts his hand on Sam's shoulder. "Sam, can you stay a few minutes? Why don't you go to my library? I'll meet you there in five minutes."

The Adventures of Huckleberry Finn awaits him at the Republic Club, and Sam is anxious to take off his dress shoes and switch into a relaxed, off-duty mode. But he makes his way to the library and settles in a comfortable leather chair set at an angle a few feet from the fireplace. Paintings and works of art of a relatively small scale hang on the walls between bookcases. Even though it is the first week of May and a mild spring evening in Manhattan, the fireplace is lit with glowing peat. These and other details in the room suggest "gentleman's library" and study, English or Irish, nineteenth century to the owner or invited guest.

Sam waits for Tom, taking it all in while musing about the "make-believe" nature of this self-consciously projected lifestyle. This is Tom's space, "English Club" flavor. He even has old lead World War II era soldiers that he probably paid a fortune for lining one of his bookshelves. Sylvie has her own defining setting on the other side of the apartment complex. Sam picks up a Renaissance book covered in yellow notes. Sylvie has banned Tom from putting sticky notes in the books in other parts of the house, valuing aesthetics over Tom's desire to learn about art.

Sam leafs through the book, finding that the stickies are all located on pages relating to Leonardo. He stands up and walks to the window behind Tom's desk, where literally hundreds of stickies are posted. In between them, Tom has made other notes on the windowpanes with a marker. Sam gets closer and starts reading the scribbles. Tom has created a sort of flow chart, a nest of nearly illegible notes that creeps up the panes as high as a man Tom's height could reach. He sees names of paintings, prices, dates sold. Something about it seems crazed. Sam wonders if Tom does this with other acquisitions.

As Sam is turning back toward the room, Sylvie steps in quietly. Her cheeks are flushed with the evening's drinks. "Sam," she whispers, getting so close to him that he can smell the drink on her breath. She puts her hands on his chest and he steps back. More than once he has found himself in a similarly uncomfortable position with Sylvie. "Tom is losing it," she says, pointing at the sticky notes. "He's going berserk." She leans in so that her small breasts are visible. "You've got to rein him in. I've never seen him this mad over anything, not even me. It's not wise."

Sam hears Tom approaching, and Sylvie rushes out through a side door; Sam collects himself.

Tom walks into the room and closes the door. "Sorry to keep you waiting, Sam. A bit of bunching up at the elevator. Last goodnights and all."

"No matter, Tom. I'm happy just watching the firelight."

"Let me put a drink in your hand before we talk."

"Absolutely," Sam replies. A bit of peaty single malt whiskey will taste good and possibly ease the experience of Tom's obsessive approach to acquiring the Leonardo. "I'd love a taste of that old Lagavulin you offered the last time."

"Right you are." Tom reaches into the liquor cabinet for the fine and rare bottle. "I'll join you."

There is a moment or two of silence as both men sniff the whiskey, slosh it up the inside of the snifter, warm the tawny brown liquid through the glass in their hands, draw the aroma into the nostrils and back of the throat. Sam straightens his shirt and remembers Sylvie's flushed face. Sometimes he tires of her antics. He has seen her leave more than one party in such shape.

"This is my favorite spot in the entire place," Tom says, breaking the silence. Sam is amazed, touched, at this rare moment of complete openness, Tom without an iota of self-promotion. Seldom, if ever, has Sam heard Tom express himself so earnestly without a shred of hype or proclamation. Both men return momentarily to their drinks. "I'd like to drink to Leonardo," Tom says.

The spell breaks.

"I've been thinking . . . Sam, have you any new ideas or hunches about that picture? I mean, could it really be what it appears to be?"

"Nothing for sure, Tom. It's only been a few hours since we discussed it. I think the answer lies ultimately in the cleaning, excavation almost, that is required to uncover the image hidden by the present surface."

"You did say, didn't you, that you and Alain agreed that there might be another painting beneath the visible surface. Right?"

Sam looks at the stickies behind Tom, not wanting to encourage this fever. "From the bit of evidence, visible with the naked eye, with a magnifying glass, under the fluorescent lights at the art storage vault . . . yes, there *might* be. But a painting by Leonardo's hand? It's a gamble." Sam pauses. "A big one. The primary issue, Tom, is that the present visible surface has to be physically removed to reveal the painted surface underneath. X-rays won't resolve the attribution question. The painting underneath, leaving aside the question of authorship, could be a wreck. And that may have prompted the repainting which someone a long time ago decided was necessary."

"I understand," Tom says quietly, peering into his glass. "Damn Ricci." Sam weighs Tom's obvious envy of Ricci and his ownership of the picture and Tom's imagined ownership of the panel, possibly the rarest of prizes. All of this adds up in Sam's mind to a familiar matter of rising obsession. Sam has seen it before. Both men are silent for a few moments, taking in the aroma and rich taste of their whiskeys.

Tom speaks first. "If that picture turns out to be a Leonardo, I want to own it." Simple as that, Sam thinks to himself, as he inadvertently lets out an impatient little laugh at Tom's insistence. Tom snaps out of his benevolent reverie over owning the presumed Leonardo. "I mean it, Sam," he says, his tone sharpened. "I want you to follow this thing closely. No more mistakes."

"But, Tom," Sam starts, and realizes he is gripping his glass of whiskey like a vise. He stares at the rich brown liquor, swirling it, trying to regain his calm. "We have to be careful. Even if it's right, the picture's story is murky. There could be provenance issues. A more naïve collector would rush in with his millions—and could be burned. Badly."

Tom swills the remainder of his whiskey, his jaw set like a student ignoring a lecturer. "I want to be there when Ricci is ready to sell it," he says, and instantly the fight goes out of Sam. "He *will* sell it."

"I'm sure he will, Tom. God only knows what he'll ask for it. I've set up an appointment for us to meet with him."

"Fine. We'll get into the matter of price when the time comes. In the meantime, keep me informed of everything you can find out about the picture. You have your sources. See what you can find out about the cleaning, the restoration—anything, everything. Get after it."

"Got it, Tom."

"I wanted to make sure you know where I stand."

Sam nods cautiously, hearing in Tom's veiled words the warning that he'll blame Sam if the picture is right and Tom for some reason doesn't get it. "I completely understand your point. But let's only go after this thing if we know for sure that it went through the proper routes to get to Ricci's hands."

Tom ignores the cautionary note, standing quickly to signal the end of the meeting. "I've got every confidence in you," he says, grinning broadly as he grips Sam's hand.

CHAPTER TWELVE

Mark Ricci hits the talk button on his intercom. "Anthea, I need a bottle of Pellegrino—lime and ice. Three glasses. Sam and Mr. Big are on their way. Oh, and Ranger needs his biscuit."

"Pellegrino and dog biscuits. Got it, sir"

Down on the street Tom and Sam get out of the car and head toward the massive iron-grill door. Sam rings the bell. The door latch buzzes and they enter the elegant, marble-walled foyer. In the corner by the staircase is a Louis XIV *bureau-plat*, behind which sits a blonde woman, smartly dressed, with fine features, somewhat patrician in her manner.

"Mr. Ricci is expecting you, gentlemen. How are you, Mr. Baxter, Sam? He'll meet you on the third floor. Go right on up." Mark views Anthea's role as to subtly generate an aura of seduction, which is a kind of prelude to Ricci's mesmerizing performances in his lair two floors above.

Sam and Tom enter the paneled elevator with its lavishly framed mirror that affords clients last-minute adjustments of vanities—ties, hair, makeup—prior to the appointed audience with the dealer. Jazz plays. "That's Art Tatum. 'It's Only a Paperless Moon,'" Tom says.

"You know your jazz," Sam replies, grinning.

The elevator stops. As the door opens there stands Mark Ricci, impeccably dressed in a charcoal gray Italian suit, graced by a lush red-and-blue silk tie and custom-made Italian black shoes. He steps back. "Mr. Baxter, Sam, great to see you. Here, Dennis, take the gentlemen's things."

Dennis disappears as quickly as he has appeared. Tom and Sam follow Ricci's gesture as he indicates the way down the hall.

"Let's first stop by my office. I have an extraordinary find I want to show you." Mark motions for them to enter his office and then leads them across the grand room.

"I just secured a little tribe of bronzes."

"Mark, you got them!" Sam says.

"I got them. Twelve little honeys."

"Dennis!" Ricci bellows into his intercom.

Dennis opens an office door. "Yes, sir"

"Can you open up the little gallery?"

"Right, Mark."

"Come, gentlemen. Show starts in five seconds."

Dennis darts ahead to open the door. Ricci shows them through a door in the corner of the office. The large oak-paneled room contains twelve oak pedestals set in a circle. They surround a larger oak stand, which supports a four-foot-high bronze figure of a young ballet dancer wearing a stiffened tulle skirt that extends a foot from her torso. A sleeveless bodice completes her costume as she stands, head thrown back, hands clasped behind her back, in a moment of alertness, as if she is readying herself to move.

Degas's ballet dancers are an astonishing find—even by Sam's standards. Clearly Ricci is trying to impress his guests, and, despite himself, Sam is in total awe of the sculptures. He could stand there all day staring at them. "Come on. On to the next show," Ricci says, gesturing for the door.

Ricci leads them out of the office and down the hall to the viewing room, velvet-lined and empty but for Ricci's massive ormolu-mounted Louis XV desk, three eighteenth-century French walnut chairs, and the easel that stands waiting at the far end of the room. The setting is rigged for drama; both Sam and Tom know that. Ricci will orchestrate the presentation and the viewing performance down to the last detail.

"So," Ricci booms, waving a meaty hand in a theatrical signal that the show is about to begin. "I want you gentlemen to have a look at the Degas pastel. The one I told you about, Sam."

"Great, bring it forward." Sam looks at Tom as he says it.

"Dennis," Mark Ricci calls to the empty doorway that opens to the painting storage racks. "Bring in the Degas pastel." And then to Sam and Tom: "So . . . mint picture. Out of an old Swiss collection. Never been on the market."

Dennis enters in a choreographed manner with the painting clad in cardboard front and back for protection, but it is also a device meant to control the first look at a valuable picture. Sam and Tom sit still in their chairs, silent, studying the pastel set upon a velvet stand from a distance of about ten feet, the only work of art in sight in the spacious viewing room. The pug hops up onto Tom's chair and sniffs his hand, and Tom jerks away.

Ricci snaps his fingers at the dog. "Dennis, turn the light down just a little. The picture looks washed out over there." Dennis does as he's told, looking to Ricci for a nod of approval. "Right."

When looking at pictures with Tom, Sam usually is the first to move. He advances slowly toward the picture under consideration, gaze fixed on the Degas. He is careful not to block Tom's view as he moves a few steps closer, attention riveted on the image. Three or four feet from the picture, he squats down on his heels to gain a steady vantage point from below the center of the image. To Sam, the picture appears to be in reasonably good condition, the strokes of chalky blues, yellows, greens, pinks, traces of strong charcoal outlines.

"Great picture, don't you think, Sam?" Ricci says.

"Tell me more about its history, Mark." Sam is unwilling to betray his impressions about quality or significance at this stage.

Ricci frowns slightly. "I *told* you. Swiss collection. Fresh to the market. It's in the catalogues. Exhibited once in Zurich in the '50s." His brusque, snappish manner irritates Sam, but he lets it go, returning his attention to the picture.

"Do we know where the picture was before and during the war?" Sam asks.

"I haven't got the history back that far. Dennis is checking on that." Ricci settles back. "What do *you* think, Tom?"

"I like it," Tom replies without a shred of enthusiasm. Tom is a master of the artful and strategic give-and-take. In the corporate world, the goal is always winning.

Tom steps away from the Degas, turns suddenly to face Ricci slouched in his Regency chair and says, "Mark, let's talk Leonardo da Vinci." Ricci abruptly sits up, looks steadily at Tom, then at Sam. Silence for a moment. Sam wishes Tom hadn't opened the discussion that way. He's never seen his client make such a misstep. In fact, Tom has been his most reliably poker-faced client. Point for Ricci.

"Harry Gordon showed me a photo, and I saw the painting with him," Sam says. "I told Tom about it yesterday. I showed him the copy of the photo that Harry got from the owner."

"What did you think?" Mark Ricci sinks deep in his chair. Sam ignores the question. "I bought it," Ricci says with unmistakable disdain. "What do you think of it?"

"I'm not sure," Sam answers.

"Well, as you looked at it and probably had someone looking over your shoulder, you might not be surprised if I say that the rendering of the figures, the style of drawing, make me think that the picture is going to turn out to be the real thing. After a lot of work," Ricci adds, "I am sure I can prove it."

Tom's eyes widen. Sam stifles a grimace.

Tom speaks up. "Mark, I'd like to ask you to keep in touch with Sam as you go to work on the picture. Depending on the outcome, after conservation and cleaning, Sylvie and I might well be interested."

Another point for Ricci. Mark straightens again noticeably in his chair. His face registers the faintest sign of surprise. Grinning, he leans over and briskly scratches his dog behind his ear.

"May we see the picture?" Tom asks. Sam looks quickly at Ricci before the dealer has a chance to reply.

"Can't," says Ricci. "It's at the restorer's." Ricci does not want to risk Tom's potential interest by showing him a picture in its worst state. "How about at another time when it's further along."

"Let us know." Sam very slightly nods his head, turning to Tom.

"Call Sam when you're ready to show the picture," Tom says flatly. "Not sure it's worth further discussion."

Ricci stiffens. He knows he has lost some control of the situation. "What about the Degas?"

"Sam and I will discuss it. I'm not sure it's for us," Tom adds, hiding his pleasure in jerking the sly dealer around. Art is another form of business, like poker or fencing. Move, bluff, feint, move.

"Sam, I've got to get back to the office for a meeting. Give you a lift?"

"Great, Tom. Thanks."

Ricci shows the client and his advisor out of his office and opens the elevator door.

"Keep in touch, Mark," Sam says. Tom nods once in agreement. The elevator starts its descent.

"Madonna," Ricci growls as he returns to his office.

In a few moments, Sam and Tom are in Tom's Bentley. Sam takes a deep breath, enjoying the aroma of the car's impeccable leather interior. It reminds Sam of a visit to an English saddle maker.

"Well," says Tom. "Another game with Ricci. But track it, Sam. I want to have first shot at the picture if it turns out to be the old boy himself."

Sam winces, turning to mask his discomfort.

Tom is undeterred. "This could be the big one."

CHAPTER THIRTEEN

Sam is lost in thought on a bright May morning as he leaves breakfast at Vaughan's, a short walk from the Republic Club on Lexington Avenue. He swipes open his cell phone and dials Harry Gordon's number. Three rings.

"Hello, Harry. It's Sam. Are you free to talk for a moment?"

"Sure, Sam. And listen, I'm really sorry about the Ricci thing the other day. That is one tough man with a long memory. You know what I mean."

Sam realizes he's in a good position to lean on Harry. He steps into a side alley where he can talk more freely. Even so, he keeps his voice low. "Harry, I should have made myself clearer than I did; I hadn't had a chance to consult with Tom—at least not enough to put a hold on the picture."

"Well, I'm sorry that you missed the first shot at it. But anyhow, as far as I can see, the painting is one big question mark."

"Exactly," Sam says. "That's what I want to talk to you about."

"I'm listening." Harry is cautious.

"A key to the riddle behind the picture is the question of its provenance. Tom is sufficiently interested in the panel to ask me to find out everything I can with respect to its history. I need you to tell me where the picture came from."

"Oh, no. Can't do that, Sam."

"Well, yes, you *can* if you wish to."

"Sam, it's out of my hands. Get Ricci to fill you in on that score—"

"Harry, Ricci is impossible in matters like that," Sam interrupts. "I give you my word I won't do or say anything that would put you in a tough spot. I'm asking you to give me the name of the guy you got the picture from. 'Old European collection' won't do."

"Sam, Ricci would kill me if I gave out any information at all. Really."

"He'll never know," Sam says. "I need this background information as part of the preliminaries that Tom and I have agreed upon as absolutely necessary to begin serious consideration of a picture, piece of sculpture—anything."

"Sam, you're putting me on the spot. You know that, don't you?"

"Frankly, Harry, we've bought a number of pictures through you. And in each case, we've insisted upon all available information as a primary requirement that precedes further study and evaluation of a potential addition to Tom's collection. I think you'll agree that our business relationship has been good and productive for all of us."

"The guy at first didn't even want to discuss the picture."

"You can be sure that I will be discreet. And I will share with you any information I get from your source."

A long pause while Sam can practically hear Harry's resolve crumbling over the telephone.

"This is against my better judgment, but okay. The dealer's name is Philip Lowder. He has a small gallery downtown on Third Avenue between 57th and 58th." Harry gives Sam the phone number.

"I'm very grateful, Harry."

Sam says goodbye and steps back into the busy street.

Sam turns the corner at 58th Street and Third Avenue; 985 is across the street. An ample show window presents a late Dufy painting depicting a scene of sailboats in the artist's frenetic composition and style. "Galerie Lowder" is announced in gold leaf on the glass door. A black limousine is parked out front. It seems unfitting for such a showy vehicle to be parked outside of an art gallery like this one. As Sam enters the gallery, a receptionist looks up from his midgallery desk and then presses the electric lock. Sam enters, smiles at the young assistant.

"May I help you?" The young man speaks with a slight accent, probably French.

"I'd like to look at your exhibition if I may."

"Certainly. Let me know if I can be of help. There is a hand list with prices." The man comes from behind his desk, handing the sheet slipped in a plastic sleeve to Sam. "There you are."

Sam looks around for the limousine's rider but sees no one. The gallery is empty. He can hear the muffled voices of two men speaking in a back room. The gallery walls are hung mainly with twentieth-century French paintings of varying quality—Dufy, Rouault, Utrillo, Vlaminck, several of the latter being examples of the artist's renderings of village roads and houses set in gray snow under leaden skies. So drab and ponderous, Sam thinks.

Sam stoops before a Rouault, a small head of Christ defined by the artist's characteristic paint-loaded brush strokes laid on paper; blacks, blues, reds, oranges are arranged to suggest a stained-glass composition—testimony to the strong influence that medieval stained glass has played in the unfolding of Rouault's style and some of his choice of subject matter. Sam glances at the price sheet in his hand. One hundred fifty thousand. He takes a closer look.

"Would you like me to take the picture down, Mr. . . . ," the assistant asks, walking toward Sam.

"Driscoll. Sam Driscoll. Yes, thanks, I'd like to see it in the daylight, if I could."

"Certainly, Mr. Driscoll. Let's take the Rouault near the front window." The young man hands the small picture to Sam. He scans the painting, noting how different it looks now. The daylight intensifies its rich hues.

"Very nice," Sam says noncommittally after a few moments. He hands the Rouault to Lowder's assistant. "May I ask if Mr. Lowder is in?"

"Yes, he is. He's with someone, though. May I be of further help?"

"No, thanks very much, but I would like to see Mr. Lowder, if that would be convenient."

"Excuse me a minute and I'll see if he's available."

Sam stands before a 1911 drawing by Juan Gris of a still life drawing of a bowl and a glass linked by drapery, the composed objects resting on a simple table, its surface tipped forward toward the viewer. Cézanne's astounding use of this innovative compositional element—repeated and developed in still life paintings of the 1870s and later—is probably the source, Sam thinks, for Juan Gris's drawing of ordinary, everyday objects.

The gallery's rear door opens and a man enters.

"Mr. Driscoll, is it? I'm Philip Lowder."

"Hello, I'm Sam Driscoll. I was just admiring this fine Gris drawing."

"A beauty, isn't it," Lowder replies, smiling and addressing the drawing as he speaks. "It comes from a private collection, then a sale where I bought it quite recently."

"I like it very much." Sam looks down at the price list. "What do you ask for it?"

"I'm asking seventy thousand dollars. Quite reasonable. A smaller sheet of similar date came up last year in Paris. It fetched the equivalent of sixty thousand. Not quite as fine as this one, in my opinion."

Sam writes the information in his small spiral notebook. He does this to gather trade information, but he also knows that such attention is not lost on dealers and other sellers. Sam's note reflects his interest, while it can also help persuade a dealer to be more anxious to draw Sam's attention to other works of art not visible in dealer exhibitions.

"I have one other Gris drawing in my assistant's office if you'd like to see it. Would you please follow me?"

"I'd be delighted to," Sam says.

"Just this way." Lowder leads him to the back of the gallery. Another reason Sam responds to invitations to go behind the scenes is that there is always the chance he will be shown other works of art in a dealer's stock. In this particular case, Sam hopes to draw Lowder out in regard to the "Leonardo" panel.

Lowder disappears into the storage shelves adjoining the small office. He returns holding a framed drawing, which he sets upon a fabric-covered easel spotlit by a track-mounted fixture. It is a rougher drawing than the one on display, much more of a "loose" sketch with forms, shapes, and drawn textures, suggesting a guitar, a newspaper, a wine bottle, a wineglass lying on its side. The classic motifs of early cubism. It is signed but undated. To Sam's eye, the drawing suggests a date of 1914/1915, his hunch based on completed pictures of similar subject and composition.

"That is a very appealing drawing, somewhat later than the one in the gallery, don't you think?"

"Perhaps." Lowder looks steadily at the sheet in front of him.

"And the price for that drawing is . . . ?" Sam turns to Lowder.

"Forty-five thousand. I don't have a lot of room in that one. It's on consignment, and the owner is not easy."

"Well, I'll keep these two in mind. I have a client who collects only drawings, and his interest is turning toward early twentieth-century material."

"Wonderful. You are welcome to return to look at these two and other drawings."

"Thanks, I will come back."

Lowder nods. He looks uncomfortable, almost as though he doesn't want to return to his office. "Do you have a number of clients? Are you a private dealer?"

"No, Mr. Lowder . . ."

"Phil," Lowder says emphatically.

"Phil," Sam continues. "I'm a private curator."

"Oh, really?"

"Yes, I spent many years in the museum field as a former director of a university art museum, and then after ten years as a curator in Boston, I decided that I was not an organization man. Now I have clients who are new as well as somewhat experienced collectors."

"Do you have a specialty, Mr. Driscoll?"

"Sam." Sam smiles graciously.

"Sam. What areas of interest do your clients represent?" Lowder glances at his office door, then back to Sam.

"Western European art from the fifteenth century to the mid-twentieth century. I've worked with European furniture and decorative arts, American nineteenth- and early twentieth-century paintings. I had eight years working in Japanese paintings of the Edo Period."

Lowder listens with pronounced attention.

"Phil, I wonder if I might ask you about another subject that I'm now quite engaged with. I would like to ask for your help."

"Please. What is the subject?"

"Leonardo."

Lowder's expression changes. He looks down at the floor and then at Sam. "I don't know that much about the painter. I don't know how I can help you." An awkward silence ensues. Lowder looks again toward his closed office door. Something about his demeanor makes Sam think he would like to talk about the Leonardo, but that he can't at that moment.

"I have a client who is most interested in a painting at least reflective of a composition by Leonardo da Vinci. It is an oil on panel of the Virgin and Child holding a cat."

Lowder listens impassively.

"The painting is now in the hands of Mark Ricci. It seems that Ricci quite recently acquired the picture from you. Through an intermediary."

"I don't know what you're talking about." Lowder turns from Sam and retreats into another office behind what appears to be his assistant's desk.

"I know the picture only through a photograph shown to me by a mutual acquaintance. I understand that the photo came from you as did the problematic panel."

After a moment of fidgeting, the dealer looks up from his desk. "I don't generally discuss my business or my transactions with anyone not involved in the subject transaction. I think you can understand that, Mr. Driscoll."

"I do understand, Mr. Lowder. I've done some routine research on my client's behalf." Sam pauses. Lowder seems tense, as if he is holding his breath. He stands up and closes the door to the office.

Sam continues. "There is reason to believe that beneath the present painted surface there is another earlier painted image probably of the same subject." Lowder, looking pale, stares wordlessly at Sam. "The picture belonged to you before Mark Ricci acquired it, did it not?"

"Yes, I have owned the picture for a very long time. It was in the inventory when I took over this business from my father."

"I'm sorry if my questions put you in an awkward position."

"You most certainly have put me in an uncomfortable position, Mr. Driscoll. I have nothing more to say about the picture. I did sell it to Mark Ricci and passed on to him the provenance that he requested."

"And that was . . . ?"

"That is not your business at this time."

"I'm sorry to press the matter, but my client is sufficiently interested in the picture that I must research as carefully as possible every aspect of its attribution, condition, and history. You can understand that, I'm sure."

"Look, Sam. You must discuss that with Ricci." Lowder sits down at his desk and reaches for a thick loose-leaf binder. He turns to a page at the very back of the binder, holding the invoice book so that Sam can see the page that reads:

"Virgin and Child holding a Cat. Style of Leonardo da Vinci. Probably 19th century. Provenance. Ray Lowder. 1950. Acquired from Mr. and Mrs. George Reinhardt, formerly of Hamburg by owners' family descent."

The dealer looks up from the book. "Ray Lowder was my father," he whispers. Then in a normal voice he says, "I have nothing to add to the painting's history. You must speak to Ricci."

"All you *can* tell me, I think you mean to say."

"Yes, 'can tell you.' All we know. Now, Mr. Driscoll, if you will excuse me, I must show you out of my office. You are most welcome to continue to view the exhibition."

"I understand. And I thank you."

The two men return to the gallery. At that moment, the gallery door opens and a well-dressed woman comes in and approaches Lowder and Sam.

"Hilda, you are early," Lowder says to his wife. "This is Sam Driscoll, an art advisor."

"Very happy to meet you, Mr. Driscoll." Hilda extends her hand to Sam.

"My pleasure, Mrs. Lowder. I've just finished a brief visit with your husband, and now I must be going." Sam turns to Lowder. "I'll keep that fine Gris drawing in mind and perhaps be in touch with you if my client has an interest in seeing it."

"Let me know . . . uh, Sam. I'll be happy to deliver it for a careful viewing. Oh . . . and . . . can you tell me the name of your client? Might I know of him . . . uh . . . her . . . ?"

"I'm afraid that I can't divulge my client's name at this point . . . Phil."

"Goodbye, Mr. Driscoll," Lowder says abruptly. "Come along, Hilda." The dealer guides his wife by the elbow toward the back of the gallery.

"Interesting," Sam mutters to himself as he steps to the curbside and hails a taxi.

CHAPTER FOURTEEN

Captain Glen Lowder lowers his field glasses through which he has scanned the slopes above the road leading away from the village of Ponte Albrizzi. There is no sign of the German troops reported yesterday to have been heading north in retreat before the swift and steady advance of the Allied Forces.

"Jansen," he calls to his burly sergeant. "Let's head for the church up that hill. We can hang in there until command decides on our next move."

"Okay, lads." Jansen gives the sign for the soldiers to move toward the stone buildings about a thousand yards away. "Haul it and spread out. And keep your eye on the church. Heintzy isn't that far ahead of us. Look alive." Fifty infantrymen start to move cautiously uphill.

The detachment has trucked and marched from Rome, their assembly and orientation point. They have intermittently traded fire with the Germans as pressure has forced the enemy northward, leaving a patchy rearguard defense against Lowder's troops. They are tough and savvy, experienced in combat. These men were chosen and assigned to Lowder because they excelled in their units, and together they bring special skills deemed necessary for their assignment. They are locksmiths, carpenters, metalworkers, museum art handlers, and packers. An unusual number of the group holds college degrees, most of those with specialization in art history; there are ten artists included in the contingent who left behind solid careers as painters and sculptors.

The initial task of Lowder's detachment is to clear and hold the city of Florence until the arrival of additional infantry, military police, and supplies, just a day or so behind. Protecting the skilled personnel embedded in Lowder's unit is the regular combat personnel's primary responsibility. The detachment's essential objective is to ensure the security and preservation of the cultural treasure that is Florence—its irreplaceable buildings, masterpieces, vast and valuable archives, and anything that illuminates or testifies to hundreds of years during which Florence, the emblem of the Italian Renaissance, brought forth genius, unprecedented experimentation, and transformation of the course of art history. First, Lowder must lead his men safely some one hundred ten miles northwest.

Some of the soldiers nicknamed Lowder "Professor" after they learned that he is a former teacher with a Columbia PhD in art history and two years of rigorous, postgraduate training in Berlin under the renowned Professor Max Schlesinger. That was before the rule of Hitler. After becoming an expert in Italian Renaissance painting, Lowder left Germany and returned to Columbia to teach. Though he was considered a star in his profession, Lowder chose to enlist when America entered the war, undertaking officer training with the goal of returning to teaching and research at the war's end.

The soldiers advance up the hill, stopping periodically on Jansen's signal to drop to the ground. Twenty minutes later, the American force gains the top of the hill. The monastic site consists of a modest church set next to a detached belfry and three outbuildings, all built of limestone ashlar blocks with tiled roofs. There is a dormitory attached to a cloister, a refectory with a kitchen, and what appears to be a small monastic library. Jansen details squads to search the buildings. Others stay grouped in case defensive action is needed.

Soon, the squad leaders report back that there is no sign of the retreating Germans or the resident monks. The disorderly state of the kitchen and the dormitory indicates the haste with which the monks left. Empty German ration packets suggest enemy troops have used the place for rest and shelter before continuing their steady, forced retreat north. Fortunately, there is no clear sign of damage within the church, refectory, or library. "Okay, guys, settle in," Lowder says to his men. "We'll be here for a while until I can get word from headquarters."

Lowder addresses his sergeant. "Jansen, post guard at the windows in case Jerry has left behind any goons. The rest of you, lie back and enjoy the sunshine. We'll be needing our energy for our next push." Mid-July is hot in Italy, and Lowder looks forward to the brief respite that will last only as long as Boot Command operations center allows, before orders to continue moving north come over the radio. Following behind the company is a supply convoy. Lowder and his company can use the rest, the first decent one since Rome. The men banter as they remove their backpacks, equipment, and weapons.

"Jansen," Lowder says, "I'm taking a walk. You're in charge. Stay alert. I'll be back at 1400 hours. Radio me if you need anything." Lowder enjoys working with his grizzled NCO, a career soldier, and he relies heavily upon his advice and instincts in their sweeps and rearguard mission.

Lowder walks from the cloister past a small burying ground over to the modest parish church. He enters through large oak doors, whose weathered planks are bound together by flat, scroll-shaped pieces of iron worn with the soft sheen of age and ancient use. The hands of faithful villagers and monks have smoothed the rings and the latches. Lowder is grateful for the soft, musty coolness that washes over him as he goes deeper into the church. He walks down the center aisle along the nave and sits on a simple pew. On either side of the altar are plain benches the monks use during daily masses.

Lowder notices that the usual cross and candlesticks are missing from the altar. Attached to the wall behind the altar is an elaborate gilt wood frame carved with lush foliate ornament rising up the sides and over the top of the surround. The frame is empty.

He gets up and walks into the choir to inspect the vacant frame. From the style and decoration of the altarpiece frame, as well as the size of the empty rectangle, Lowder speculates that the missing picture must have been of some significance to warrant such embellishment. Occasionally, ordinary churches were given fine paintings and other "embellishments" to honor a donor's favorite religious image, to venerate a patron saint, or perhaps to acknowledge a miracle that touched the donor or a family member. The ornate surround appears to be of a late seventeenth-century date because of its style, condition, and quality of the gilding; Lowder is certain that it is not a later reproduction copying an earlier style. He estimates that the displaced picture is at least three feet wide by four feet high. There is no indication that the frame was ever altered, as the ornament is uniform on all sides and corners. When complete, the altarpiece must have displayed sharp contrast to the simple interior and furnishings of the church.

Lowder retraces his steps down the nave and moves outside into the jarring sunlight. He pauses in front of the church and, shielding his eyes from the high noon sun, walks down the road. Why such an impressive altarpiece in a simple monastic church that also serves the small community as a parish church? Who would have taken the picture? A German soldier? For what purpose? Will it be recovered or abandoned by an enemy in flight?

Down the road a little beyond the church lies a farmhouse, a shed, and what looks to be a small barn—all built from local stone. A white horse paces rapidly up and down within a narrow fenced paddock, barren of grass. Lowder sees no signs of anyone in or around the farm buildings. The horse is clearly hungry. He watches him pause briefly at one end of his track, turn, and nervously jog down to the other end, keeping his head and shoulder expectantly to the fence. Lowder surmises that the horse was left in the paddock when the monks and villagers fled before the arrival of the Germans. He lets himself into the enclosure and enters the barn, leaving the top half of the barn door open so that he will be able to see in the shadowed musty building. Through the gloom he sees on the right some farm implements: a plow, shovels, pitchforks. Hung on the walls are the harnesses and tack with which the farmer had many times—judging by the worn state of repair of the horse fittings—rigged up the horse to open and harvest the ground.

To the left, Lowder can see two large bins stuffed with loose hay. *Feeding a horse on a deserted farm in the middle of a war zone.* He shakes his head, smiles, and moves over to the hay bins to gather a few armfuls for the horse. Lowder carries one load to the door of the barn, opens it halfway, and pitches the hay out in the middle of the small paddock.

As he returns for another bunch, his hands strike something hard in the middle of the bin about waist high off the floor. He reaches down into the tangled hay, and his hands feel a thin straight surface—wood, it seems—with pronounced edges. He lifts it up through the hay and over the edge of the hay bin. What he sees coming out of the hay is a rather large rectangular piece of wood, dark with age and slightly bowed, which he gently lowers, standing it on its edge on the earth floor. Lowder leans the panel against his legs and then picks it up, one hand on each side, lifting it on a slight angle. He uses the bin edge as support and rotates the rectangular board. Lowder catches his breath. His eyes are watering, his mouth dry. He whispers, "Holy Jesus Christ!"

Before him, within arm's length in a dusty, middle-of-nowhere Italian barn, is a startling painting of the Madonna and Child. Lowder is dumbfounded. The artist has depicted the infant Christ seated upon the Virgin's lap, reaching in a way as might any child in the same position, in a spontaneous, impulsive gesture, for what astonishingly is a beautifully observed and modeled cat. He's stunned. Remembered comparisons, related images appear and flit away in his mind. The trained art historian's instinct begins to analyze composition, the subject matter, and the one-off invention of the cat as the object of the Infant Christ's attention. He recalls the surviving drawings of the same subject that he knows so well and has studied carefully. Lowder's initial conclusion is that the inspiration for the image painted on the panel could have derived from no other source than the superbly inventive, complex mind of Leonardo da Vinci.

"My . . . God." He estimates that the size of the empty space of the frame in the church and the size of the painting before him are a match. The monks must have cleared the church of valuables for fear that the approaching German soldiers would take them.

On a hunch, Lowder walks over to the second hay bin and reaches down into it. His hand touches metal. He withdraws a simple silver cross, and, reaching down further, he discovers the communion service—chalice, cruet, and paten—in a plain fitted wooden box. Lowder puts those hidden pieces back in the bin where he has found them. He has studied and researched the work of Leonardo in some detail during the years of his postgraduate work, and after he continued his studies in Berlin before the war. He has seen the early *Virgin and Child with the Vase of Flowers* in Munich and also the "Dreyfus Madonna" in the National Gallery in Washington, both probably painted in the 1470s while Leonardo was in Florence. He has carefully studied photographs of other Leonardo paintings of the 1470s, and he knows other drawings attributed to the master. Lowder is unaware of a painted version of the Madonna with a cat, which only adds to his growing excitement.

The barn is dusty, and Lowder blinks to clear his eyes to better see the painting. Is this a sixteenth-century copy of a lost original by Leonardo? He is aware that many such Leonardo-related pictures exist that point at once to the legendary artist's influence as well as to his extraordinary wide range of inventions.

Indeed, to Lowder's eye, there is a pronounced unevenness and lack of integration in the elements of the painting and in its spatial conception. There are areas of flatness in the rendering where a sense of volume is called for. Student work? Clearly a good deal of the painting is occluded and distorted by the cloudy, dirty varnish applied many years ago. A later copy? How much later? Only careful research and technical analysis will perhaps bring some clarity. Someone should take this on, he thinks to himself. Lowder considers the inhabitants of the village who obviously consider the panel important enough to have hidden it in a hay bin. If he puts it back where he found it, the picture might be returned to its frame and to its position as a devotional object in the church. It might . . . but what if it doesn't? What if someone else accidentally finds the picture as he has just done? Or what if the Germans return or some strategic shift in this campaign brings destruction to the area?

Lowder looks at his watch: 1345 hours. Word of further orders will be coming in soon. He has to move. He hesitates and then rises and puts the panel back in the hay bin. He rearranges the hay so that the panel is well hidden, and he leaves the barn. That picture needs care, he hears himself saying. It needs saving. *If I march out of here, turn my back on it, that may be the end of it.* His rising need to do something—anything—works on him. He starts back to the church.

"Ray!" Lowder says quite loudly to himself. *Ray*, he thinks. Ray should see that picture there where he saw it. Ray Lowder, Glen's younger brother, is an art dealer who runs a small gallery in New York. He was denied enlistment because of chronic asthma. Ray and Glen are bound together by a brotherly bond and also by a common interest in art. Ray, the dealer, natural dealmaker, an eye for a buy; Glen the scholar, the guy with the theoretical mind, a tireless investigator of style and history. Would Ray agree that the panel should be taken out of here? Glen tells himself it is probably just a school piece, that there are many of them. Why else would it have been here in this village for so long? His mind circles the dilemma. The picture is a fascinating image, a bit rough, an interesting document, probably not worth a lot. How could he get it out of here? To Florence while they're chasing Germans? How could he get the picture to his brother?

Lowder's mind won't let go. He doesn't hear Jansen calling to him as he approaches the cloister where his men are sprawled with fatigue, many dozing in the afternoon sun.

"Captain?" Jansen calls out.

Lowder still has that image in his head.

"Captain! HQ wants to talk with you. They're on the radio in five!"

"Got it, Jansen, I'm there." Lowder snaps back to the present, walks over to his signalman, who is standing by for the call from HQ.

The camouflaged electronic box squawks; the signalman cranks the handle and hands the receiver over to Lowder.

"Echo, Lowder," he speaks loudly into the radio. "Over."

Headquarters advises Lowder that the Germans are still moving steadily north sixty miles from Lowder's position, definitely indicating retreat. The US strategy resembles something of a herding operation, like driving cattle into a box canyon; only the canyon wall in this case is a well-armed, well-prepared superior force south and west of Florence that will intercept the Germans in the next couple of days. Colonel Miller at Command north of Rome gives Lowder the good news that Echo Company can settle in until the next day and await the resupply convoy on its way from the south before Lowder's company will be ordered to pick up the march to Florence. Miller also tells Lowder that the convoy will transport some of his men in trucks and most of the way to Florence before Echo Company joins the rest of the battalion, augmented by two more for the push to Florence, which is still lightly occupied. The coming operation there is considered complicated and somewhat delicate because of the historical importance of the city. Lowder considers the project—liberating Florence—to be like the most demanding task of a surgeon, ridding that city's vital body of destructive elements without unduly sacrificing its integrity or endangering its cultural value.

When Captain Lowder gives the good news to his men, they cheer. He finds Jansen and goes over the sentry requirements and other security matters.

"The guys need a time-out," Jansen says, offering him a smoke.

Lowder accepts, taking a light from Jansen's battered Zippo.

"I guess we'll be seeing resupply and your buddy, Colonel Benson," Jansen says, his face lit up.

"Yup."

"How do you know Benson again?"

"Grew up together in New York City. Used to fish for bass and bluefish off the Long Island coast with my brother Ray. We lost track of one another after the US entered the war, but man did we have a reunion when we met up in Rome over the Fourth at the Officer's Club in Piazza Novana." Lowder contemplates how Benson was deployed as commander of the 43rd Quartermaster battalion, charged with supplying the sizeable US military commitment detailed to drive the Germans up the boot of Italy into the large force that awaited them. The story Benson told him was amazing: Benson said that after opening a food market chain, he enlisted in the Army, leaving a trusted cousin in charge of the food business. He was commissioned as a second lieutenant, was assigned to the Quartermaster Corps, and rapidly rose through the ranks to colonel because of his considerable experience in distribution systems and comestible management. Benson was recognized for his quick mind, personnel skills, gift of gab, and apparently miraculous ability to make what was needed available. He could move things through the Army labyrinth utilizing his limitless contacts, a ready list of favors owed to him which he called upon frequently and repaid in kind—not to mention his boundless energy and riotous sense of humor.

"I heard that early on in his rise, he could produce a chilled bottle of Dom Pérignon in the middle of the driest, humblest rural countryside," Jansen says.

"I don't doubt it. I'm looking forward as much as anybody to the QM's supply trucks and Benson's arrival," Lowder says, putting his cigarette out on a nearby rock and taking a moment to lie back on the ground for some rest.

It is late afternoon when the lookout in the monastery bell tower spots the eagerly awaited convoy from Rome. A cheer hails the trucks as they pull in and park in a field next to the church. There are sixteen trucks, one carrying infantry troops, two APCs providing protection for the trucks and personnel, and a jeep whose occupants are Colonel Benson and his top sergeant, a clever old career NCO named Mahoney. As the jeep rolls to a stop, Colonel Benson bounds out and hoots, "Lowder, you layabout. How do you expect to win the war idling about in quaint little villages?"

"We were waiting for your home cooking," Lowder says as he walks up to Benson and slaps him on the shoulder.

Benson puts his arm around Lowder's shoulder and takes him over to his jeep. In the back is a cardboard box with wine, coffee and cheeses—heavily wrapped, still cool. Benson hands Lowder a few large cigars.

"After supper." Benson winks. Lowder eyes the treasures hungrily but then beckons Benson toward the road.

"Frank, let's take a walk," he says. "I've got something to show you."

The two men walk to the enclosure where the white horse is dozing under a tree in the late afternoon heat. Lowder unlatches the gate. Benson shoots his friend a puzzled look.

Lowder leads the way into the barn and turns toward the hay bins. "Grab some hay." Lowder reaches into the bin and pulls out the painting and hands it to Benson.

"What's this?" Benson frowns.

"Gently. Get it down on the floor, the other side facing you."

Benson does so and then stands back from the panel, stares at it, says nothing further, and turns to Lowder, mouth agape, looking for an explanation.

"It's from the church up the road, from the altarpiece. The monks must have removed it to hide it from the Nazis. I found it a few hours ago. By accident."

"Do you think this is something important?" Benson asks.

"It's an old picture. I know for sure its composition, style, and subject matter derive from Leonardo da Vinci."

"Da Vinci?" Benson scratches his head.

"This may be an old copy by a student or follower. There are some things about it that don't add up."

Both men stand before the painting, the late afternoon light giving way to shadows and the setting sun. "I want to get it out of this war zone, out of this barn, and somehow to New York with Ray so I can study it." Lowder looks over at Benson for some sign or response.

Benson shakes his head. "Are you suggesting . . . ?"

"You can get it to New York through your network." Lowder looks hard at Benson.

Benson remains silent.

"I can't leave it here to be eaten by rats. It would be unethical. Listen, after the war we can figure out what to do with it, return it to the Italians, whatever needs to be done."

Benson is quiet, a bit subdued. Both men are a little unsettled.

"If you can find a way to get the picture to my brother," Lowder says. "I'll write Ray and tell him to put it away out of sight."

"You sure this sleight of hand is worth it?"

"Let's put the picture back in the bin for now," Lowder suggests. "After chow, we can come back and wrap it and put it in one of the deuce and a half's under a tarpaulin."

"Lowder, my ass could end up in a sling. You could get thrown in the slammer. Getting this thing to Rome is just the beginning."

The two men hoist the panel back in the hay bin and leave the barn.

By eleven that night, the picture is wrapped in official-looking cardboard, marked "maps," and protected and hidden in an extra canvas tent fly. It will be in Rome in a few days and on its way to New York shortly thereafter.

The next morning, Lowder and Benson finish coffee together. The resupply convoy is due to load up the mess tents and field kitchens before heading north with Lowder's men in additional trucks that have arrived at Ponte Albrizzi during the night.

Benson reaches his canteen cup toward Glen Lowder and clanks Lowder's cup in a toast.

"We're in it now, Glen"

"Thanks, Frank."

"I hope you're right that the picture will be better off." Benson pauses. "And I hope I'll be wearing colonel's leaves when I see your crazy mug again."

Benson sloshes out his cup with water from his canteen, salutes his friend, and heads toward his jeep. In a few moments, the convoy begins to move north. Lowder climbs into the cab of the lead truck, and the US Army leaves the little village of Ponte Albrizzi.

On September 14, Ray Lowder receives a large cardboard box containing a painting on a wooden panel depicting the Madonna with the Child on her lap reaching for a cat. There is no accompanying information except that it has been forwarded through the US Army Quartermaster system at the request of Colonel Frank Benson. It is delivered by Frank Benson's cousin into whose hands the package was placed by two QM enlisted men driving a small truck attached to a supply depot in New Jersey.

On December 10, the US Army informs Ray Lowder that his brother, Glen Lowder, has been killed in France.

Frank Benson, Colonel, US Army Quartermaster Corps, dies near Paris shortly after the liberation of the city in an automobile accident following a good deal of celebration of the Allied victory in France.

CHAPTER FIFTEEN

Sam takes the stairs up to the reading room of the Frick Art Reference Library. He once more requests the Leonardo monographs and several volumes illustrating Leonardo's drawings.

"My," the young man in charge of circulation says, "there sure is a lot of interest in Leonardo these days."

Ricci's people, Sam thinks. "The best-known artist in the Western world, I heard once or twice."

The librarian smiles. "We'll have these ready in about ten minutes."

"Thanks very much. I'll be at the far table in the corner."

"We'll find you."

The books arrive, and Sam notes again that among the drawings that survive in various collections are eight that explore the theme of the Virgin and Child with a cat. Additionally, one of those is clearly a larger image, more carefully drawn, possibly closer to a finished composition. To Sam that drawing seems more deliberate and resolved, sure in the definition of the image in comparison to the looser, more exploratory studies of the same subject. And, comparing it to the photo of the panel, it is generally closer than the others in the arrangement of its main elements. Gloomily, Sam considers that Ricci's research assistants have most likely noted the same similarities based on the same references spread before Sam on the library table.

Sam returns the books to the trolley and thanks the librarian. Outside, he steps into the warmth of spring in New York; every available planter on Madison Avenue bursts with tulips, daffodils, and hyacinths. A carpet of neat rows of red, pink, and orange tulips unfolds down Park Avenue. Sam looks up and sees the very same model of limousine parked outside the Frick as the one that was parked outside of Lowder's gallery several days before. The door opens and Ricci steps out.

Sam's stomach turns. There is a lot that Sam would rather do than play games with Ricci. However, with Tom's interest in the panel Ricci now owns, the stakes are high.

Ricci sits down on a park bench and pulls out a cigarette. As Ricci settles deeper in the bench, he crosses his legs. Ricci is "dug in." His advantage. Ricci knows that Sam has seen him. Sam has no option but to approach the man.

"Were you researching the panel?"

Sam clears his throat. "Mark, Tom is quite interested in it."

Mark Ricci fixes his gaze on Sam. He presses his fingertips together, a parody of hands in an attitude of prayer just touching his chin, his cigarette dangling from his lips. He stares at Sam, silent for several beats.

"Are you following me?" Sam asks.

"I got wind that you have been stomping all over town rooting up the provenance on my painting."

"What, do you have the Frick wired?"

"Be careful about prying too much into the provenance. I am protective of my paintings. You visited Lowder the other day, didn't you?"

"Yes, that was a routine call for me."

"If you want this painting, you have to play by my rules. Do we understand each other?"

"I'm not sure I do," Sam says, keeping his voice casual.

"I don't want you speaking to Lowder again. If you speak to him again, Tom loses first rights to the panel."

Sam stares down at a red tulip that is drooping in the early summer heat.

"Sam, I have a hunch it's the real thing. I said so the other day, and from what George Wilson is finding beneath the surface of the painting, I'm becoming more and more convinced."

"What is he finding?"

"X-rays clearly show another image beneath the visible one that differs in small but clear ways from what you see in the picture's present state."

"What about infrared reflectography?" Sam asks.

"I sent the picture over to the Met last week with five thousand dollars for some lab equipment they need. The radiography confirms an image under the visible surface. Just as I expected," Ricci purrs.

"How far has Wilson gotten with his work on the top surface?"

Ricci ignores Sam's question. "And the panel is poplar, with a clean split down the middle."

"How fa . . ."

"Carbon-14 tests place the panel at 1500 plus or minus one hundred years. As I said it's poplar, always a good sign, and so is the cradle. It tests out too. And Wilson found a small burned-in stamp with initials on one of the battens. PM or RM—hard to read."

"Mark, I'd like to have a look at the panel at Wilson's studio."

Again, silence, the contrived pose of the hands. "If there is serious interest, I'd say okay. Two conditions. Tom doesn't see the picture in this state of conservation. You know what you're looking at. Tom wouldn't understand what's going on. Second condition: you back off on Lowder."

"Agreed."

"I'll ring Wilson and tell him to expect your call." Ricci writes something down on a piece of paper. "Sam, I'd better prepare you. If this picture turns out the way I think it will, the price will be astronomical."

"What do you mean by astronomical?"

"Think one and a half, two hundred million, more." Ricci has always felt slick to Sam, but in that moment his voice sounds almost threatening. As if Ricci can sense how he's coming across, he changes tack. "But it's way too early for that kind of discussion. Have a look and let me know what you think. If a Picasso 'Rose period' picture fetches one hundred four million . . ." Ricci rises up off the bench and extends his hand. Meeting over.

Wilson works in a brick building just off Third Avenue. The building also houses a large upholstery shop and a distributor of small electronic devices—tiny flashlights, beeping key finders, and other necessities that US buyers did not know they needed until they saw them advertised on TV. All of this is good cover. In fact, Alain Bovin's restoration studio is in a similar setting on 83rd off Third Avenue.

Sam takes the elevator to the third floor where George Wilson's studio is located behind a triple-locked door just down the hall from the electronic gewgaw business.

Wilson comes to the door and starts the series of key turns and the release of the standard thick-doweled steel door jammer, capable of preventing a tank from gaining unauthorized entry.

"Sam. Come on in. I'm taking a small break from chipping away on that bloody panel—come and look."

George leads Sam through a short maze-like path past and around several easels with paintings in various states of "undress." He stops in front of the panel of the *Virgin and Child with a Cat*.

"Well, there she is. The 'cat lady' slowly giving up her secrets."

Wilson has opened up four areas on the painting surface; the largest is approximately eight inches square. That one is at the lower right corner of the panel where the Madonna's blue drapery eddies on the edge of the platform upon which Mary sits, falling to the lower limit of the picture. Another "window" is at the junction of the Child's hand and the body of the cat, which he gently restrains. A third opening is at the junction of the Madonna's left shoulder where the dress meets the baby's skin between shoulder and neck. The fourth and slightly larger opening into the image below is the edge of the Mother's forehead where it meets the darker background, picture right.

Wilson directs Sam's attention to a small beaker and a circular metal container in which a cluster of cotton swabs are set like a bouquet of small white blooms.

"That is a very gentle solvent which, when diluted and applied with a swab ever so gently, causes the top layer of paint to soften somewhat and loosen some of its adhesion to the primary painted surface below."

"Sounds like the conservator's magic elixir. Have you used it before?"

"No, not in this reduced strength. Too strong, it can dissolve an area of paint. Too weak and nothing really happens. It's too soon to determine the ongoing chemical reaction and future result. I might add that age has naturally consolidated the old paint surface that we see. It has been subjected to change and stress from changing atmospheric conditions that the level just below has not been exposed to over the years."

"You're saying that the top layers of paint over many years kind of petrify as living wood does."

"Yes, kind of like that." Wilson nods. "And I've used one other little trick to lift the top surface off the painting below."

Sam is spellbound by the insider look at the craft.

"Just before I take a little off the top surface, right on the spot I've dabbed with diluted solvent, I wait about thirty seconds, then apply a little spritz of liquid nitrogen, which atomizes when it is released into ambient air. The nitrogen freezes the small section, just a dash of the stuff. It causes the target area to contract, to shrink a bit."

"Dermatologists have been removing skin cancers and whatnot this way for years," Sam says.

"Exactly. Anyway, the spot of paint that I want to remove with the scalpel picks off a bit more easily. Understand? Look, I'll show you."

Wilson applies his secret method in the quadrant in which he had been concentrating. After about thirty seconds, he carefully picks at the edge where the undersurface is exposed. Sam watches as less than a centimeter of the covering layer comes away, falling lightly into a trough of soft white paper attached to the easel, its upper edge flush with the panel surface.

"Wow," says Sam in astonishment.

"It's not risk-free," Wilson continues, "but controlled application of this sleight-of-hand method seems to work quite well. A bit of a high-wire act."

"But you seem encouraged and confident for the moment that the picture will not dissolve before your very eyes."

"So far." Wilson holds up his crossed fingers. "I'm going to give it a week's rest to make sure that this remedy is stable and can be controlled."

"Ricci will be breathing down your neck."

"I have no doubt," Wilson says, shaking his head ruefully. "If he doesn't like this cautionary program, he can get someone else to take on the picture. But he won't—I think we've got a winning solution here."

"Will you let me know what happens in a week's time?"

"I will," Wilson says softly, preoccupied, gazing at the panel as if it exerts some kind of magnetic attraction upon him.

CHAPTER SIXTEEN

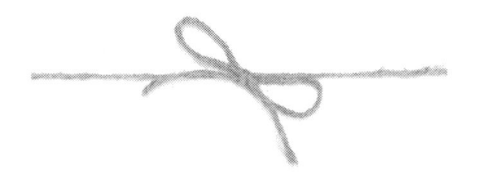

Sam and his friend Ken Taylor tack as they make their way out from Stonington's harbor aboard *Silkie*. Sam pulls in the mainsheet and Ken hikes farther out to windward to help keep the boat flat. There's a nice breeze blowing—ten knots easy—and you can see the whitecaps beginning to form way off in the distance. Sam feels better out there on *Silkie* than he has in a long time.

"*Silkie*'s a fine vessel, isn't she?" Ken says. Sam appreciates the easy conversation, counts Ken as one of his dearest friends. They met quite a long time ago when Ken was lecturing about Italian mannerism in a gallery that Sam visited. Sam was carried away by the NYU professor's stirring analysis of a Pontormo painting, and they've been friends ever since.

"You see that seal?" Sam points at a dark spot on the water several meters in front of the bow.

"You sure it's not a porpoise?"

"Could be," Sam says. "I didn't see a fin, though." He eases the mainsheet out as he heads downwind, and he instructs Ken to let out the staysail and the jib sheets. The boat flattens out and picks up speed, gliding along effortlessly. "We could buzz the lighthouse if you want," Sam says.

"Let's do it." Ken grins.

Sam listens to the waves hitting the bottom of the boat. It is a sound he could listen to for days on end and never be bored.

"How much does it cost you to keep her going from one year to the next?" Ken asks.

"I don't know, maybe two, three grand a year."

"You got the upkeep on that cabin in Wyoming too."

"I know. It's worth it, though."

"Mr. Big must be keeping you flush with cash."

"Depends on your definition of flush."

"When are you headed out there next?"

"Fall's my favorite time. I love it when the elk are rutting. Back in the fall's when I used to go there hunting; it felt like that cool air wanted to slice you apart. I swear, being on a hunting expedition is like being reborn all over again. Somehow it cuts you open into someone different, perhaps even gentler. You know what I mean?"

"No, I guess I don't. Maybe the closest I've come is skiing. But no, never had anything cut me apart at all, aside from being a father. Being a father will change you."

Sam nods.

"Sam, tell me about the painting you've been researching."

"Sure." Sam cleats the mainsheet and leans forward to take a folder out of his Gore-Tex bag. He hands the folder to Ken, who sits deeper in the cockpit as he opens it. One of Wilson's photos documenting the changing state of the picture sits on top of the file. There are close-ups of the openings in the top surface showing sections of the painting underneath.

Ken emits a long, low whistle as he stares at the photo. "Am I looking at what I think I'm looking at?"

"Depends." Sam watches the mainsail and adjusts his course slightly, aiming for the southern end of Hog Island.

Ken looks up and gazes at the water. "Let me have a minute," he says. The wind is whipping the water apart in a million different angles. As he watches the water, his mind clears. Finally Ken says, "Okay, Leonardesque. Somebody like Francesco Melzi. Not nineteenth century. First time I've seen this subject as a painting."

"Keep going," Sam urges, smiling.

"Drawings of the Virgin and Child with a cat, several early on usually dated before the old boy goes to Milan the first time . . . 1478, 1480 or so. Okay. Some in the Uffizi. Three? Three in the British Museum."

"There are also sketches of cats—just cats—as late as 1515," Sam adds.

"Okay, let's see." Ken pauses in midsentence. "This looks later than the 1480s. It also looks like a Leonardo follower, but more derivative than close. Do you know what I mean?"

"Exactly."

"Are you worried about the saltwater getting on these?"

"A drop won't matter, but good God man, keep them dry." Sam laughs.

With his back to the water, Ken flattens one of the pictures out on the bottom of the cockpit and stares hard at it. "So what is going on in these openings on the present surface? From what I can make out, and it's very little, the patch shows Leonardo-style drapery, intense blues, certainly that ultramarine lapis blue. And from what I can see based on one, two bits of drapery fold, I would be open to the possibility that there is an autograph Leonardo underneath the top surface. How am I doing?"

"You're on the money, as I expected you would be." Sam's skin is warming where the sun strikes his arms. It feels good.

"Any more surprises?"

"Yes." Sam keeps his eyes on Hog Island. "Just that the painting was photographed, infrared imaged, X-rayed once a few days ago. And then Wilson has a pal at Mt. Sinai Hospital who is a radiologist who never got over his undergraduate plunge into art history. They have this new technology that allows a deeper kind of scan than an MRI scan. Wait for this."

Ken is entranced by the photograph. "Go on."

"This machine can distinguish animal, vegetable, mineral layers—metal, plastic, rock, you name it. The people who do this can scan each level separately."

Sam changes course slightly and pulls the mainsheet in by several inches. "Wilson, risking Ricci's wrath, a lawsuit, calamity, certain death, wound the panel in bubble wrap, tied it with a string handle, and schlepped it over to the hospital radiology lab."

"A milestone in the evolution of secure art handling," Ken says with a smirk.

Sam nods as he watches a boat tack in the distance. The breeze looks better out there. "Anyway, Wilson's friend took pictures during a slow moment at the hospital yesterday. Wilson showed me the films this morning. There is a painting beneath the second layer, a shadow, but readable."

"God."

"When have you heard of a picture, possibly by a great artist, bearing three renditions of the same subject on one canvas or panel?"

"Counting the top surface, which we agree is the work of a Leonardo follower," Ken answers. "Three campaigns? Not ever in the case of a major master. There are old icons that were occasionally painted over and over on the same support, but that's all that I can come up with."

"Same here."

"What did the films show?"

"Level one, working up to the top layer, is clearly an image of the Madonna and the Little One, who holds a cat. Somewhat similar to the Hermitage Benois Madonna in pose. The Virgin inclines to viewer's right, the Child to viewer's right. The Baby holds a seemingly agitated cat, who also faces right. In the background right, you can make out a double-arched window, can you see?" Sam leans into the cockpit, reaches over to the folder, turning the color print of the panel in its present state facedown. Now Ken sees a photocopy of a Leonardo drawing. "Somewhat like this drawing in the British Museum. Look."

He studies the radiograph image of a Leonardo drawing resembling Sam's description. Paper-clipped to it is a small color reproduction of the Benois Madonna in the Hermitage in St. Petersburg.

"Next scanned image Wilson shows me is a different arrangement, similar to this drawing."

Sam flips over the British Museum photocopy, careful to keep it dry despite the moisture coming in off the leeward side of the boat. "That one," Sam points to another image, "which differs from the preceding one. This one shows the placement of the Virgin looking down and viewer right, the plump and healthy Child looks left in pronounced *contrapposto* as he holds the cat, which is apparently leaning toward viewer right, itself perhaps in a *contrapposto*."

"I follow you," Ken says. "So level two resembles the drawing in front of me."

"Yes, that one is in Florence, the Uffizi. I think you'll agree that it is nowhere near so sketchy as the first I showed you. For that matter, it is more direct and sure than any of the other sketches of the subject that I can find."

"I would agree with that," Ken says, closing the folder and beginning to make a sandwich out of a piece of salami and cheese that he pulls from a small cooler. "Amazing how good food tastes out here on the open water, isn't it?"

"Yes, agreed."

Ken wipes his hands on his shorts. "So to clarify, the second scanned image suggests a composition similar to this Uffizi drawing, which in turn corresponds fairly closely to the panel that Wilson is working on—this image at the beginning of the file here. The top level that we see now should most surely be considered as being after Leonardo. Fascinating puzzle. Never seen anything like this," Ken says, staring at the Wilson photo.

"Nor have I." About twenty feet out a Boston Whaler buzzes by. A young man waves and Sam and Ken wave back.

"What about the first image beneath the others? Is Ricci aware of it?"

"I think he might suspect it's there. That's what he hired Wilson to find out."

"Sam, what do you think about all this?" Ken opens the folder again and studies the photo of the picture in its present state.

"I think that the justification for the removal of the Leonardo follower's picture is sound, Francesco Melzi or not. After all, it's been photographed, and the image survives as an important document." Sam is cutting the shoreline close there, and they can both hear the sound of the waves lapping the big rocks.

"I agree," Ken says. "Relieving the top layer will reveal what will probably be a beautiful and terribly important autograph picture of what may have been one of Leonardo's favorite subjects, and it will probably end up being in excellent condition—because it has been covered up since the late fifteenth or early sixteenth century. And we have proof of the nature of the original composition."

"Leonardo hits a triple. Art history wins." Sam turns his gaze back up to the mainsail.

"What do you think of Wilson's plan to keep the evidence of the first composition all to himself?" Ken asks.

Sam pauses for a moment. "Tough call. But I think Wilson's plan is inspired and courageous. He's doing a service to the history of art, to students and museum goers."

"What do you *really* think?" Ken asks with a big smile.

"I think Ricci would screw the picture up."

"Well, such as I know and have heard of the man, I agree."

"I've dealt with Ricci for years, Ken." Sam looks around to make sure there's plenty of water beneath them. "There have been stories about people who stepped on Ricci's toes."

"Does he negotiate?"

"Yep, some." Sam takes a bite of the cheese Ken hands him. "I think he and Tom enjoy the sparring, the contest." Sam adjusts the tiller.

Ken lays into his sandwich. "These paintings bewitch us. They dare us to do everything we can to enable them to talk. We're stuck in present time, yearning to see and understand as did artists, patrons, society in the days when they were made. Ultimately, I don't give a damn what the picture's worth, what it cost, what it will sell for. What it *has* sold for."

"You've hit a sensitive nerve here, Ken." Sam stares off toward the lighthouse. They are closing in on it now. "Really. I feel that more and more strongly. It's as if the painting or work of art has too often been kind of monetized, so that its commercial value becomes the primary consideration. This is why I go to the Met or the Frick and just look at things without the distractions of negotiating, the buying and selling. The bullshit."

"I do the same thing and for one other reason."

"That is?" Sam asks, glancing at his compass.

"I get to look at a picture, let's say, and I concentrate on the *facture*, the gestures, strokes, painterly responses, a heavy passage, a flick of the brush."

"Kind of as if the painting dissolves in a way, then recreates itself." That is what the waves are doing in that instant.

"Exactly, Sam, exactly. And then you can experience it in a way deeper than just the perception of an artifact or an artistic . . . journey. Here it is, sum of all parts, the result of countless small and greater gestures in a painterly sense. And knowing the artist's ways in many cases, you can intuitively experience those smaller and larger actions of the picture, not only as a finished result but also as an evident process of conscious and unconscious actions—events—as many as it took to bring the picture to the state you see before you."

"I get it, Ken, and that way of looking, searching, exploring, focusing even—opening to empathy in the truest sense—is ultimately why we keep discovering, why we do what we do and feel we must try to do it."

"This is none of my business, but . . ."

Sam interrupts the question that Ken is about to ask. "One hundred fifty to two hundred million for openers."

Ken whistles softly in reply, shaking his head. "Do you ever worry you might be in danger? That's a lot of money."

Sam looks away. "Well, for example, what I just told you, Ken, I never told you."

"No question about that, Sam."

"So back to the provenance. Frankly, I think what little I've learned is made up. All I have is 'old European private collection.' To an American dealer in 1947. To Ricci less than a month ago."

"Not much." Ken adjusts the jib. "Sam, I've got an idea."

"Say on . . ."

"I know this priest in Florence. He's a Jesuit and a damn good art historian. He teaches in Florence, knows the archives, and has access to a lot of information, including where a lot of things are located."

"Sounds invaluable."

"I know him quite well. He's helped me in the past with questions about Masaccio, for instance, and another bunch of research I was doing on Verrocchio. He keeps up with current scholarship, research on all levels. I could put you in touch."

"Please do." Sam pauses. "To protect my client, could you describe my project as having to do with a broad interest in Leonardo's early and midlife pictures?"

"Yes, that would be all I'd need to specify your focus."

"Could you get in touch with him . . . soon?"

"Yes, of course." Ken holds his arms out as if to embrace the lighthouse as they go blasting past it with the wind.

CHAPTER SEVENTEEN

Sam sits in the boardroom adjoining Tom's office. It is a gray day. The dense clouds envelop the glass-walled building. From the forty-seventh floor, the outlook toward the Hudson is obscured. Sam feels the clouds crowding in on him.

"It won't be time wasted," Sam says.

"What'll you do there?" Tom asks.

"Perhaps the most valuable part of the trip will be spending time in the Florence and regional archives, not to mention visiting with the archivists."

"What's in the archives?"

"The possible mention of a name, an event, a transaction, the chance that something turns up that has not yet been considered in the context of Leonardo, or the appearance of paintings of a Madonna and Child—common enough—but in this instance accompanied by a cryptic third presence: the cat."

"What does the cat signify?"

"I wish I knew. That feature is rare even when you consider the iconography of the Madonna and Child in all its various representations."

"What do you mean by . . . iconography?"

Sam pauses. "Basically, the term means the study of imagery expressed in the form of sculpture, painting, decorative arts, and manuscripts."

"Go on," Tom says.

"That's about it. The term most frequently refers to religious imagery. Christian, Jewish, Buddhist."

"I get it. I should know these things. Bottom line, Sam, I don't think this trip is necessary."

"Why not? We don't have anything pressing here. I could do it in a week. Meanwhile, Wilson will have removed a good deal more of the top surface."

"No, I don't want you dredging up any information that would put this deal in peril."

"But if there is any such information, wouldn't you want me to find it before you close the deal? If there's information that I could come across, it means the Italian authorities—anyone really—could also come across it."

"No, Sam. I'll handle this risk."

"But, Tom, I think that's a little reckless. If this turns out to be a Leonardo, and if you buy this painting, the Italians are going to be crawling all over their archives to see if they can get it back."

"I said no, Sam. I want to buy this thing. If you dredge up something that would upset Sylvie or prejudice the deal, this whole project could go under. That's a hard no."

Sam steps back toward the gray wall of clouds behind him.

"Oh, and Sam, give Ricci a call and make sure that our first refusal is in place."

"Tom, I'm sure that he—"

"Call him. You never can be too sure with Ricci."

"Okay, Tom. Okay. If you don't hear from me, assume that the agreement, such as it is, is in place."

"Right," says Tom brusquely, turning to leave for a meeting.

Sam can just imagine Ricci licking his chops.

CHAPTER EIGHTEEN

Sam stares out the train window. The press of buildings starts to give way to flashes of water in the distance. Gradually, longer stretches of the edge of Long Island Sound replace the urban sprawl. Sam takes his cell phone out of his pocket. He stares at it like it's a coiled snake, looks out the window. Then he dials Ricci.

"Mark, Tom would like me to confirm that we have first right of refusal on the panel should it turn out to be a Leonardo."

"I told you and Tom that you get first crack at the picture—if it turns out the way I think it will."

Sam hates these calls; they only make Tom look desperate for the painting. Another score for Ricci. "Oh, one more thing, Mark." Sam can't help himself. "Anything to add to the question of the painting's history?"

"No, Sam, I've told you more than a few times now. All I have on the provenance is New York trade acquired from a European couple who brought it to the States after the war. There is no more."

"Do we know where the couple sold the painting to the trade and when?"

Ricci takes a moment to answer. "I've told you all I know, and you already know from your own snooping who the dealer was."

"One dealer, or was it passed on to another dealer after the first one?"

"I never said there was another dealer involved."

"I never said you did. I was just asking. The provenance is a little spare."

"You have all the provenance I can give you, Sam. I suggest you drop it."

"It's part of my job to learn about provenance."

"Suit yourself."

"Okay, Mark, I'll pass this on to Tom."

"Be my guest. Sam, the point here is the painting. Nothing will change that. I've got another call." Ricci hangs up on him.

The long views extending east continue as the train heads north to Stamford and then New Haven. Sam starts to relax. In two days he will be on his way to Florence to meet with Ken Taylor's good friend, the art historian Father Anselmo. He had already booked the tickets before Tom told him "no," and he is hell-bent on going. Sam feels strangely at ease with his decision to ignore Tom. He's never done anything like it before, and yet it feels right. The repetitious sounds of the train underway and the fast-forward play of the familiar landscape unfolding at over a hundred miles an hour are hypnotic. Sam puts aside his current copy of *Art and Auction*, draws a deep breath, and closes his eyes, knowing that the conductor will gently wake him as the train pulls into New London.

The tinkly, electronic reproduction of a fragmented Schubert theme sounds, then repeats itself as Sam gropes for the phone in his briefcase. "Hello." Sam can't cobble together any cheeriness.

"Sam, it's Ken."

"What's up?"

"Good news. I got a hold of Father Anselmo and gave him the dates you're planning to be in Florence, told him that you were coming over to do some research on a painting that seems to have to do with one of the scores of Leonardo followers."

"What was his reaction?"

"Well, as I told you he is a pretty decent, sensible, and serious art historian. So the mention of that 'L' word didn't seem to excite him particularly."

"No notable reaction?"

"No, not at all," Ken says. "That's him—a straight shooter whose job in the church universe is that of an art historian and teacher."

"Ken, it would be great if you could skip school and sneak off to Florence. It would be a treat to look at pictures with you."

"Nothing would please me more, Sam. I'm feeling overwhelmed by my administrative duties, though."

"Solidarity, my friend."

"I envy you—free as a bird, no committee meetings, performance evaluations, and on and on."

"Ken, I'm losing the cell signal a bit."

"Hey, I've got one more thing for you."

"Say on, professor."

"Well . . ." Ken pauses. "It's like this. One of my graduate students did a really good seminar paper on Leonardo's followers last year."

"Oh?"

"Well, I was going back over that paper, and I looked hard at one of the illustrations supporting her discussions of Leonardo links, possibly lost pictures by the old boy, you know, that line of inquiry."

Sam's excitement rises.

"I needn't send you the whole paper, but as I was going over it again, I came across one image that grabbed my attention. I've scanned it and emailed it to you. Have a look at it when you get home," Ken says.

"But I can't wait that long. Apologies for my . . . my mania."

"At least it's not absolute monomania." Ken laughs.

"Yes, there are things that give rise to monomania—single malt whiskey, beautiful, intelligent women, simple yet superb Italian cooking . . ."

"Whoa, you've got the first two and are about to set yourself up for the third. Hey, how are you and Cassie doing?"

"Ken!" Sam says. "Describe the damn thing to me. Please."

"Just teasing you. Okay. Typical Leonardesque Virgin, very Leonardesque face, figure turned slightly to viewer's left. She holds the child Christ, also very

Leonardesque features, also inclined to viewer's left. The Christ embraces a lamb, almost as large as the Child. The Virgin has a hand on the lamb as if also embracing the animal."

"Symbolizing St. John the Baptist," Sam interjects. "Christ as the Lamb of God, the sacrificial Lamb, et cetera, et cetera, traditional and at that time current iconography."

"Yeah, but wait. First, the composition in this photograph before me is close to the British Museum Leonardo drawing of the Virgin and Child with a cat, which was among the reproductions you sent me."

"Fascinating. I wish I had the file with me."

"There's more, Sam."

Sam frets. How long will the damn cell signal hold up? Sure enough, the signal gives out. He looks out the window then keeps glancing back at his phone to see if he can get the signal back. A couple bars pop up. A text appears on his screen with an image Ken has sent him. Sam's heart picks up speed as he enlarges the image. The lamb in the picture is three-quarters the size of the Christ, maybe a little less. His head is weirdly twisted to align with the Child's head, as if the animal's head was cranked completely around, even as one sees the hind legs and tail of the lamb facing to the rear of the picture.

To Sam, the body of the lamb looks quite unlamb-like. The beast seems, at least from the reproduction, gray rather than white and furry rather than woolly.

Sam calls Ken. "Ken, I opened the photo."

"Can you believe it?"

"Astounding."

"You ready for the last whopper of a revelation about this picture," Ken asks, "by *uno seguace di Leonardo*?"

"*Certo. Da me tutto*," Sam says. "I'm running out of signal bars on my phone. Quick!"

"This picture is in the Brera, the Pinacoteca room XIX. I've got the catalogue in front of me. '*Virgin and Child and the Lamb*. Tempera and oil on panel. 68 x 52 centimeters. Acquired in 1891.' I'll email the entry, but not before I quote a passage from the catalogue:

The composition is, in fact, based on the drawings by Leonardo for the *Madonna with the Cat* (British Museum, London, and Uffizi, Florence), which are characterized by notable dynamism. The cat struggling to free itself in Leonardo's drawing is replaced here by the lamb, the symbol of Christ's sacrifice. Nevertheless, recent X-ray analyses have demonstrated the existence, under the layer of paint, of a previous version of the picture, in which the form of a cat is visible. Thus the artist who painted this picture, which is remarkable for the gentleness and grace of the Virgin and the enamel-like surface of the paint, had evidently seen Leonardo's paintings. This may have occurred in Florence, towards 1505, when we know that a certain "Ferrando spagnolo"—Fernando de Llanos, or perhaps Fernando Yáñez de la Almedina, who was responsible for a similar painting now in the National Gallery in Washington—was one of the assistants working with Leonardo on the *Battle of Anghiari*.

Silence.

"Sam, did I lose you? Sam?"

"No, Ken, I'm in shock."

"I imagined you would be. I guess you'll be off to the Brera on your Italian odyssey."

"Now we can at least propose with some evidence that Leonardo may well have executed a composition of *The Virgin and Child with a Cat* of which the Brera piece may be a later repetition. Aye-yi-yi."

"Aye-yi-yi is about right, Sam. So now there is even greater significance for your Leonardo project: expanded context suggesting that these sketches of the Virgin and Child with a cat that you sent me were probably not mere doodles with no further development. They led somewhere, and that somewhere may be the picture that Ricci is sitting on."

As Ken talks, Sam gazes at the approaching shoreline that points to home. For him, this is what working in the art trade is all about.

CHAPTER NINETEEN

Home at Stonington after the train from New York, Sam sits at his desk texting a massive letter to Cassie. She is always pushing him to further his art career, and he wants her to understand the things in his career that have disillusioned him. He needs her to get it. It seems vitally important. With the dogs lounging at his feet, he continues to write:

> Cass, aye-yi-yi. Saved by a glass of wine, I was at an opening earlier today—a show which presented a much heralded (before the event) buzz of critical babble presented by shoulder-to-shoulder, belly-to-back attendees looking at walls. Everywhere the clogged gaggle of chatters in three rooms, maybe one or two attendees looking at the installation. Boxes. 51 used and damaged heavy cardboard vegetable and fruit crates in a 3-room gallery. That was the installation. It was a much hyped debut of an unknown whose fix in this event was, as the show title suggests, empty containers. WHAT A CHALLENGE for the eye and mind of the beholder. Well . . . I guess. Perhaps the challenge was even greater

for the artist person who claims to have hauled the boxes in after some unspecified period of usefulness out in the world. There was evidence of wear and tear on the boxes, so I can guess about the unknown history of same—not mentioned in the 23-page illustrated catalogue (fitted with cardboard box covers) bearing visible words and numbers surely rescued and genuine.

I can imagine, say, one of the, uh, pieces carefully packed and protected headed for California, in a large cardboard box cozily packed with another in a sturdy wooden shipping container.

I have visions of Leonardo wandering into the gallery instantly aware that no one is looking at the boxes. They are just yammering and chattering, sloshing down cheap champagne. Horrified Leonardo turns back through the door through which he wandered. The place and its crowd are a vision of hell. God, Cass, I've worn out my texting thumb and I have a sense of how screwy all of this is. My next book is going to be my view of where art is going after all these centuries since Lascaux (caves of Lascaux).

Sam stares at the screen, surprised by what he has written. He had no idea how badly he wants to leave New York. He could go on about how he feels about having to work for people who are so concerned about art as trophy, but Cass has heard all that too. Sam has not yet told Cassie about the upcoming trip to Italy because of the urgency that has given rise to that project and Tom's opposition to the idea. And yet now that he has written and sent the text, he feels somehow more intimate with Cassie. He wants to invite her on the journey. He decides to call her.

Sam turns and sinks into the old leather easy chair, beside which the phone rests on a rugged table of silvered oak. He remembers the warm spring afternoon in the Cotswolds when, on a wander with Cassie, he discovered that piece in the back of one of the many antique shops on a village high street. It was the silverish color and patina of age, its roughhewn form, probably just a plain farm table—maybe built to support a chopping block in a humble seventeenth-century farm cottage—that seduced him. For two hundred sixty pounds, he brought it home to stand here next to his favorite chair. Sam loves the honest simplicity of that table neatly joined and pegged. He feels close to Cassie when he looks at it.

Sam dials Cassie's cell phone number. Two rings. Then, "Hi Sam."

"Hi Cass. How's it all going?"

"A five-ring circus, complete with unruly crowds and occasional power failures." Sam has always felt that she has a penchant for calamities and a need to demonstrate that she will prevail over them.

"So the show goes on," Sam says.

"The show goes on," Cassie repeats.

"Did you get my text?"

"Yes, it's huge, too big to read now. I've just got a moment. They're setting up the gambling tables and the chip booths and briefing the actors. Las Vegas in the middle of Boston."

"That *was* great when you put it on last summer. And those pencil-thin mustached guys with slick hair and top hats. And the babes with cantilevered breasts and net stockings. Your clients loved it, as I recall."

"They did."

"Whatever works," Sam says. "Cass, I've got to go to Italy tomorrow, for about a week, maybe more."

Silence on Cassie's end. "Just like that? What's going on?"

"Well, the lure of Leonardo. Baxter doesn't want me to go, so I'm paying out of pocket. Florence is the target. Ken Taylor has hooked me up with a Jesuit art historian who may be able to lead me to information, images, archival stuff that might illuminate what we've got in this mystery panel and fill in some of the questions about its history. Mark Ricci has not been particularly diligent in his research, or at least he hasn't volunteered any revealing or confirmed findings."

"But Tom doesn't want you to go?"

"No, he's afraid of what I may uncover."

"So why upset him, Sam? He's your best client. Without him, you could never buy the art you buy. The game you're in is astounding, and he's the key to you getting to play."

"But, Cass, what if there's something in the provenance that's shady?"

"Do you really want to unearth that?"

"Yes, I do. Listen, Cass, I was hoping you would come with me to Florence."

"Sam, that's crazy. I can't leave my work for that long. I have a big event coming up."

"You've always got a big event, Cass. Come on. Get one of your assistants to pull it off. I want the romantic you that wants to run off for five days to Florence with me."

"Sam, I've got the German pharmaceutical guys this weekend, and then the think-tank people early next week. If you want me for five days, book me a year out."

"God, Cassie. Where's your sense of adventure?"

"Work is my adventure. You'd bore of me lounging around the way some of your friends' wives do." She pauses. "But seriously, Sam, consider the last time we were together. I told you I needed space."

"Yes, you did say that. So here we are."

"It might be good for us, the space."

"Well, I don't know about the space, but I've got to dive into this mystery picture. It can only be done in Italy. The time is now."

"Sam, I wouldn't do this if I were you."

"I bought my tickets."

"All right. Good luck then." She pauses. "God, I'm just feeling pulled in too many ways. Like your Flemish painting in your old museum."

"You mean the *Martyrdom of St. Hippolytus*. Yes, Flemish, about 1400. Four horses headed in four directions pulling ropes tied to the guy's hands and feet."

"Sam, I've got to go. I'm holding up my own show."

"Okay, Cass. We'll talk when it makes sense."

CHAPTER TWENTY

A litalia 250 New York JFK to Milan. Transfer to Florence. Arrival in Florence: 10:50 a.m.

Sam boards with Zone 3, makes his way to 21A, a window seat. He settles into his seat, noting that so far the aisle seat is unoccupied. Good book in his lap (James Salter, *A Sport and a Pastime*). Also at hand: a cadre of pens, red, blue, black, a yellow highlighter, and a folding leather portfolio equipped with a standard-size yellow lined pad, a smaller one, stickies, and more pens. The portfolio is worn and handsome in its patina and significance. It was a gift from his late sister Julia, who died suddenly in Ireland, cause unknown. She was a gifted poet and a constant champion of Sam's own extracurricular writing, mostly poems and ragged attempts at fiction. He has always wondered whether Julia's attentions arose mostly out of their mutual affection, or whether she truly believed that her brother showed promise as a writer that he himself has never really felt.

Sam is deep in his seat, two pillows behind the small of his back. The door has been closed, cross check performed, and 21B is empty. "*Miracolo, miracoli,*" he mutters. The plane takes off. Sam watches the ground fly off beneath him. He feels like he is looking back on his life: an entire adult life designed to do the right thing in a field where principles frequently wobble. He is tired of doing what others want of him. He has tried to explain to Tom what his ethics dictate. Now he must take action on his own.

Looks so simple from up here. The compulsions down there are so powerful. Way up here, above all that, *here* in infinite space Sam is convinced is power, energy more compelling than that which emanates from the buildings, warrens of hyperactivity lining the mazes of stone and steel canyons of cities like New York.

Sam eases into sleep.

Five hours later he awakens. He sees the unbroken cloud-covered floor below, the surface slightly dimpled, no cloud towers, now with subtle valleys running into the far distance casting so many faint shadows, which remind him of the shallow brooks across high plains he has looked down on from Wyoming's mountain prospects.

The captain comes on over the public address system to tell the passengers to begin preparing for their descent. Nearly ten minutes at a downward incline and the plane punches through the clouds. On the other side is Florence, its red tile roofs and grand churches making themselves known above everything else.

CHAPTER TWENTY-ONE

At ten-thirty-five, Sam enters the arrival hall of Peretola, the small airport a half hour from Florence. Sam leaves the terminal with his carry-on luggage and walks to the taxi rank.

"Buon giorno, signore," the taxi driver says.

"Hotel Donatello, via dell'Oche, please."

"My pleasure, sir."

It is a bright spring morning, cool and green. Sam leans toward the open car window. He hasn't been back to Florence in eight years, as none of his clients have been interested in Italian art. This has been regrettable, and except for a long visit to Rome four years ago, leisure time in Florence has not seemed possible.

"You here on business, signore? Fun?"

"Business, which will be a pleasure, I expect."

The rest of the trip passes in silence, except for the sound of the driver singing to himself. As they near the city, Sam can begin to make out Il Duomo rising above the other red tile roofs. They cross the Rio Arno. Sam feels a deep sense of relaxation and good fortune. They pass by an outdoor market where he can smell the newly oiled leather goods. The air is still moist and comfortable, a few weeks before the rise of summer heat.

"Driver, could you please drive by Orsanmichele before we go to my hotel?"

"Certainly, signore."

"Grazie."

"Do you know the Oratorio, signore?"

"Yes, I studied it many years ago. I've never forgotten it."

"It is very beautiful. The perfect sculptures by the great old masters. Donatello, Ghiberti, who also made the golden doors at the Baptisterio, you know them?"

"Yes, I have always admired your great sculptors—and your painters."

The taxi slows to a stop in sight of Orsanmichele. The church is one of Sam's favorite monuments, if not because of the building's architecture, then surely because of the feature of niches on the lower story, each of which contains a sculpture by a different Renaissance master—Donatello, Ghiberti, and others of equal fame.

"Would you like to look, signore?"

"Another time, yes. I'll come back and spend more time here. I just wanted to say hello."

"Yes. The sculptures are old friends to many."

The taxi driver drops Sam off at the nineteenth-century stone building, where Sam has stayed before. He checks in and finds that little has changed about the building, a lesser palazzo dating back about five hundred years. His room is in the back overlooking the little garden. He sits in the cushioned wicker chair by the big double window. Sun floods the spacious, high-ceilinged room. The room phone is blinking. He picks it up and finds a message from Father Anselmo who, in his message, suggests lunch at one-thirty at Trattoria Fabiani, via Ghibellina 48. Sitting on the edge of the bed, Sam gazes out the window on the clear spring day. Despite the travel fatigue, he is eager to get to the heart of the Leonardo matter.

If Sam is quite comfortable with the authenticity of the Leonardo—the result of scrupulous observation, state-of-the-art technical examination, and expert restoration—there is still something disturbing about Ricci's claims and the dealer's behavior when he speaks about the Leonardo, something that triggers Sam's intuition yet defies his voices of instinct upon which he has relied for so long. He picks up the phone, eager to meet Father Anselmo.

CHAPTER TWENTY-TWO

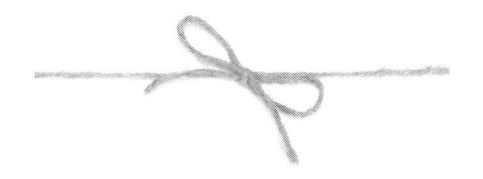

Trattoria Fabiani is packed, as one might expect in a European country accustomed to lengthy lunch hours. Just beyond the door are several bentwood and wicker chairs underneath a giant Technicolor poster proclaiming an Italian soccer championship of some decades ago. Seated at a small table staring contemplatively beyond his knees to the floor is a priest in a black vest and white collar, which, in their traditional sobriety, contrast with a tasteful plaid jacket woven of Italian wool. He is in his midfifties, graying hair, narrow face, aquiline nose, kindly demeanor, with an air of quiet but acute intelligence. Sam makes his way toward the cleric, and Father Anselmo lifts his eyes to greet Sam's, rises slowly, and smiles warmly at Sam, extending his hand.

"Mr. Driscoll? I'm Father Anselmo, Paolo Anselmo. I've been looking forward to meeting you."

"My great pleasure . . . Father . . ."

"Paolo, my friend. May I call you Sam? You don't mind?"

"Not at all. You're kind to make time for me on such short notice."

"How could I not meet with you to talk about the painting? Shall we refer to it that way? The painting?"

"Yes, good idea."

"Come, let us go to the table I reserved. If we get special treatment, it's because the owner is my cousin's wife, you see."

Sam smiles broadly. He already likes this. He appreciates Father Anselmo's pleasant, direct manner.

At the table, Father Anselmo sits back in his chair, hands clasped on the table edge, saying nothing, studying Sam. Sam glances down at the menu, uncomfortable with the silence and the priest's gaze. He is about to open the conversation when Father Anselmo says, "How long will you be staying?"

"I've planned for four days, but I'm prepared to . . . I would gladly stay longer if necessary."

"I understand. You've chosen an excellent time to visit, well before the city becomes crowded. Not to mention the heat, which increases every year."

"To be honest, the timing arises out of my need to investigate the painting."

Father Anselmo smiles. "Yes, I am somewhat familiar with the painting of the *Virgin and Child with a Cat* but I am less personally knowledgeable with the documentation and the physical research that I understand has led to these stunning connections to Leonardo himself."

"Father Anselmo . . . Paolo, I have brought with me a dossier of all the pertinent documents—X-rays, microscopic photos, conservation logs—everything that I have gathered since I first saw the painting three months ago."

"Fascinating. I would be most interested to learn what you have to . . . relate. Sam, may I suggest we order? Also a little wine. I could make some recommendations if you would like."

"On all counts, yes."

During the course of almost an hour, Sam relates his long involvement with the picture from the moment when he was first shown a photograph, through his research and close attention to the restoration process. He is careful not to reveal too much about his client's identity, but he does tell the priest of Mark Ricci's questionable behavior.

Father Anselmo listens intently, only occasionally interjecting a clarifying question. "It is clear that an apparently rare work of art has stirred a pot of power and ego. Not surprising."

"It's as if the picture has achieved an aspect of star quality which I don't believe it had when it was painted. And it's generally understood that Leonardo's renown as a painter was in his day challenged by his reputation as an engineer, an inventor, a scientist, a theorist. Furthermore, this may very well be done by one of his followers."

"Yes. That is true," says Father Anselmo, "and the subject of the painting we speak of is hardly grand like a portrait, or an elaborate sacred subject, such as *The Last Supper* in Milan."

"Certainly, *The Virgin and Child with a Cat* is quite an intimate painting in its subject and size."

"I *have* seen the beautiful drawing of the subject in the Uffizi," says Father Anselmo. "It is so very exquisite."

"To see that lovely sheet will be one of my great pleasures while I am here. I only know it from photos in the catalogues. As you may be aware, there are a number of other related drawings in the British Museum, one in the museum in Bayonne in France, another possibly in a collection in New York. A few of them are simply the young Christ with a cat."

"Yes."

"Ken told me that in Milan, at the Brera Gallery, there is a painting by a follower of Leonardo."

"Yes, Ken shared that with me too," Father Anselmo replies, sipping his wine. "It's an artist who is obviously influenced by the style of Leonardo, possibly painted during his lifetime. It depicts the Virgin and Child in a landscape. And the Child holds a lamb. Quite recently, X-rays revealed that at some time the lamb was painted over what is clearly the figure of a cat, held in a way that resembles the pose in some of Leonardo's early drawings."

"But why, Paolo, was the Brera painting changed by replacing the cat with a lamb?

"We'll never know for sure, Sam, but the lamb, as you know, is the symbol of John the Baptist. And Leonardo later explored the painted themes, which included the infant Christ and the young John the Baptist, with the lamb. Certainly followers and copyists of Leonardo's work knew of his use of lamb imagery."

"But what does the cat *mean* in the context of the Virgin and Child?"

"Sam, who but Leonardo could have imagined the Holy Virgin and her Son, who turns away from his mother to embrace a cat? Thinking that in Renaissance Florence or Milan was blasphemy. We can assume from what we know that Leonardo was headstrong, totally unorthodox in most aspects of his life, and above all an inventor."

"But you know, in scholarly discussion of Leonardo's drawings, it has been thought that a legend about a cat giving birth to some kittens in the manger at the moment of Christ's birth may have been the source of Leonardo's conception in his early sketching of the Virgin and Child with a cat," Sam says.

"I'm not familiar with that legend, though I must say it is a charming one."

"Well, it is possible that Leonardo knew of some legend of that kind, or that it was an element of folk tradition of the time which has been lost."

"How wonderful it would be to be able to communicate with some of the great minds and spirits of the past." Paolo swirls his wine.

"It never stops, the pursuit and the pleasure of the truth. In life and in art."

Paolo grins. "Amen."

"There's one other little thread, Paolo. Will you indulge me? Maybe it's the wine."

"No, please, Sam . . . I'm quite engaged."

"Well, there's still another legend that relates to the Virgin and Child with a cat. It has to do with the cat as protector and the enemy of evil traditionally appearing in the form of a snake."

"Ah! Excellent point. That would invoke the tradition of the Virgin, Queen of Heaven, as the new Eve and the snake as the evocation of the evil serpent in the Garden of Eden." Paolo is clearly excited.

"And I know of only one image, more than two hundred years later, that uses that same iconography. It's an etching by Rembrandt."

"Incredible!" The priest is spellbound.

"The inclusion of the cat didn't cease with the death of Leonardo," says Sam, pleased with his captivated audience. "Giulio Romano painted a picture of the Virgin, Christ, St. Anne, and St. John the Baptist, grouped together with Joseph in the distant background. A cat is prominently represented to the right of the main figures."

"Joseph does always seem somewhat lost."

"Yes," Sam replies, "and in the sixteenth century, Federico Barocci painted a charming picture, now in the National Gallery in London, showing the Virgin, Joseph—here he is included—the infant Christ and the infant St. John the Baptist. The smaller Christ Child watches, fascinated as a baby would be, as the infant Baptist holds aloft a goldfinch, seemingly tempting a cat."

"I would like very much to see that picture. Now, Sam, I'm sure you are aware of the miraculously restored painting by that same artist, which is a pride of our Uffizi Gallery here in Florence. That picture also includes a cat."

"Yes, *The Madonna della Gatta*. I long to see it while I'm here."

"I must be returning to my duties shortly. But I would like to invite you to join me on a visit tomorrow to a small village not far from here, perhaps a half hour's drive. Would you be free early tomorrow afternoon?"

"Yes, I would be delighted, Paolo."

"I should not tell you the object of our visit except that I hope what you will learn tomorrow will be of greatest interest in regard to your search for the painting's provenance."

Sam smiles. "I may have trouble sleeping tonight in anticipation of our adventure."

"All will be revealed and a door will be opened. You will see." The priest chuckles and stands up. "Now I am becoming obsessed with cat imagery. God forgive me. The Holy Church discourages obsession." Sam shakes his hand and they bid each other farewell.

Sam sits back down and cradles the wineglass in his hand. He feels a glow of wine and good fortune. Here he is in Florence drinking a rich Barolo, poised to plunge into research on a puzzle that *is* an obsession; he has met a sympathetic friend, he is off tomorrow on another trail. He is filled with a sense of well-being.

CHAPTER TWENTY-THREE

Father Anselmo hands a stack of file folders to Sam. His face is merry as he starts the car and turns into the narrow street.

"Do read the papers now if you wish. They are a gift in appreciation of your integrity and your industry in regard to the newly revealed Leonardo. They have been translated by a scholar who is my acquaintance."

"Thank you, Paolo, I will." Sam opens the folder, puts on his reading glasses, and begins to read. What he sees appears to be a facsimile of a sixteenth-century document in Italian accompanied by a typed translation describing how the panel was discovered deep in the woods and how it got to a church in Ponte Albrizzi.

"Holy." Sam whistles.

Father Anselmo is beaming. "I thought that would interest you."

Sam sits silently attentive but obviously stunned by what he has read. "This is incredible." There are three pages from one of Leonardo da Vinci's notebooks describing how the painting came into being, how it was lost in a caravan on his way to Milan and how a man named Piero Mazza rediscovered the painting. Sam is silent as he rereads the translation.

"Paolo, these pages focus beams of light onto the questions of the painting's provenance. You have no idea."

"I think I do."

"'PM' Piero Mazza, the initials on the cradle of the New York painting. I've run into his name in the literature. There are one or two Leonardesque pictures attributed to him, nothing closely resembling Leonardo's style. But I didn't know that he was something of a restorer or repairman. I wonder whether the overpainting on top of the Leonardo in New York may be Mazza's work."

"And now that painting on top of the alleged Leonardo is being removed completely. Am I correct?"

"Yes, though high-resolution photos were taken before the cleaning and removal of the top image. The true identity of that painter will, I'm sure, remain a mystery for a while—until the frenzy of interest in the 'great man' subsides. I'd like to plunge into that attribution question myself."

The priest nods. "The great man will always be in the spotlight, even though relatively few are really aware of Leonardo's work other than the *Mona Lisa* and the Milan *Last Supper*."

"Paolo, it seems clear that the original home of the new Leonardo is pretty much beyond doubt."

Paolo nods again and continues driving in the direction of Ponte Albrizzi, which lies not far from Florence, northwest about fifteen kilometers from Prato, once a prosperous town in the fifteenth and sixteenth centuries—and now restored as a textile center.

For the next half hour Father Anselmo and Sam chat about Sam's work, the staggering rise in the world art market, life in New York City, and Father Anselmo's assignment as an assistant librarian in the Institute of Renaissance Studies.

Sam sees the outlines of Ponte Albrizzi up ahead with its many original buildings and a few new ones. It is a farming village with perhaps a thousand occupants, maybe less, set on a hill. They cross the old bridge that spreads itself over a small river below the town.

"One could assume with good reason that the present bridge was built at the expense of Giovanni Albrizzi or an ancestor," Father Anselmo says. "Unfortunately, little is known of Giovanni Albrizzi. He is known to have been a *condottiere* of some repute. He must have had some wealth as a result of his adventures, how gained it is not known." He points out the ruins of a *castello* not far from the village, which may very well have been a country retreat for Albrizzi. The priest then guides Sam's attention to the church of Santo Stefano and a monastery, still active, with a religious community numbering about twenty. The rest of the town consists of possibly fifty houses, barns, a few shops, two taverns. There are farms spread out on the hillsides around the town. Sam can make out a tractor up on a terraced hillside near the *castello*.

Father Anselmo turns into an open, gated entrance to a large house built in the early years of the last century. On the other side of the lot is a plain chapel. A sign to the right of the door to the house announces that this is a home run by the diocese for retired priests and monks. Sam's puzzlement rises as he follows Father Anselmo up the short flight of steps and through the heavy wooden door. Just beyond the entryway is a long corridor to the right of a stairway leading to the upper floor of the three-story stuccoed building. The passageway is dark except for minimal light all the way to the end. Five doorways on each side open onto the gloomy passage. Some are open, some closed. Murmured conversation, a thin reedy voice, the faint trail of static and operatic music, occasional coughing, and a thin wailing sound are all that suggest life in the place. The air is stagnant. Sam feels a touch of claustrophobia.

Father Anselmo takes his elbow and explains in a low voice, "This is a diocesan retirement, an old-age home for servants of the church from our district and near regions. Come, we will go to the end of the hall."

Approaching a door on the right, Father Anselmo knocks softly. "Yes, enter please," a female voice answers. Sam follows Paolo into a narrow room with a single window for light. Through the gloom, Sam can see a bed, a night table, and a small dresser, upon which stands a short, simple cross fashioned from branches and joined by ordinary twine. Next to the cross is a tattered Bible. Worn yellowed paper slips mark many pages of the thumb-worn holy book.

Set back a foot or so from the window is a scarred wooden rocking chair in which sits a white-haired man with skin like parchment. He is dressed in a black cassock. There are cushions beneath him, one supporting his back as he leans forward to accept a spoon full of puréed vegetable held by a portly nun, who attends the ancient priest with obvious authority tempered by devotion. The priest's gnarled arthritic hands are clasped in his lap, laced together with a string of worn rosary beads.

"Brother Andrea," Father Anselmo says in Italian before entering further into the room, "may I come in? I have brought a friend. Sam, I will have to translate for you."

The old cleric instantly answers. "Oh, oh, Father Anselmo, your visit brings strength to this old heart." His voice betrays a tremor, yet is robust at the same time. "Of course, come in, come in."

The monk's hand trembles as he gently pushes the proffered spoonful away. "Welcome, welcome, good Father Anselmo. You are so welcome. I am never too busy to see you. I eat too much anyway." He grins. "Come in. Yes, come closer."

Father Anselmo guides Sam into the room to face the chair in which Brother Andrea is tucked. The old man is taller than average, once perhaps physically powerful. His big-boned face shows the hollows of age. Bushy white brows animate blue eyes, which are unusually bright for a man in his mid-nineties. Baldness has left a permanent tonsure, and the ring of snowy hair, clearly trimmed, partially covers large ears, which haven't shrunk with the years. Brother Andrea peers through round wireframe spectacles at his visitors.

"Father Anselmo! You don't come often enough to see me. Shame on you." The old man chuckles. Letting the rosary rest in his lap, the monk reaches both shaking arms toward Father Anselmo, gripping the priest's hand as if to raise a victory salute.

"Dear Andrea, I want to introduce you to a new friend. From America. Sam Driscoll."

"Brother Andrea, I am very happy to meet you," Father Anselmo translates for Sam.

"Thank you, my young man, and I you. What brings you to our little town, to my small room to visit? You've come a long way, my son."

"I've come to Florence to do some research and to study some of the art treasures there."

Sam waits while Father Anselmo translates.

"Ah, you are an artist? My sister was an artist and a photographer."

"No, Brother Andrea, I am interested in the history of art. I have studied for many years, most particularly European art of the Middle Ages to the twentieth century."

Brother Andrea listens, eyes alight, looking between Sam and Father Anselmo, his mouth open in concentration while the priest translates.

"Ah . . . a historian of art, I see. So . . . yes."

"I hope you can imagine my great pleasure to be in Italy, particularly in Florence where there are many wonderful treasures."

"Brother Andrea, our friend Sam has come a long way not only to visit Florence and its marvels, but also to learn what he can about the church at Ponte Albrizzi and particularly about the painting that was once above the altar. The beautiful picture of the Virgin Mary with the Child holding the cat."

Brother Andrea, sitting forward in his chair up to this moment, slumps back against the supportive cushions. His eyes go dull. The old monk shakes his head slowly. He closes his eyes. "O Blessed Virgin of Mercy, pity the lost souls who took away from Santo Stefano Thy Holy Image and that of Thy Child and the Cat of the Sacrifice. May those misguided ones return the sacred image to its rightful place in our humble church. O Blessed Virgin, I beseech Thee."

Brother Andrea sits, as if crumpled, wordless.

"Paolo, he seems heartbroken. Should I tell him about the painting in New York, about the documents you have given me about . . . can we?"

"This sweet old man was in service at the monastery in Ponte Albrizzi. In his heart, he lives with the image of the Holy Virgin and Child. It was once the centerpiece of a shrine above the altar of the church. Just wait, my friend."

"My God . . ."

"That is why I brought you here. I wanted you to hear the story that Brother Andrea has to tell."

"I understand, I . . ."

Brother Andrea sits up in his chair. "Father Anselmo, you are talking to the young American about Ponte Albrizzi. What are you saying?"

"Andrea, I've just told him that you spent most of your God-given life in service to Christ at Santo Stefano in Ponte Albrizzi."

"Ah, yes, yes. May God grant me another life to serve again, and in that life with God's help, I will find the most beloved picture of the Virgin stolen during the terrible war. With God's help."

Father Anselmo turns to Sam. "As the lost painting was and is his passion, there is a risk that disappointment might injure this poor man's spirit a second time. It might kill him."

"I see, Paolo. I do understand. But with the documents that you have just shown me, the Albrizzi document, the *PM* on the painting's cradle, the Leonardo notes, the apparent certainty that the hand on the painting is Leonardo's—all of that indicates the New York painting is Brother Andrea's painting."

"Suora, what are they saying?" Andrea pleads with the nun who had been sitting quietly in a corner of the room while the men talked. "They use my name, they say 'Albrizzi.' Who is Leonardo? Anselmo, please tell me?"

Father Anselmo goes to Brother Andrea's side, places his hand on the monk's shoulder, and raises his index finger. "Andrea, we were just talking about your painting. You can explain all to my friend Sam in just a moment."

The monk nods in agreement, is still. A little calmer, he stares out the window.

Father Anselmo returns to where Sam has been standing. "Yes, Sam, the art historical and documentary evidence seems to connect the painting you've studied with Ponte Albrizzi. But it is in New York you say, and it is now probably owned by someone who knows nothing about Ponte Albrizzi. And I suspect would care nothing about the painting's history or original home."

"Yes, Paolo, that's true and . . ."

Brother Andrea suddenly, impulsively rises just barely off his chair, turns slowly toward Sam and Paolo. The nun sitting by Andrea's side has not said a word. She places her hand on Andrea's, which is gripping the arm of his rocking chair. She looks anxiously at the old man.

"Anselmo," Brother Andrea says, pleadingly. "I can't understand what either of you are saying."

Sam turns to face Paolo. He lowers his voice to a whisper. "Paolo, I believe the painting should be returned to Italy, to Ponte Albrizzi. And there are international laws and treaties . . ."

Paolo looks silently at Sam for a moment. "Yes, I know that, Sam. And the Italian authorities are beginning to look into these matters, as I told Ken Taylor last week."

"Yes, he mentioned that."

Paolo turns to the old priest. "Andrea, do you have the little box of photographs you showed me the last time I visited you? Do you remember?"

"Oh, yes, yes. Suora, please fetch the cigar box in the drawer of my little bureau. Thank you, thank you."

Andrea is clearly relieved to be recognized again. The sister brings the rubbed and tattered cigar box to the monk, who takes it from the nun's hands almost as if it were the sacrament, a precious relic.

"Andrea, would you be willing to show our American friend the photographs?"

"Of course, Anselmo, with pleasure. Please, young man, come closer to the light."

Brother Andrea opens the box and removes a small packet of snapshots, bound with a string, resting on top of a bundle of yellowed and thumb-worn letters.

"Ah. Now here they are." The monk takes the small stack of photos and places them in his lap. "Suora, please help me untie them. Yes, yes. Now these were taken by my sister. She lived in Prato. You remember I told you that, Anselmo? She came often to Ponte Albrizzi to visit and bring fresh bread and, when she could find one, a hare or a duck. Food was so scarce. Especially during the time the German soldiers started leaving Italy when the Americans were after them."

Sam takes the photos gingerly as Andrea hands them to him, each accompanied by explanation.

"Yes, and here is my sister . . . and me standing in front of Santo Stefano with Brother Tommasso, Brother Timotheo, oh, and there is Brother Francesco, you can just see his big smile—he's laughing. I remember. He was always happy, too seldom serious. The abbot often spoke harshly to Brother Francesco."

Sam graciously, but also with genuine sympathy, takes each photograph, nodding as Brother Andrea hands each one with a nostalgic description.

"Ah, ah, yes. Oh, and here are two pictures taken by the grocer in our little town. He had little to do then just before the Germans passed through. He had no groceries to sell. We were all out in the fields picking beets. Even fat Brother Timotheo was getting thinner every day. Watery soup and bites of bread during those days of approaching armies."

"I can imagine how very difficult those days were, Brother Andrea." Sam wipes the corner of his eyes as he listens.

"Yes, my son. So much suffering during those war days."

Andrea offers more photos to Sam. "Ah yes, and here are the pictures of our Blessed Virgin and the infant Christ with his cat. Here, see. My sister made these pictures when we took down the Holy Image to put it away in a safe place to protect it from the soldiers. She had them made in Prato just before she came back to visit . . . before she disappeared . . . my dearest Alma. We were so close."

Sam holds himself back from snatching the pictures out of the monk's hands. He is transfixed as he slowly shuffles the snapshots. One picture shows a painting being held by four monks who stand in full sun just outside what seems to be the double wooden doors of a church. The second photograph is a picture of the whole painting with the fingers of those who are holding it clearly showing, while the third photo is a close-up of the middle of the painting, showing the Virgin, from below her lap to the top of her head, as she holds the infant Christ, who in turn embraces a cat

Sam cannot speak, does not wish to speak. He stands on the window side of Brother Andrea's rocking chair, back to the light, looking intently, again shuffling one snapshot, then another and another. Then again.

"It is a beautiful painting, isn't it, young man?" Brother Andrea asks almost in a whisper.

"Yes, Brother Andrea, it is one of the most beautiful pictures that I've ever seen." Anselmo translates.

"Yes, I feel that too," says the old monk. "I can tell that the Holy Image would have . . . would have touched you very deeply if you had seen her in her shrine over the altar in our church. Several people experienced miracles standing in front of her. We few who remained . . ." Brother Andrea is weeping. He struggles to speak.

"We took her and hid her in Ponte Albrizzi . . . two days later . . . after my sister left to return to Prato . . . we hid her in a barn, in a manger under the hay. We thought the Virgin and her Holy Child would be safe there." Brother Andrea lifts his trembling hands and holds them to his lips in a prayer pose. He bows his head. Tears seep from his eyes, down his cheeks, onto the back of his hands.

"We prayed . . . we prayed that Our Lady would be safe and that the Germans or the Americans . . . we were told they were a few days away from us . . . we prayed to the Virgin and the Saints that the soldiers would not find her, that they wouldn't take away our blessed Madonna and the Christ Child. Oh, how we hoped, how we prayed for her and our church."

The nun gently places her hand on Brother Andrea's arm. Father Anselmo kneels down before the rocking chair, lays his hand on the old man's knee. Sam is lost in the monk's account of those days when the Germans, pursued by the American infantry, marched up the spine of Italy.

"We could not know whether the soldiers would be coming to our little village. But when we heard explosions and the sound of guns below and off to the south of our town, those of us who had decided to stay in the village, we hid deep in the woods beside the road to Pistoia. There were more than twenty of us. Most of the brothers, a few women, more men. For three days we waited. Then . . . then we could hear engines, trucks we thought. Then that noise stopped. Yes, early the next day, another several hours of engines. We were afraid. One man dared to go to the edge of the woods. It was the Americans. That man, he was called Piero, came back to tell us that it was safe. We went out to the road. A truck stopped and gave us food in packages. We had not eaten in three days, and the only water we had was from a little stream in the woods."

Brother Andrea brings his hands together again in the gesture of prayer, his fingers extending over his mouth and nose. His head is bowed, his eyes closed; tears fall down his cheeks as he nods his head gently. "She was not there when we returned. She was not there . . ." He is still. "Not there," he whispers.

Brother Andrea is transfixed. Father Anselmo, Sam, and the nun seated next to the monk sit motionless, profoundly moved by what they've heard. Sam looks toward Father Anselmo, who has been softly translating Andrea's account of those terrible days when the Italian campaign touched Ponte Albrizzi.

"May I?" he asks, catching Father Anselmo's attention.

"Yes, Sam. I think you should. You must," the priest says with a kindly smile and a nod.

"Brother Andrea," Sam kneels down beside Andrea's chair. The old man raises his face from his attitude of prayer. "Brother Andrea, I want to tell you . . . I believe your precious painting of the Virgin and Child is safe. It has been found."

"Oh, please young man, oh you must . . . please tell me the truth . . . that the Holy Image is safe . . ."

"It is safe, dear man. It is in America. I have seen it. I know it. I have studied it. It *is* the picture that disappeared from Ponte Albrizzi. I am sure of it."

Anselmo translates again. The monk's face, eyes still wet, is suddenly touched with joy. He looks from Father Anselmo to Sam and then back to Father Anselmo.

The priest nods in affirmation. "Yes, Andrea. The Holy Image from Santo Stefano is safe."

"And she is in America?"

"Yes, it is she."

"The Holy Image has been missing so long, so long. Will she ever return to our church where she belongs?"

Neither Sam nor Father Anselmo answers. Brother Andrea looks from one to the other, his expression one of profound concern. Sam rests his hand on Brother Andrea's arm. A few seconds pass. He thinks of his former loyalty to Tom, but that all feels so far away. He doesn't know whether to speak, but then he does. "Yes, I think she will return to Ponte Albrizzi. I cannot say when. But I think she will return to her home."

"Oh, thank you, my dear young man." Andrea smiles, looking from Sam, still kneeling by the chair, to the priest. "Yes, your words of hope come straight into my very heart. I have thought about Our Lady every day since we hid her away." He adds wistfully, "I pray that she will come home."

Another moment of silence. "As do we," Father Anselmo says, turning to Sam. "It appears you have a dilemma, Sam. You are loyal to your client, and yet

I believe the return of the Madonna and Child is only right. You may have a role to play in that outcome."

"I will carry your message in *my* heart, Brother Andrea," Sam says. "In my heart, in my mind when I return to the United States in a few days."

"I hope you will, my son. I hope you will."

CHAPTER TWENTY-FOUR

On a chilly, damp day in Florence—it is March of 1476—the twenty-four-year-old painter sits lost in thought on a three-legged rough-hewn stool, a cast-off milking stool, now cracked and peeling paint though serviceable. The seat is humble as is the rude chamber in which it stands. Leonardo is temporarily housed in a tiny building in Via Ghibellina belonging to his teacher, old Verrocchio, who has allowed his brightest and most talented student to use the space as shelter and studio.

High up on the stuccoed wall is one north-facing window. Good chance for an artist. Hardly more than a cubicle. Fit for a monk, there is room for a bed of sorts, a wooden plank, set on timbers a foot off the floor, shoved lengthwise across the width of one end of the tiny chamber; laid upon the roughly assembled platform is a rough canvas bag, flattened, filled with straw. Next to the bed is a simple, small table. Along the wall opposite the window is a row of large pegs that serve as hanging space for Leonardo's spare tunics, pants, long cotton shirts, and two cloaks—the heaviest barely adequate for these rainy late winter days.

Leonardo, from the town of Vinci, is of medium height, slender, with a handsome face, shadowed by the early growth of brown mustache and chin hair. He sits motionlessly, stares as if in some sort of trance. At this moment he should be going to Verrocchio's studio where he is expected. Before him is a door through which he has just entered after taking his meager breakfast at a nearby tavern.

By six-thirty each morning, Leonardo is regularly at work in the alternately hushed and raucous *bottega* presided over by Andrea del Verrocchio, painter, sculptor, teacher, well known, respected, and successful in Florence and beyond. Verrocchio generally admits a dozen students, mostly around Leonardo's age. The older artist and teacher—he is forty-one—keeps his little crowd of assistants busy at menial tasks when they are not busy on commissions awarded to Verrocchio. The boys and young men can be unruly, and the master cracks down on them, sometimes rapping them with his painting stick. He depends upon them to prepare sizing and glues, to grind pigments—just up to the point at which the prematurely grizzled Verrocchio takes over, adding his touch and secrets to colors and other workshop recipes known only to himself.

Leonardo is more fortunate than most struggling artists in a city that is a magnet for would-be artists, students, and practicing painters, sculptors, craftsmen, as well as patrons—the *maecenases*, lay and religious, the Medici, the Rucellais, and other great families; the guilds—the monasteries, churches, and confraternities. The young man's father, Ser Piero da Vinci, has recently been appointed notary in the city government. This position allows Ser Piero a good standard of living, affording modest comfort for himself and his mistress, the mother of the illegitimate Leonardo. The father's diligence and newfound fortune permits him to extend to his son a modest stipend for his maintenance, an extension of the parent's ongoing fascination with Leonardo's talent and precociousness, which Ser Piero noticed very early in his son's life and, to his great credit, has encouraged since Leonardo's earliest days.

Leonardo has rapidly assimilated the training in craft of the aspiring professional painter. He has mastered the preparation of surfaces—panels, canvas of all types and weaves, paper for studies preliminary and finished. He excels in the application of glues, gesso, and other primers laid on the grounds for the supports—wooden panels, canvas, and the like. He is as expert as his master at the grinding and preparation of colors from rare minerals to earth colors, and he has made his own versions of the secret recipes previously known only to Verrocchio and unveiled only to Leonardo. Some of these unorthodox confections would surprise the viewer or patron of a given painting if they were made aware of the bizarre ingredients.

Now the moody apprentice, who lacks the playfulness and propensity for mischief characteristic of many of his studio mates, is frequently at Verrocchio's side painting shoulder to shoulder. More and more often, the master leaves Leonardo free to paint passages of major painting commissions without supervision. Leonardo's master has allowed—sometimes depended upon—him to develop compositional layouts or adjustments to design in the work that goes out to the world as autograph Verrocchio.

As a consequence of his advanced standing as a student, Leonardo is frequently immersed in self-directed artistic exploration, interrupted when necessary by his master, who might need to engage him in finishing a final sketch for an altarpiece, a portrait, the modeling of a relief, or a maquette for a monumental sculpture that needs to be worked up in clay or plaster before it is cast.

Important to the course of his study is the copying of Verrocchio's drawings, or those of other contemporary and deceased artists, which Leonardo collects as he has done insatiably for years. Even more, Leonardo draws tirelessly from nature, from skeletons, often from wax-impregnated drapery produced for the purpose of having on hand a ready, motionless model. And sometimes he accompanies his master to executions or, occasionally, to dissections at the pleasure of an old doctor friend of Verrocchio's.

Several of Verrocchio's paintings out of the *bottega*, delivered since Leonardo's arrival, installed on site, carry Leonardo's imprint unknown to the patron. These include an attendant angel in an Annunciation, significant portions of painted portraits, or ranges of landscape background in a variety of paintings. A few pictures are almost completely by Leonardo's hand working in the master's style. Outside the studio, the patrons and the well-trained admirers of the work by "Verrocchio" are never the wiser.

The training and growing responsibility conferred on Leonardo by his master has encouraged the young man to believe that he will, in a reasonable timeframe, go out on his own and pursue his own artistic career—hopefully with Verrocchio's blessing. He dreams that such a career will eventually produce steady patronage and independence as an artist of high reputation and a man of knowledge.

His intention to study and learn sets him apart from his young, aspiring contemporaries who don't yet live in Leonardo's visionary way. Ever since his earliest youth, Leonardo has been consumed by ceaseless curiosity, almost without regard to subject matter. He remembers his father's accounts of his fixation on questioning and knowing. His father has recalled countless examples of the child bringing home animals alive and dead—mice, bugs, lizards, birds, tiny minnows. They sometimes bore clear signs of the child's own crude dissections. His parents better tolerated the countless varieties of leaves, flowers, vines, stones, clumps of earth attached to moss that he dragged in. This manic curiosity has not ceased. The young artist guards packets of notes and detailed drawings, which he has made since he could hold a pen and then later a rudimentary brush.

And these fixations continue to this day, the only difference being that with the expanding intellectual and observational range of his rising years, Leonardo feels a tireless need to reach, to explore, to seek into fields and subjects that are frequently beyond the grasp of his contemporaries of any age, including respected scientists, philosophers, and theologians. He is truly alone in his seeking knowledge in a multitude of subjects: anatomy—he has sneaked into dissections on his own; optics—he incessantly studies perspective. The universe and its laws in all their magnificent ordinariness cause him to wonder and question in ways that no one in his sphere of acquaintances, or in the circles of learned men that Verrocchio has described to him, is accustomed, aware, or apparently able. Consequently, Leonardo is most of the time lost in his thoughts and speculations. And his extreme introversion—characterized by melancholy, withdrawal, moodiness, and impatience—is the root of his demeanor. To say he is merely precocious is inadequate. Leonardo seems unaware or unconcerned about the nature of his eccentricity. Leonardo lives to work.

Here the boy sits, absolutely still, struck with somewhat troubled introspection. He is totally fixated on a dream he had last night, several times over. He writes about it in his journal. It feels to Leonardo more like a vision than a mere dream. He saw in the night the image of the Virgin holding the infant Child. Typical enough. But the image of his dream and the image as it filled him changed, shifted, became a living image. The vision was of the Virgin and her infant Son together with a cat. The cat was a common tabby, in itself hardly an oddity in a city filled with cats in every narrow street, in the marketplaces, in the cemeteries.

It was an image he'd never seen before, certainly never in the myriad of current representations of Mary and her Child, representations governed by orthodoxy, assumption, habit, custom. Leonardo has never seen such an image of Mary, Christ, a cat, never imagined it. A hallucination? An inspiration? Here he sits puzzled, transfixed, and submerged in a sea of deep emotions. The dream seems as if recent. A few moments ago? Oddly, the picture burned into his mind seems strange to Leonardo, but at the same time familiar, as if he has known it forever, as if he has witnessed the scene. As if the apparition and that trinity were as well known to him as the routine images of Mary and the Child which dour-faced clerics are always invoking when they rant from the pulpits or the streets, wherever there is a crowd willing to spare a few alms in return for the promise of salvation.

Galvanized by the strange and wonderful dream, Leonardo lights a candle, and as he sits in stillness, his lingering shock begins to shift to mental images, which he imagines as drawings that he could and will set down. He has drawn and painted in part countless images of the young Virgin, based on models from humble families. He's practiced transforming them into the Madonna, holding and adoring the chubby infant Christ. In fact, he has worked hard on a panel of his own of a Madonna who holds a simple flower as her sweet downward glance meets the attention of the naked tousled-haired Christ Child. This particular study, for which he has made a number of drawings, has been admired not only by some of his studio mates, but also by his old master Verrocchio. In that painted panel, Leonardo has pictured the Mother and Child in a room with a double-arched window in the still fashionable late gothic style on the back wall of the composition's right-hand side.

A few moments pass. Leonardo finally breaks his reverie and focuses on leaving for the *bottega*. He rises from his rumpled place on the crude bed against which he has been sitting—for how long?

He will spend the day sketching his night vision of the Virgin and Child with the cat. He will drop everything, talk his master into allowing him today to recover his dream images on paper, elaborate upon them, explore them. Perhaps in doing so, Leonardo will discover some deeper meaning of those startling images.

The young man rises hesitantly, all but tearing himself from his entranced state of meditation and reflection. He takes his warmest cloak off the peg, rubs his stubbled chin, and makes his way to the *bottega*. In moments, he will join its waiting noise and energy. His mind clings to the image as he strides toward Verrocchio's studio, three doors down from his own shabby entryway. Leonardo feels now again that he is *there* in the image place, not here in this noisy street.

CHAPTER TWENTY-FIVE

Alitalia 157 is two hours out of Milan heading for New York. Drowsiness stays his hand even as Sam, being offered a slice of chocolate torte, abandons that idea and instead asks for Sauterne and assorted fruit. He reclines his seat to its limit, sinks back, picks lazily at the grapes. Gazing up ahead, Sam listens to the hushed lazy current of prominently Italian mind talk. He drifts in that stream of unbridled delight in the sensory, and of course the sensual. Then his mind spins off to the people rooted in their ancient history since Rome when the French were still Gauls.

Sam thinks wistfully, while a bit muddled because of the rich Barolo that he chose with the veal scaloppini a half hour ago. *God, we Driscolls, we were wearing skins, and torcs on our biceps, all of us. Picts, carrying clubs and rude spears, screaming down hills trying to terrify Caesar's legions while his decked-out, squared-up troops were coolly advancing.*

Sam, are you feeling the second glass of wine a bit? Beautiful women, boundlessly inspiring Florence, Piazza Signoria, the light on the stone at sunset as I just sat last evening, just watched the light by myself. By myself. Four days changed me. I will go back there sooner rather than later. To the Uffizi. And to the countryside. And Prato, Ponte Albrizzi. Yeah, and to Rome. Four days touched my heart, my spirit. No ruts for a change. No bullshit, hype, gargantuan egos. Didn't call Cassie. Forgot about her. Didn't think "clients" much. Just uh-oh, how will Tom take to the reality of the Leonardo matter? Two hundred seventy-five million dollars for Leonardo da Vinci's painting of Christ's mother watching her Baby hugging a tabby.

What now can only be described as the Leonardo—without question. The art world will be agape; it will unhinge itself. Not a desirable circumstance to represent Tom. There will be a volcano of chatter, hype, hubbub, posturing, the art world at its most dynamic.

I have waited for this moment in my career, for whether I will lay my stake for art as game or art as an affair with what is most true. Fragile old Brother Andrea—hope, repatriation of the Leonardo, the old man's dream, the wine make it all seem so possible. Ricci, who is determined to sell the painting, and Tom, who clearly seems bent on owning it. Just look *at the picture, Tom, Ricci, world. Just see it, for God's sake, get in it, listen to what it says, what Leonardo, the wizard man of mystery, is telling you . . . Christ, I'm not even absolutely sure what he's really saying. Cat, kittens born when Christ was born? That legend? But where did he get that idea? He wasn't an old man in 1478; he didn't borrow the image from Verrocchio. The cat wasn't exactly an approved feature of the Virgin and Child pictures of the time; Leonardo wasn't exactly orthodoxy personified either, Sam.*

God, that Barolo was delicious. Velvet in a glass. I'd like some more . . . shouldn't. Airplane headache is the worst. Wish I could turn this big jet around. Ask the flight attendant to show me the insider's Milan. Wonder how Cassie is doing. Remoter and remoter. She used to be interested in all of these kinds of things; damn we're drifting apart. Been there . . . .And Piero Mazza? When Mazza told Leonardo about his repair mentioned in the document Paolo gave me, I wonder if Leonardo suspected more than Mazza told him. Don't think Leonardo would have cared. Always on to the next thing, no matter that he was involved in ten other projects at the same time.

The lamb. Symbol of the Passion, Lamb of God, Agnus Dei, or just a note of John the Baptist, the Prophet of the Child's arrival. But the cat. A protector? Maybe I should talk to a psychic. I wish I were psychic. I am tired. And I've had a bit too much wine and Sauterne, and these last few days were utterly rich. And I'm going home to see the dear dogs. God, New York in two days. Rather be headed west to Wyoming. Maybe I will. The dogs would like it.

Sam's head sags to the left.

CHAPTER TWENTY-SIX

Sam sits in a chair in Tom's office riffling through the *New York Times* looking for the art coverage. What he sees as he passes through the obituary section slugs his consciousness, sets his heart racing. He sits forward in his seat, eyes fixed on the page.

"Christ. Good Christ," he says to empty, uncomprehending space. "Art dealer found off Montauk, apparent drowning victim," he reads aloud. "Police say cause of death uncertain." Then the column reads:

> Philip Lowder, a well-known art dealer, was found by local fishermen on Wednesday, an apparent victim of accidental drowning. The U.S. Coast Guard later located his bass fishing boat adrift several miles from the location of Lowder's body, which was taken aboard a commercial fishing boat five miles from Montauk Harbor. Lowder . . .

"Holy God," Sam whispers, reading the remainder of the obituary in silence. "Philip Lowder dead." He stares out the forty-seventh-floor glass wall, silent.

A half hour later, Angela opens the door, pokes her head into the library. "Time . . ."

Sam slowly rises, still reeling.

In Tom's conference room, Sam settles into one of a dozen chairs pulled up to a conference table with a north prospect over Central Park and beyond. Five minutes later, Tom comes in. "Sam. Great to see you!" Tom's gusto is genuine and warmly meant. Sam is convinced that despite his power and following, Tom, in his guarded, unfathomable heart, needs to be loved and appreciated. But Sam is also aware of just how off-putting his client can be in his zealousness to succeed and stand out.

"Tom," Sam begins. "I went to Italy." He knows he has to start with Italy. There is nowhere else to start.

"I told you not to." Tom's voice, eyes, go cold.

"It was beyond any expectation that I had," Sam interrupts. Tom's face tinges red. "And what I learned, I would not have believed possible."

"Oh?" Tom leans forward in his boardroom chair, hands clasped so tightly that the tips of his knuckles are white.

"Tom, it *is* a Leonardo."

Tom straightens up in his chair—for a rare moment, speechless.

"How do you know?" Sam has never seen him so carried away. He feels an opening to Tom, a kind of sympathy for him.

"I met a priest, an art historian . . ."

"Go on."

"The priest is an expert in Italian Renaissance painting. He is an unmatchable source of information concerning Italy's artistic heritage. And he is a defender of the same."

"Yeah . . ."

"Father Anselmo introduced me to an old monk who, in his younger days, was assigned to a Tuscan monastery in a town called Ponte Albrizzi, where our Leonardo panel was installed above the altar until the last months of the Second World War. The picture had resided there since the day it was donated in 1491."

Tom straightens in his chair. "Shit, Sam, so does that really prove that the painting Ricci is asking two hundred seventy-five million for *is* Leonardo da Vinci? Where is the proof of Leonardo's hand?"

"Such questions are particularly tricky given the fact that the artist is dead, no one left to testify. But there *are* documents, related works of art—sketches, as you know—and other kinds of evidence."

"So where is the proof?"

"The proof is in two forms."

Tom stands up and writes a 1 and a 2 on the whiteboard behind his chair.

"In addition to the stylistic evidence that the ongoing cleaning has already revealed, the style of the painting underneath the overpainted image is arguably equivalent to the style of accepted Leonardos of the period proposed for the original. The stylistic judgment is corroborated by three physical pieces of strong, hard evidence."

"And they are?" Tom turns away from the whiteboard and back to Sam, his voice almost giddy.

"Two are documents, the other is a simple monogram inscribed on the back of the Leonardo panel, which itself is linked to the documents."

"I don't . . ."

"I'll read you the documents. The first one is a later copy of what was a document contemporary to the gift of a painting by a little-known nobleman to a church in the town named after the nobleman's family. The town is called Ponte Albrizzi."

"Ponte Albrizzi," Tom says almost in a whisper, and again, "Pon-te Albriz-zi."

"Tom, are you with me?"

"Right here, Sam." Tom straightens, crossing his arms across his chest, assuming a posture of rapt attention.

"Okay, so document one."

Sam looks down at the paper in his hand that Father Anselmo translated from the original. "May God bless the custodians of our church as I bless them for their goodness and their prayers. From my sinner's heart, I ask God's grace, and honor His Son and the Holy Virgin. In their names I present to our church a fine and admirable panel of wood (three braccia by two braccia) with the painted image of the Holy Virgin with the Holy Infant Savior who holds a small cat. The painting for which the woodworker Alessandro Ciofagni will make a suitable shrine to be raised above the altar of the Church of Santo Stefano in honor of the Blessed Saint and the Miraculous Holy Virgin, this relic given in thanks to the most Blessed Mother for granting the humble prayers of Giovanni Albrizzi for her Grace and Providence at the birth of two fine sons who shall be raised to honor Her Sacred Name and to serve the everlasting Church as does their Father in all humility." Sam looks up from his copy of the document. "The document is dated 1491."

Tom is quiet, absorbing what he has just heard. "Something quite moving about what you just read, that document. Somehow as you were reading, I was drawn back in time to the real people, real events. To the origin of this picture."

Sam is struck by Tom's totally unpredicted *aperçu*. Never in his fifteen years working with Tom has he experienced this kind of reaction from his client. "There's more to read," Sam says, not wanting to break the spell.

"Please go on, Sam. I'm right with you." Tom settles back in his chairman's chair, his hands folded in his lap like a student.

"On the reverse of the panel, Tom, as you've seen, is a cradle, a grid of wood pieces attached vertically and horizontally to the panel, glued and notched, which inhibit the panel from warping or curving into a concave or convex shape because of changes of atmosphere or, say, rising and falling humidity levels. Such a cradle—it's an old device—can mean the difference of a split or completely fractured panel and the ruin of a painting."

Tom says not a word, mesmerized by Sam's account.

"On the rib of one of the outside battens there is an old carved inscription: 'PM fecit.' PM, it is believed, is the initial signature of a man named Piero Mazza, a painter of modest accomplishment from whose hand a few pictures have survived. He is better known as a sometime repairer of panels and pictures."

"What is known about the man?"

"Nothing, except a few pictures carrying his mark or brand on his panel and its cradle. He was clearly enterprising, a jack of several trades and respected."

Tom nods.

"And," Sam continues, "there is a mention of Piero Mazza in Leonardo's strange and wonderful, occasionally chaotic notebooks which he had started to compile when he went to Milan from Florence, we think, in 1481. The mention in Leonardo's notebook indicates that Leonardo knew or at least had met Mazza in Milan where Leonardo went, as I mentioned, in 1481 to work for Ludovico Sforza, the powerful Duke of Milan."

"I don't quite understand . . ."

"Let me read you some brief notes that Father Anselmo got from the archives." Sam shuffles through papers. "Okay, Mazza may very well have done work for Leonardo as a joiner or repairer, or at least have been involved somehow in one of the projects Leonardo was working on in Milan."

"Do the notes get specific?" Tom asks.

"There are two fragmentary references. There's a journal entry and marginalia along the edge of the notebook pages dealing with the construction of armatures and reinforced molds as he was thinking about a monumental sculpture of Ludivico's father. Never completed."

"So read me, please, what you've got."

"Simply this. I quote, 'Mazza came by to see the framing for S. Francesco . . .' There's another note. 'Mazza two lire, three soldi . . .' and then 'Mazza repaired Madonna, Christ and a Cat in country . . . Albrizzi.'"

Tom is clearly astonished.

"Finally," Sam continues, 'my dream? . . . lost caravan.'"

"God," Tom whispers.

"Right. It's beautiful—that flash of suggestion from the fifteenth century. A sense of what happened—partial, but something. Art history at its heart-stopping best."

"So, I wonder. Leonardo never regained the picture?"

"It would appear not, Tom. It would seem that the reference to 'lost caravan' and *its* link to 'Madonna, Christ, and a Cat,' and 'country' and 'Albrizzi' indicates that the picture was lost to Leonardo and never returned."

"You mean, someone found it and then at some point it ended up in the church in Ponte Albrizzi?"

"That would appear to be the case. One lost picture, mentioned to Leonardo by sheer chance by a painter-framer acquaintance named Piero Mazza. What are the chances?"

"And Leonardo didn't care," Tom says almost in a whisper, as if to himself. "I wonder what he meant by 'my dream?'"

"We'll never know."

Tom straightens up as if he is pulling himself out of a dream. "Listen, Sam, what you've discovered in Italy tells me all I need to know. There is no reason for you to root any further into the provenance."

His abruptness catches Sam off-guard. "But, Tom—"

"No, I mean it, Sam. I want this painting." Tom points at his chest. "At this point, I don't want you uncovering anything that could prevent Sylvie and me from purchasing it. You are not to do any more investigating into this matter. If you do, I will take you off of the Leonardo altogether, and I may consider other measures too that would have significant financial ramifications for you." Tom stares intensely at Sam, letting the words sear through him.

CHAPTER TWENTY-SEVEN

Three blocks from the Lowder Gallery is South Tower, a well-built prewar apartment building offering comfortable two- and three-bedroom apartments, attractive and well maintained, but far more "real world" than the over-the-top luxe units preferred by Sam's clients. As Sam passes the gallery, he notices a man step out from a side street. The man starts walking unusually close behind him. Sam looks over his shoulder. The man is dressed in a black suit. His eyes are cold. Sam speeds up as he approaches the door, which a smartly uniformed doorman opens for him. The man who is trailing Sam walks up the steps after him and then abruptly pivots away. The doorman gives the man and then Sam a confused look.

Sam, unnerved, introduces himself to the concierge—young, Spanish, impeccably dressed—who picks up a phone and speaks to Philip Lowder's widow, nods at her reply. "I'll send Mr. Driscoll right up."

"Mr. Driscoll, twenty-four. Elevators just over there."

Sam proceeds to the elevators, and one opens. He presses button twenty-four. The elevator is old and Sam feels uneasy. He dreads paying this call to

Lowder's widow, but there is something more to his uneasiness. Lowder's recent death has made him jumpy. There is malice in shadows. Familiar streets seem menacing. He wonders if the man on the street was following him, or if he's just imagining things. And he knows that this meeting with Hilda is precisely what Tom doesn't want. And yet somehow discovering the truth seems more important than Tom's interests. The elevator glides to a soft stop on the twenty-fourth floor. Sam follows the signs indicating that D, E, and F are to the left. In a moment, he stands before the Lowder apartment door, taking a deep breath before pushing the doorbell. He hears the sound of slow footsteps, and then the door opens. The woman standing before him looks frail.

"Mrs. Lowder? Sam Driscoll."

As Mrs. Lowder steps away from the door, she nods and gestures for Sam to enter. He follows her down a dark hallway. The whole place feels cold.

"Won't you have a seat on this sofa?" The widow points toward a comfortable wide sofa facing a seldom-used fireplace, above which hangs a superb Schiele graphite and gouache of sunflowers painted around 1911. It is of impressive size.

"I'm stunned by the Schiele," Sam says, not taking his eyes off the picture. "I am fascinated by his work. I wish I had a client who might understand and appreciate his work. Such an amazing sense of line, unerring, silence."

"My husband also acquired several nude studies, a few rather blatantly erotic." She picks up a drink umbrella from a bowl full of them on the sideboard.

"Those nudes can be off-putting to some people."

"On the other hand, some buyers will be attracted by Schiele's obsession with the erotic and miss the point of his extraordinary command of his medium." Hilda opens the little drink umbrella and twirls it absentmindedly as she gazes at the painting.

"Yes, you're right about that, Mrs. Lowder."

She folds the umbrella back up and puts it in the ornate bowl from which it came. "Mr. Driscoll, it may interest you that I will perhaps have to sell the Schieles and some other things in addition to Phi . . . , to Mr. Lowder's stock. He left a sizeable debt, which I cannot carry."

"I'm sorry to hear that, Mrs. Lowder. That prospect must be painful for you."

"You have no idea." Mrs. Lowder's words fade off as she gazes at the Schiele and then out the south-facing window.

The silence is heavy. Sam does not know how to begin the conversation again.

"How may I help you, Mr. Driscoll?" Mrs. Lowder says as she turns back from the window to peer at Sam.

"Mrs. Lowder, I'm grateful that you have agreed to see me . . . I'm sure you're wondering why I am here. I have a client who is very interested in the painting of the Virgin and Child with a cat, which your husband sold to Mark Ricci a few months ago."

"Sold? At this point it seems ridiculous to say that he sold it."

"Well, I'm determined to find out everything I can about that picture so I can represent my client's interest in the painting and provide him with any and all available understanding of it."

"Of course," Mrs. Lowder says. She falls silent again.

Sam is growing more uncomfortable. The house feels like it is closing in around them. Somewhere an antique clock ticks ponderously. "Please, Mrs. Lowder, I know this is a very sad and difficult time for you. If you'd prefer, I could come back at a later time . . ."

"No, no, Mr. Driscoll. But there is very little that I can tell you. Philip kept enormous files on the pictures he bought and sold, not to mention that he also kept, I guess, every photograph or transparency of pictures that he saw or considered. I've hardly had a chance to look at those files, as you might imagine."

"I can understand your husband's wanting to hold onto those images. From my visit with him—the day I met you briefly—I sensed that he was a man who loved images."

"He was, to distraction. He would bring files and transparencies home and pore over them until dinner. Often, he would return to his study and settle in until bedtime."

"I know the feeling," Sam says. "Paintings, works of art—even small things of no great value—capture my attention. And I can't throw away the photos and transparencies, for love or money."

"Yes," Mrs. Lowder says abruptly. "That's the way he was."

"I wish I'd known him."

"You would understand." Mrs. Lowder pauses for a moment, her eyes showing tears. "Come, I'll show you his study." She rises, beckoning Sam to follow. They return to the corridor leading to the entry. She stops before one of the doors and unlocks it.

"Be prepared for chaos on the other side of this door. Philip wouldn't allow anyone in the study. Never the cleaning lady," she says, turning to Sam as she unlocks the door.

"Philip knew where everything was, on which pile he had left a photo or a document." She opens the door. Filing cabinets, eight of them, along one wall. A long table with stacks of side-cut folders stuffed with papers and photos, transparencies. Another long trestle table, a computer attended by a comfortable-looking high-backed office chair. More stacks on either side of the computer. No apparent room to write. "He seldom left the world of art—the images themselves—behind. He would sit in here and look at pictures on his light box. Night after night. Unless there was baseball on the television. Phil was a Boston Red Sox fan."

"In New York. Now *that's* dangerous. Your husband was a man after my own heart."

Mrs. Lowder smoothes her skirt with her hands. "How can I help you, Mr. Driscoll?"

"Sam." He reaches to pat Mrs. Lowder's arm, but she moves her hand up to grasp the silver pendant hanging off her necklace.

"Sam, I'm Hilda."

"Thanks, Hilda. Is there any reason to believe that somewhere in his files your husband might have noted additional information on the Leonardo panel?"

Hilda straightens up, perhaps alarmed at Sam's question. "I wouldn't have any idea. I've never sat down with his files. Phil never talked business when he got home from the gallery. He would just go into his study and close the door for an hour or two almost every night."

"I understand, Hilda. It's just that there are questions—gaps—in the matter of the picture's history, its provenance. All we know is that your husband's father, Ray Lowder, acquired the picture from a European couple, along with a few other paintings. One would love to know where and when the European couple acquired the picture."

"Why isn't the known history of the picture enough to satisfy the prospective buyer? My husband, it seems, didn't need to know more than he did."

"Because such an important picture deserves scrutiny and stirs up questions that can lead to complications. For instance, it is quite possible that the Italian authorities may question the provenance and even try to lay claim to the picture as a lost national treasure."

"On what basis?" Hilda asks, a little sharply.

"Hard to say, but I've already heard, on good authority, that the Italians are moving in that direction."

"Philip never mentioned that," Hilda says. Her mood has changed. She seems to Sam a bit defensive and testy.

"Well, as I say, it's not definite yet, but I heard of the Italian government's interest a few days ago from a reliable source in Florence."

"Well . . . Sam, how can I help you at this moment?"

"Do you know of anything in this house or in Philip's office that could help me identify the provenance of the painting?"

Hilda looks at him in a way that makes Sam think she is estimating his worth. Her edge softens. "I was looking through some files in my dear Philip's desk. He has . . . he had a drawer of files in his desk as well as those filing cabinets along the walls in his office. He saved everything, you see. He just couldn't throw things away. He never would let me straighten out his office. Sometimes he'd stack files on the floor around his chair."

"I can relate."

"Yes." Hilda sounds as if she is on the verge of tears. "Well . . . I found two things in a file. The file is marked 'Ponte Albrizzi.'"

"That's where the picture was located from the fifteenth century on."

"There was a photograph of the Leonardo painting, an eight-by-ten that Phil must have taken recently. And stapled to that picture is a smaller one, a little bent and faded, of the same painting with . . . 'Ponte Albrizzi' written on the back. It doesn't look like Philip's handwriting."

"No other information on the back of the photograph?" Sam can feel his body tensing.

"No. I did find a letter in the same file, though. It's addressed to Ray Lowder, Philip's father. It was written by Glen Lowder, Philip's uncle who was killed in Italy."

"Does it mention the painting?"

She walks over to a manila envelope sitting on the end of a bookshelf. "Let me see; here, Glen Lowder mentions to Ray the town of Ponte Albrizzi. He writes that his unit finds the town virtually deserted, he describes the town as beautiful."

"Go on," Sam urges, hoping for some clue relative to the Leonardo painting.

"Here. Let me read this. Yes. Glen writes of a fine church, 'left as if someone had suddenly taken away a few of the things which one expects to see in an Italian church—the candlesticks, the cross, and the painting, which must have been removed from the elaborate empty frame set above the main altar.' Hilda pauses. "Then Glen writes, 'The Krauts must have taken them.'"

"Later, the picture turns up somehow in the hands of Ray Lowder, who passed it on to your late husband," Sam says, walking over to take a better look at the documents Mrs. Lowder has pulled out of the envelope. The paper looks dated, the color of an old linen sheet.

The doorbell rings and Hilda sets the manila envelope down. "Excuse me a moment, would you?" He hears her walk down the hallway and begin talking to someone. They apparently know each other—they go on at length.

Sam glances at the stuffed manila envelope sitting precariously on the end of the bookshelf. He picks it up, his pulse quickening, and finds a second letter. Scanning quickly, he sees it's one in which Glen Lowder writes to Ray Lowder indicating that he found the panel of the Virgin, Christ, and cat in Ponte Albrizzi and that he believed it was a Leonardo. Sam listens for Hilda. She is still talking by the door. He moves fast, opening the photocopier and sliding the first letter onto the glass surface, closes the lid, and quickly hits the copy button.

He hears Hilda shut the door; he fumbles with the second letter and quickly copies it, hoping the sound of the machine doesn't carry, and puts the originals back on the shelf and stuffs the photocopies in his briefcase. He steps hurriedly out into the living room. She is carrying a flower bouquet.

"A neighbor brought these by," she says, a weak smile on her face.

"It must be terribly hard," Sam says, smoothing his coat.

"Yes, I miss him." Her eyes turn back to tired. "What more can I do for you?"

He feels uneasy plying her for more information. "Simply, if you happen to discover any more relevant information on the Leonardo picture, I would be very glad to know about it." Sam glances back toward Philip Lowder's study. "I will certainly understand if Mark Ricci has expressed the same request—"

"He hasn't," Hilda Lowder cuts in. "Besides, I'm afraid of him and don't trust him. I heard . . ." Her voice trails away; she puts a hand to her lips as if frightened of what she might say.

"What did you hear?" Sam urges gently.

"Nothing. I'd prefer not to discuss Mark Ricci or have anything to do with him." She looks around, scanning the corners nervously.

"Has he been here?"

"No, I've told the concierge not to ever let him or any of his underlings in here."

"I understand," Sam says in agreement. He'll leave it alone for now.

"Mr. Driscoll . . . Sam, I will let you know immediately if I find anything related to the Leonardo picture."

Sam grips his briefcase a bit tighter. "I would be most grateful, and I thank you for letting me visit with you today."

Hilda guides him down the hallway toward the front door. They stand in the hall. Sam clutches the briefcase. He produces a card from one of the pockets. "Here is my private cell phone number, in addition to my office and home numbers." He thanks her and turns to take the stairs down.

As soon as he steps outside Hilda Lowder's building, his phone rings. It's a member of Tom's staff, summoning him—with a note of urgency—to the office. Sam feels a rock in the pit of his stomach as he hails a cab.

CHAPTER TWENTY-EIGHT

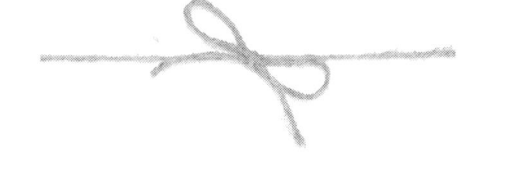

"Sometimes you're pretty hard to get ahold of," Tom says as he walks into the conference room where Sam waits for him. No greeting, Sam notes. He means business. Sylvie walks in behind Tom, looking similarly disgruntled. He has never seen Sylvie in Tom's office before. "Gone for a week to Italy, now out of touch for a morning," Tom says. "This isn't just your usual week at the office, Sam. We've got a two-hundred-seventy-five-million-dollar deal to do this week."

"Tom, I told you the painting's not worth more than two hundred twenty-five million."

"I know. I'm trying to talk him down to two hundred fifteen million. Do you have any idea how much money that is, Sam? This is exactly when I need you to be available."

"Look, I know this is going to upset you, but I was visiting with Hilda Lowder, the widow of Philip Lowder, the man who sold the Leonardo to Ricci."

"I told you when you proposed the Italy trip to cut out your research. I told you that again once you got back."

"I know, but as your art advisor, it is my business to look into Hilda Lowder or to go to Italy if it's in your interest." Sam turns toward Sylvie to see if she is tracking him, but she is gazing steadily at Tom. The scarf that Sam and Tom picked out for Sylvie is wrapped around her shoulders. Of course, she doesn't have a clue that Sam helped pick it out.

"I have revoked your permission to determine my best interest on this painting, Sam."

"As I mentioned, the Italians are starting to suggest that the picture is important cultural property and that, absent clear title by an American owner prior to Lowder and Ricci, they—Italy—can claim ownership. I felt it was important to find out more."

"What can the Italians do about it?" Sylvie says, cocking her head dismissively.

"They can bring the matter to a governmental level. Between the Italian government and the US State Department."

"That's concerning," Sylvie says, turning to Tom.

"It's not *that* big an issue," Tom says.

"Tom, there are precedents, and with the Internet, attention to protection and recovery of cultural property is increasing. It has been increasing for some time."

"What can they do, Sam? Bring in the military?" Tom smirks. "Come on."

"Tom, listen to him," Sylvie says as she bunches up the scarf she is now holding.

"All I'm saying is that times have changed. What was possible, what someone could get away with twenty years ago, is less possible now, given the priority and importance assigned to works of art that define a nation's culture."

"It's not as if Italy has no works of art by Leonardo da Vinci."

Tom is like a bulldog, Sam thinks. He can't read Sylvie either. "Right, and Leonardo is one of the greatest figures in the entire history of art. I was involved in such a dispute in my curatorial days. A museum trustee smuggled a small Italian Renaissance picture into the States . . . twenty-eight years ago. The Italians claimed ownership and illegal export. The State Department got involved. The Italians won. The picture is back in Italy. The trustee resigned. The director was fired."

"Sam, all this is beside the point. I told you to stop researching the provenance. I told Ricci that I will make an offer on the Leonardo. Apparently, someone else is considering an offer too. Simply put, I am going to have that painting, no matter what."

Silence. Sam cradles his chin in his hand looking at Tom. "I know what you're saying. This Leonardo represents a collector's dream. Unprecedented."

"Right, Sam. You agree."

"Tom, I'm saying that the painting's ownership may very well be challenged. Even if Ricci agrees to sell it for two hundred fifteen million, the new owner is in line to prove clear title if the Italian government chooses to pursue that question."

"Sam, we don't know what the Italians are up to."

"That's the point, Tom. There's tremendous risk. It's Ricci's problem at this point. Let Ricci—"

"I've built this company on risk. I'm not about to back down from this opportunity because of a dustup over ownership. I've taken on organized gangs and contrary-minded stockholders."

"Governments work a little differently, I think," Sylvie says. "We don't want to lose two hundred fifteen million and our reputation on this."

"Sam, you believe this is the real thing, don't you?"

"I do."

"Well. Get out of the way then."

Sam recoils and stares at Tom. Sylvie's cheeks are tingeing pink. Pulling out the letter from Glen to Ray would be decisive, but Sam thinks better of it. Tom's made it clear he doesn't care what the provenance says.

Turning his swivel chair away from the conference table, Tom gazes out the window. Not a word. Finally, "Sam, if you are not 100 percent behind this project, I'll have to continue to deal with Ricci directly."

Sam turns to Sylvie. She perhaps could stop Tom, but she looks away toward her husband. "All I'm trying to say, Tom, is that I would hate to see you in the position of holding property subject to seizure, having acquired it through Ricci, who will want to hang on to your money."

"You don't trust Ricci, do you?"

"No. Any good dealer is something of an opportunist. Ricci is someone I would describe as . . . sharp, extra sharp. Should it come to an actual claim, I think you would have a tough job getting all your money back if the sale of the Leonardo is declared null and void."

"Do you trust Ricci?" Sylvie asks her husband.

"I trust him in that I think I can use him to get me what I want."

Sylvie nods. "We've both decided we want the painting." She stares at Sam. "Are you willing to work with Ricci?"

"I'm not entirely sure I am, at least not on this one. The stakes are high."

"You've made your point, Sam," Tom says. "You see risk and problems. You're blind to the reward. I am not."

"The possibility of risk, Tom."

"Sam, we've done a lot together. Now I think we've gone far enough."

"What?"

"I never thought I'd be saying this to you." Tom abruptly gets up, striding toward his office through the adjoining door. "You're fired."

Sylvie stands up and follows after him.

CHAPTER TWENTY-NINE

"Me to the woods," Sam says, quoting Robert Frost almost in a daze as he climbs the steps to the front entrance of the Met. After his morning with Tom, he's craving some restorative time in his temple.

His cell phone rings. It's Cassie.

"Sam, hello, it's me. My meeting was canceled so I can do lunch early. Are you free?"

Really he would prefer to postpone the whole thing, but Cassie's so rarely in New York for lunch. "Cassie, can you give me an hour?"

"I can give you that."

"Let's meet in the Met, say in the restaurant in the Decorative Arts wing where we met last time we were at the museum together."

"Fine. See you at one o'clock." She clicks off her phone.

Sam feels woozy; the facade of the museum swims in the sunlight. The last thing he wants to do is meet with Cassie, and yet he knows he has to. After checking his briefcase, Sam walks into the huge entry space and heads to the right-hand doorway leading toward the Egyptian collections. Deep in the corner of a small gallery, his eye seeks a familiar glow livened by an overhead spotlight. The shape is dear and precious to him. It is that of a fragmentary portrait head carved from precious jasper, which reflects auraed hues of butterscotch and orange. The fragment evokes elegance and mystery. It's the one that Tom hired someone to make Sam a copy of. Because of the sculptor's choice of jasper as a medium, the head stands apart from the limestone and basalt sculptures with which it shares its space.

The anonymous carver has divined a queen, or perhaps the favorite of a Pharaoh—in any case an image of an unknown rendered with exquisite grace and presence. All that is necessary to communicate the essence and power of haunting beauty is there—an elegant mouth defined by full sensuous lips, the taut curve of the cheek, the lingering traces of the nose. This apparition has drawn Sam countless times to visit it. Always he is profoundly stirred by his frequent wonder at what was lost, the woman's identity, her history, her fate, the story of the sculpture's destruction, the saga of her arrival in this gallery, in this museum. And here he is before her now. Seeing how she has withstood all these centuries always generates in Sam a deep sense of well-being.

He walks through several galleries until he comes to the Chinese Sculpture Collection. At one end, set on a high platform, is a Sung Period gilt-and-polychrome wooden figure of Kuan-Yin. She is the symbol in Chinese Buddhist lore of beneficence and mercy. The deity sits surveying an assemblage of Chinese figures with a benign gaze, yet with a slight *hauteur*. A large figure, this personification of compassion commands not only space in the gallery, but also seems to hold the other ancient figures in the thrall of her presence. Sam is filled with a sense of hushed awe. Before this extraordinary carved wooden sculpture, he is always moved by a sense of peace and calm.

When he can no longer put it off, Sam enters the museum restaurant. Cassie is comfortably unaware at a four-top, gazing across the dining room out the window at the pond behind the museum.

"Cass," Sam calls softly as he reaches the table edge. She is striking when she is still and her attention is focused far from where she is.

"Cass," Sam calls again. She turns to him, smiling brightly. Sam leans over to kiss her forehead. "Hi. How are ya?"

"Fine." She smiles still. "I'm fine."

"Good to see you. Nice surprise, meeting up like this for lunch."

"Is it?"

"Yes, I mean it." He bites his tongue. All these subtle ways he lies to Cassie and Tom to please them are why he feels so betrayed by himself now. He has no idea how he got himself in a place where he was fired from a career where his love of art fueled his client's greed.

"Good, I'm glad. It's been about two weeks."

"I know."

The waitress comes to the table. "Ready to order?" she asks pleasantly, looking at Sam, then Cassie. He wonders if Cassie has ever experienced being fired. They quickly give their order. Sam orders automatically, not from appetite but from habit.

"How'd it go with Tom today?"

"Poorly."

"Did you tell him about your trip?"

"Yes." Sam doesn't want to divulge this information to Cassie.

"I never responded to the text you sent me from the cardboard box exhibit because I didn't know how to. I am trying to understand your problems with the field, but, Sam, you're at the top of the art advisory world. You deal with the richest and the best. Why jeopardize that?"

Cassie's misunderstanding of his profound disappointment in the art world flips a switch in Sam. He is suddenly, strangely, at ease. He pauses for a moment, gathering himself. "I'm not sure I care about 'best' anymore, Cassie. That's what I was trying to tell you. Not if it's at the expense of my own integrity."

Something flickers on Cassie's face. Alarm? Disdain?

The waitress arrives with their salads. Sam picks up his fork. He can see that there's no point in getting into how he feels about the art world with Cassie. They have fundamentally different orientations toward work. Cassie seems to sense his thoughts. She turns her head to gaze out the nearby window and swallows, compressing her lips in a hard, determined smile.

"Cass," Sam says gently. "There's this, I don't know, this shift in the way we are together. Or at least I feel there is."

Cassie is staring down at her napkin folded in front of her. She lifts the edge slightly, lets it fall into place, totally attentive to that small gesture . . . then silence. Sam looks at her downturned face as she says, "I'm feeling stretched thin. I'm feeling that this—our relationship—is taxing. Maybe that's not the right word, but that's how it feels."

Sam leans back in his chair, looks beyond Cassie across the dining room to the large picture windows. Then his gaze finds her. "How can we do this differently? A better way for both of us?"

"I don't know," Cassie says almost in a whisper. "Maybe some time apart."

Sam turns back to his salad and picks through the lettuce. He feels kicked in the stomach for a second time in one day. Yet there is something else—a relief bubbling up from deep inside. He can see it all so clearly.

CHAPTER THIRTY

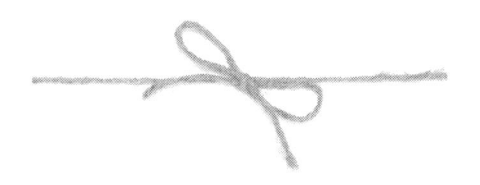

It has been three days since Sam left New York. Neither Tom nor Sylvie nor Cassie has called to ask to change their course. Sam sits at the desk in his study staring out through a large picture window over the marshland and beyond to the blue expanse of Long Island Sound. The phone rings and he picks it up.

"Hello?"

"Yes, this is Hilda Lowder."

"Oh, hello. I'm glad you called."

"I wanted to thank you for visiting me. Are you coming to New York again soon?"

"I have no immediate plans. Is there something I can do for you?"

"No. But I have something to share with you that I think will interest you."

Sam sits straight up in his chair. "Oh?"

"I'm not sure whether to convey it by phone."

Sam thinks of the mysterious death of Lowder and wonders if Hilda suspects her line could be tapped. Surely a quarter billion is enough money for Ricci or even Tom to tap a few phone lines.

Hilda Lowder is silent. After a moment she says, "I was totally unaware about the history of the Leonardo painting, and Philip didn't have any idea of the importance of the picture when he sold it to Mark Ricci."

"I understand," Sam replies.

"Do you really understand? Phil was furious with Mark Ricci. That man took my husband for a ride. You know what Ricci is asking for that painting? The whole world knows," Hilda says bitterly.

"I can imagine how your husband felt." Sam pauses, not knowing whether he should instead say what he's about to say in person, but really it's nothing no one else doesn't know. "Ricci cheated Phil and Phil knew it. It may well turn out that Ricci will not be able to sell the painting."

"What's to stop him?"

"The Italian government. It's not unlikely that the authorities will file a claim on the painting, if they can prove illegal export." Sam stands up with the cordless phone and walks over to a drawer, pulls out a map of Italy. He looks at Ponte Albrizzi and then at Sicily—Ricci's homeland.

"Phil got the picture when his father died and left the business to my husband. Phil didn't know how the picture came to America, or when."

"Well, perhaps you're right. If he'd known the truth about the painting, he certainly wouldn't have sold the painting to Ricci for the price he asked."

"Just before he died, he told me that he didn't trust Ricci. I overheard him arguing with that man two days before he went fishing that last time."

"What did you hear?" Sam says, setting the map down.

"Phil was angry. I could hear his voice."

"Could you hear what he said?"

"Yes." Hilda pauses. Sam thinks he can hear her swallow nervously. "I heard him say 'Ricci, nobody knows. Nobody has to know. There's no proof.'"

"Did you hear anything more?" Sam's whole body is alert.

Hilda hesitates, then says in a half whisper over the phone, "He . . . he . . . said 'Mark, please. Get off my back.' That's all I heard. Phil must have hung up then."

Sam feels a heavy weight on his chest. "Did you report that conversation to the police when they brought you word of your husband's death?"

"No. No, I didn't think of it then. I was in shock."

"Of course you were. Do you have the name of the policeman who visited you?"

"Yes, I think so. He gave me his card."

"Hilda, I think you should call him and tell him what you heard," Sam says, putting the map away.

"What could it mean to the police? Philip's . . . gone."

"The word threaten is pretty strong." He shuts the file cabinet drawer a little too hard. "I think the police should know about that argument. For the record. Did your husband say anything about it?"

"No, nothing. After he hung up, he stayed in his office for some time, an hour or so. And when he came out, he was very remote. He hardly spoke during that evening before he went to bed."

"Did the police tell you anything about your husband's death, the cause or perhaps the circumstances?"

"The lieutenant said that Philip drowned. That somehow he tripped or stumbled aboard the boat, knocked the back of his head, and fell over."

"Mrs. . . . Hilda, I have the feeling that what you've told me should be reported to the police." Sam listens intently to the silence on the line. Is there a nearly inaudible static, or is it his imagination? He worries he is crossing into dangerous territory advising Lowder's widow about this matter.

"Sam, what are you suggesting? Do you think Phil's death was . . . was not an accident?"

"I know nothing about that, but a violent argument with threats in the middle of business between seller and buyer, involving a two-hundred-seventy-five-million-dollar painting without a complete history or provenance, which the owner sold for two hundred fifty thousand, is perhaps suggestive."

"I don't understand," Hilda says.

Sam masks the hint of frustration he feels at this willful sense of denial. "Give the police this account you've just given me."

"Yes, but who will I speak to?"

"Call the NYPD." He checks himself. "It's probably nothing, but it's worth a phone call for the record."

"I suppose you're right. Now I must say goodbye. I'm tired, and the strain of the last ten days has been awful. Thank you for your concern, Sam." He hears the click as she hangs up.

Sam settles back in his comfortable, high-backed chair. "Well, there it is," he says out loud, staring off into the Sound. He thinks of Tom. If Ricci really did kill off Lowder, then Tom could be in trouble too if anything goes wrong with the painting. He knows it's unreasonable, but after sixteen years with Tom, he still feels a sense of responsibility for his interests. Sam decides he must call Tom.

"Mr. Baxter's office."

"Angela, it's Sam. Is it possible to speak to Tom?"

"Yes, I'll put you through."

Tom picks up.

"Tom, I spoke with Hilda Lowder this morning. She, as you remember, is the widow of Philip Lowder, who sold the Leonardo to Mark Ricci."

"Dammit! I told you to stop talking to people about this painting."

"Listen, Tom, please. She told me that Ricci threatened her husband."

"So?"

"So, her husband turned up dead."

"And?"

"And Ricci has a two-hundred-seventy-five-million-dollar painting out of this. I think you should be careful, Tom."

"Sam, this is preposterous. You're really losing it now. I've already sent Ricci a check for two hundred fifteen million today. My lawyers say that if you tell anyone anything that you've learned about the painting's provenance, you'll be in breach of our contract. If you breach our contract, I'll have the right to sue you for everything I lose on this painting, and I'll drag your name through the mud. *Capisci?*"

"Yes, I understand."

"And now I'm going to formally ask you to please stop calling me." The line goes dead.

"For Christ's sweet sake," Sam says aloud, rubbing his forehead. He puts his feet on the desk, leans back in his chair, and stares out across the marsh to the water beyond.

CHAPTER THIRTY-ONE

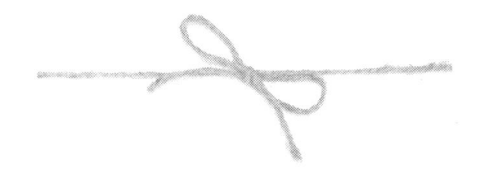

"Donahue." Lieutenant Jim Donahue is on the phone at his direct contact number in Precinct 24, access to which is limited to internal police business and a few of Donahue's best friends. The detective Hilda spoke to earlier about her husband's death has passed her along to his number.

"What can I do for you today, ma'am?"

"Well, it's about a threat followed two days later by a death—my husband's death, Philip Lowder. Are you familiar with the case?"

"Yes, I believe that was the one we deemed accidental. I'm so sorry, ma'am." For Donahue, this is the worst part, talking to the victim's relatives.

"Yes."

Hilda relates the published facts of Philip Lowder's death off the Montauk coast, the recovery of the body followed by the drifting boat. She explains the details of the heated exchange with Mark Ricci two days before this death and the fact that Ricci paid Lowder a pittance for what has turned out to be the most expensive work of art ever sold.

"Okay, let me talk to Gill, the investigator who worked on that case, and I'll get back to you."

"Thank you, lieutenant. Maybe I'm making too much out of an overheard conversation."

"Can't be too careful, Mrs. Lowder. A threat is a threat. Look, I'll run this one down immediately, okay?"

"I'm grateful, lieutenant."

"Of course, Mrs. Lowder. I'm on it."

Hilda Lowder places the phone on its cradle, leans back in her chair, and begins reading an art magazine. Since Phil passed, she is forcing herself to learn more about art in order to sort out his collection.

Barely half an hour later, her phone rings.

"Mrs. Lowder, it's Lieutenant Donahue. I talked to the detective who investigated your husband's death. It was filed as accidental drowning. Actually . . ." Donahue pauses. "Before we go any further, are you okay with a few graphic details?"

"Yes, I have had to suffer through quite a few in the last couple of weeks. I can handle it."

"All right." Donahue continues. "Let me know if you need me to back off at any point. The coroner found a—and I'm quoting a report they emailed over—a severe wound on the back of Philip's head that they couldn't quite figure out. On the *back* of the head. Probably knocked him out cold. But what makes this suspicious is that if he fell over backwards aboard his boat, he likely would have been found *in* the boat."

"It would seem so. Lieutenant Donahue, where does all this lead?"

"Again, I'm not certain, but we are going to open an investigation. This Mr. Ricci. Who is he anyway?"

"He's a powerful art dealer who bought a masterpiece for a song, as I told you, and is about to sell it for two hundred seventy-five million dollars."

Donahue whistles at the enormous sum. "'Money is the root of all evil,' my father used to say."

"I'm feeling somewhat like that myself," Hilda says.

CHAPTER THIRTY-TWO

"Mark, there are two gentlemen here to see you. A Lieutenant Donahue and a Sergeant Petrocelli, from the New York Police Department." Anthea grips the phone at her desk, talking to Ricci while she takes in the police officers' impassive faces.

"What are they selling, raffle tickets?" Ricci brings his free hand up to his silk necktie and straightens it.

"No, Mr. Ricci They would like to have a word with you."

"It won't take but a couple of minutes," Donahue says to Anthea.

"Mark, the gentleman says it won't take but a few minutes."

"Well, send them up."

The two plainclothes policemen enter the elevator. At the top floor, they exit. "Mr. Ricci?" Lieutenant Donahue calls out in the hallway. "Mr. Ricci?"

"Down at the end of the hall!" Ricci calls out.

The policemen look at one another as they come to the doorway to find Ricci on the phone seated behind his desk. On the easel at the end of the room is a large painting of a Renoir, *Nude Bathing,* which Ricci told Dennis to put up while the elevator rose from the ground floor. As the men enter the office, the dealer sits in his chair with the phone to his ear, nodding as if in agreement with the voice on the line. "Let's buy it," he says into the phone as the two men stand, looking puzzled, if not annoyed, at the casual reception Ricci is giving them. Ricci speaks into the phone again. "Okay, I'll get back to you." He hangs up and turns to his two visitors. Without standing, he motions to two gilded silk upholstered chairs. "Make yourselves comfortable, gentlemen."

"Mr. Ricci, I'm Lieutenant Donahue, NYPD. This is my associate, Sergeant Petrocelli. Sergeant Petrocelli has been assigned to the investigation of the death of a Mr. Philip Lowder."

"I read about it in the paper. Was it three weeks ago?"

"Yes. That's right, sir," says Petrocelli. "Did you happen to know Mr. Lowder? We understand that he was an art dealer."

"Uh . . . yes. Not well. I did a little business with him, that's all."

"A little business? What would that mean?"

"Oh, one transaction during the last year."

"One transaction?" Petrocelli asks.

"Yes, that's all." Ricci leans back in his chair and stretches.

"That's all? Could you tell us about the transaction, Mr. Ricci?" Donahue says.

"It was a European painting." Ricci looks out the window as he speaks. "You know, I can't really remember. I think it was a painting, possible sixteenth century, a Virgin and Child. A common subject."

"Can you tell us how much you bought the painting for?" They are both staring at Ricci, but he gazes up at the ceiling in a studied show of casualness.

"Well, I don't generally make public the numbers and values of our deals . . . transactions, gentlemen." He laughs jovially as if talking business with old buddies at his country club.

"Mr. Ricci, this information is not for the public. This is an official police investigation. I hope you understand." Petrocelli sits forward in his chair.

"I do, but what does this have to do with Mr. Lowder's death? It was an accident wasn't it? I read . . ."

"That's what we're trying to determine, Mr. Ricci," Donahue says.

"Ah."

"So how much was that deal—transaction—that you mentioned? The sixteenth-century painting?"

"Let's see . . ." Ricci pauses.

"Would you like to look it up?"

"Yes, if you can wait a moment."

"Take your time," Petrocelli says.

Ricci picks up the phone, buzzes Dennis.

"Dennis. How much did we pay for that sixteenth-century Virgin and Child we bought a while ago?" Pause. "I'll wait." Ricci places his hand over the mouthpiece. "My assistant will look it up."

"Hard to keep those figures straight, I guess. Business must be going well, right, Mr. Ricci?" Petrocelli says.

"Yes, it is. And business is not bad, thanks."

Ricci keeps his ear to the phone. Silent, looking perplexed. The policemen look across the room at the Renoir. They exchange glances, Petrocelli smiling, raising and lowering his eyebrows. Ricci still holds the phone close to his face. Suddenly Dennis appears at the door. Ricci now looks pleasantly at the officers.

"Mark, the sixteenth-century Virgin?" Dennis asks. "You mean the Leona . . . oh, sorry. Excuse me."

Donahue and Petrocelli turn from Dennis to Ricci then to one another.

"That would be the Leonardo da Vinci that the whole world is talking about. Would that be right, Mr. Ricci?" Petrocelli says.

Ricci slowly, with apparent discomfort, places the phone on the receiver.

"Yes . . . we . . . I bought the painting, and later we discovered—it was quite a shock, as you might imagine—that a painting by Leonardo . . . da Vinci was hidden underneath the visible painting."

"And how much did you pay for that picture, Mr. Ricci?" Donahue asks.

"Is it really relevant to your investigation? I can't see why you're interested in the minutiae of my business. Perhaps my lawyer . . ."

"I think it would be best if you left questions of relevancy to us, Mr. Ricci. However, if you'd like to consult with your lawyer . . . Or perhaps we could all go downtown and finish our interview there, if you'd prefer." Donahue stands up and folds his arms across his chest.

"I paid two hundred twenty-five thousand for the painting," Ricci says sullenly. Dennis has quietly backed out of the office.

"And the seller was . . . ?"

"Philip Lowder," Ricci snaps, looking at Petrocelli.

"And the press is saying that the present selling price is two hundred fifteen million." Donahue continues to stand across the desk from Ricci. "Quite a return on your investment."

"It isn't sold yet," Ricci answers in a low voice.

"I understand."

"Mr. Ricci, did you have contact or conversations with Mr. Lowder subsequent to your remarkably fortuitous purchase?" Petrocelli asks.

Ricci looks out the window, as is his habit. After a moment he says, "I don't remember. Possibly. Once, maybe after the sale."

"Just once?" Petrocelli asks.

"That's what I said."

"Do you recall the substance of that conversation?"

"No, of course not. It was weeks ago."

"Nothing?"

"No. Oh, maybe some small detail about provenance or something like that."

"Did Mr. Lowder seem . . . depressed or angry, in your opinion?" Donahue interrupts.

"No, it was a routine call."

"Nothing more?"

"Nothing more."

"You never had an argument with Mr. Lowder during that conversation . . . or any other?" Donahue asks.

Ricci, clearly startled, hesitates. "No, of course not. Why do you ask?"

"Just wondering," Donahue says.

"What's this about? I've told you all I can."

"Thank you, Mr. Ricci," Donahue says. "That's all for now. We'll let you get on with your day."

Both policemen get to their feet and start toward the door. Donahue turns back toward Ricci, still seated and looking a bit frayed.

"Mr. Ricci, if in the next couple of weeks you have plans to leave the city, would you please give me a call?" Donahue hands the dealer his card. "Here, take my card. I'm quite easy to reach."

CHAPTER THIRTY-THREE

At three in the afternoon an armored car parks in front of Tom Baxter's address on Fifth Avenue. It is preceded and followed by unmarked cars carrying private armed security personnel who augment the armed driver and occupants of the armored car. Parking space has been cordoned off for the small convoy, and police officers are grouped at the curb and the door to Tom's building.

A chauffeured limousine pulls in just behind the last security car. Ricci and his assistant, Dennis, proceed from the limo directly to the entrance of the exclusive apartment building. Out of the secure carrying space of the truck appears a sizeable crate with "Fragile, This side up" stenciled top and bottom on both sides. Ricci, like a symphony orchestra conductor, ever the maestro, directs and commands as four men cautiously carry the crate through the building entrance, then head for the large freight elevator. Two armed guards, Ricci, Dennis, and four porters will accompany the crate up to Tom Baxter's penthouse apartment.

The elevator rises slowly. The passengers are silent, watching the floor numbers flash above the door. Into the large quiet elevator cab, Ricci says before the last number comes up, "Finally. I made it." Puzzlement shows on a few passenger faces.

The elevator stops and immediately Gerhard, the Baxters' head butler, opens the door. Just behind him stands Tom Baxter, beaming.

"Mr. Ricci! I must know you from somewhere! Have you brought me a present?"

"A small one," Ricci says with an expansive gesture. "A tiny painting by a minor master."

"Well, bring it in. Welcome. You security fellows may stand down. I think the risk is over."

"Are you sure, sir? We'd be glad to stay if you need us," says one of the guards.

"No, no thanks, officer. We've got quite the security system here."

Ricci's men bring the crate out of the elevator into the back hall and place it gently on the floor. With power tools they remove the screws from the top of the box.

Ricci, standing next to Tom, watches his men like a hawk. "Careful! Both of you lift the lid slowly."

Tom is tense with excitement, expectation.

Inside the crate are custom-fitted Styrofoam corner braces. A painting is visible through two layers of airtight wrapping and small cushion bubble wrap. The men, one seeming to hold his breath, carefully lift the package from the crate and rest it on a padded shipping blanket spread out on the floor. Now the delicate part: the removal of the four layers of wrap. Tom crosses one arm across his chest, the other one supports his chin, covering his mouth. He feels both excited and anxious. Ricci continues to direct his experienced art handlers every step of the way. The last wrap falls away, revealing *The Virgin and Child with a Cat* in all its idiosyncratic beauty and mystery.

Tom does not speak, cannot speak. Ricci stares at the Leonardo with a smile of satisfaction.

"Well, Tom, buddy, how does it feel to own the most valuable painting in the world?"

Tom looks silently at the painting supported on each side by the art handlers. "You know, Mark? It feels . . . magnificent. I never imagined . . ."

"Well, let's get it installed. Guys, let's get to work." Turning to Tom, he says, "What time do your guests arrive?"

"Seven."

"We'll have plenty of time. Shouldn't take more than an hour. I'll want to check out the atmospheric control system you had installed."

"Have at it, Mark. I'll show you to the Leonardo room. We took out the wall between a closet and a bathroom to create space just for the Leonardo."

The art handlers carrying the painting follow Tom and Mark to the reconfigured room that has been painted in a subtle stone-gray color complemented by gray carpet. The small gallery is equipped with low-heat lighting and vents for the state-of-the-art atmospheric control system designed to maintain the stability of the wood panel and its ancient painted surface.

"I'll leave you men to your work. I've got a conference call. Ask Gerhard to come and get me when you're finished. Don't drop the painting, for God's sake," Tom says with a smile.

An hour and a half later, summoned by the butler, Tom returns to the Leonardo Room as he has decided to call the small newly minted gallery.

He stands at the door. *The Virgin and Child with a Cat* is bathed in a moderately low light, glowing against the soft gray background, projecting toward the viewer as if radiating an inner glow.

"Breathtaking. Simply breathtaking," Tom almost whispers. He so rarely feels such awe.

"How many collectors can say they own a Leonardo, Tom?" Ricci is ever the cheerleader.

"How many dealers can say they collected two hundred and fifteen million for a painting, Mark?" Tom's smile isn't exactly glowing.

"Tom, I did give you a break, didn't I? We started at two hundred and seventy-five if you remember."

"Was that what it was?"

"There is no precedent . . ."

"We've been through that. It's unlikely that the world will ever know what you paid for the Leonardo." That subject strikes mortal fear in Ricci's heart. He swallows hard.

"Well, most sellers don't declare their purchase prices to the world, Tom, old buddy."

"Wrong, Mark. Our business is closely regulated. Most of our transactions are by law a matter of record. Full disclosure."

"Let's not argue. You're standing in front of a masterpiece. Any collector would give . . ."

"How much?"

"Many collectors would give anything to own that picture." Mark points at the painting, raising his voice. "It's . . . it's a trophy!"

"We'll let it go at that," Tom says quietly, taken aback by Ricci's shrillness.

"I guess we'd better," Ricci says morosely. Both men stand looking at the Leonardo.

CHAPTER THIRTY-FOUR

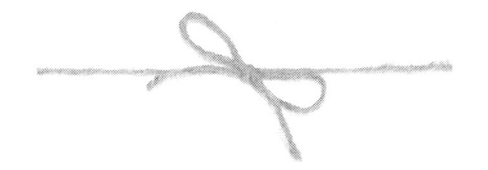

Late May weather in Wind River country is still cool, but there is no trace of snow as Sam covers the last section of his road trip from Stonington to Dubois, Wyoming. His long-bed truck with its cap, home for the large gray dogs for the last three days, has carried him at a brisk 60 mph well past Lander.

Before leaving on the trip, the Italian government began discussions with Sam, hoping that he would testify as an expert witness. They say his testimony is crucial. Soon thereafter, Sam received one death threat in the mail. The police haven't traced it. They have recommended that he not testify in person in the matter, out of an abundance of caution. Since being on the road, he hasn't seen any evidence of Ricci's people following him.

All his fears over Ricci seem as though they burned off back in South Dakota's Badlands. Holding his attention in the distance is Crowheart Butte, noble and solitary, rising up from the flat land, legendary site of a hand-to-hand fight between the Crow and Shoshone chiefs in 1866. It is a beacon for Sam, less than an hour from the ranch his father left him. The ranch, since Sam turned fifteen, was home during winter holidays and many summers. Twenty miles from Dubois, tucked well back off the road, a lodge building, three cabins, and corrals sit by the East Fork, a tributary of the Wind River.

Dan Forman lives in a comfortable cabin set apart from the group of ranch buildings by the river. For twenty years he has been caretaker, hay man, wrangler, as well as independent outfitter and hunting guide. Dan is older than Sam by twenty-two years, once married, divorced long ago. Sam considers him family in all but blood. Dan is quiet and wise as men are who live alone and are immersed in and dependent upon the seasons—loners who have few acquaintances and yet are close to animals, horses, and wild game, feel profoundly connected to wind, weather, nature in all its guts and aspects.

Sam is eager to settle in to the stillness of this peaceful land for a while. He seeks to distance himself from the titanic energy, the frequently dysfunctional ethos of New York. Central as the city has been to his professional life, his aspiration, and his practice, he is at this moment in full flight from that world. It is a joyful retreat.

The golden light of the descending sun washes the arid land, turning the sandstone cliffs and outcroppings and the wintered grass rich ochre. Sam passes the two-hundred-yard-long settlement of Crowheart, marked by an old-growth stand of trees lining the road and a general store housing the post office for the outlying ranch population. He presses the accelerator to seventy.

"Got to keep up with my soul," he says out loud, shutting off the satellite radio that has kept him company over the long distance from the East Coast.

Looking into the rearview mirror, Sam sees the dogs standing in the capped truckbed. "You know where we are, don't you, guys?" Their attention is riveted on the country they have come to know in the same way twice a year for the past seven years.

Twenty minutes after passing Crowheart, Sam turns down the gravel county road that leads to the ranch entrance ten miles to the east. Pulling up to the double swinging gate chained and padlocked, he gets out of the car, stretches, shakes the cramps out of his legs, and opens the lock. The ranch lies at the end of a narrower gravel road that curves down a steep sagebrush-covered hill.

Dusk has settled into this dell in which the ranch buildings were built sixty years ago. Stopping the car, Sam feels the tension of driving subside as he sits in the silence, cheered at the sight of lamplight shining through the windows of the main house.

He doesn't move for a few moments. Then he opens the window. Almost utter silence, except for the whisper of water a hundred yards away. He can smell the river. Slowly, Sam gets out of the car, stands still for a few moments, listening to the whispering of the East Fork.

"Lordy, lordy." He lets the tailgate down. The dogs leap from the truckbed and start their patrol.

Sam takes his bags to the lodge, enters the large living room, its walls hung with deer, elk, lynx, bear, and buffalo skin trophies, which came with the ranch when his father bought it years ago. Dan has laid the fire. On the rustic 1920s pine-and-log table is a note in handprinted pencil:

"Sam. Welcome back, boy. Store-bought roasted chicken and some greens in the cold box. See you, Dan."

Sam lights the fire, freshly kindled with kerosene-soaked sawdust. The electric heat that Dan turned on early in the afternoon has brought the lodge up to a comfortable temperature, and the fire that soon catches on dried pine logs roars and animates the shapes of well-stuffed worn leather furniture and some of the trophies in the dimly lit, high-ceilinged room. The dogs settle in front of the fireplace near a deep leather easy chair set at an angle to the hearth. They perk their heads as Sam comes toward the chair carrying a short glass of Laphroaig and hot water. He sinks into the soft leather, watching the fire. Settling. He raises his glass in toast.

"Thanks, Dan. Dogs, we're home again."

Eight-thirty in the morning, Sam is at the door. "Come, dogs, time to eat." Night's breath of frost glazes the new grass. The dogs set to their large food dishes while Sam lays strips of bacon in a cast-iron skillet, rich with patina.

As he is cracking eggs to scramble, he hears a knock on the door.

"C'mon in," Sam calls, turning from the counter toward the front door. The latch clicks open. Dan walks in, closes the heavy, double-planked doors, and wipes his boots on the brush mat.

"In the kitchen, Dan. Coffee's on."

"I'm ready for it." Dan comes through the kitchen door. They shake hands; Sam puts his free arm around Dan's shoulder.

"Too long, Dan."

"That's what I keep telling you."

"I know, I know." Sam shakes his head with a grin. "A man's got to earn the rent."

"I suppose. So how are you? Can I sit? Knee's a bit off."

"Good friend, you're at home. Coffee?"

"Dying for it." Dan sits on a stool. Dundee clacks into the kitchen, trots toward Dan, noses between the cowboy's neck and shoulder, reaching to nuzzle his ear.

"Good old dog remembers me. Hey, Dundee, you big baby," Dan says in a sweet half whisper, scratching Dundee's ear.

"Eggs? Scrambled over easy, right?"

"Save my life," Dan says, resting his hand on the back of the adoring dog. "Had a biscuit with peanut butter and jam before I came over. Kind of figured you'd be whipping up something good."

"Good timing. I'm glad to see you, Dan. Coming back here, being here and seeing you, listening to all the blessed silence around—it's a lifesaver."

"Glad you're here, Sam. You come a long way." Dan pulls a pocketknife out of his back pocket and opens it, peers at a raw spot on his hand. "How's the drive? God, I couldn't do it."

"You know . . . it just happens. It seems like that. I head the car west and it's almost as if it's on automatic pilot."

"I hear you. Like Quest. I get on him, head him out. He just knows where we're going, knows where we are, where we been. I'm just sitting following him." Dan pulls a thorn out of his hand with the help of his knife. "Been trying to get that sucker loose from my hand for a week," he says as he closes the knife and puts it back in his pocket. He gets up and throws the thorn in the trash.

"That horse of yours is one of a kind," Sam says.

"Well, maybe, but I've seen lots of horses like that. Depends on what they think you're looking for. If you think clear, they'll get it, and if you listen to them and with them, you'll get it and you'll get there . . . and back."

"Wish I could ride all the way back from the roads. Better yet stay here."

"Well, you and me can go out while you're here. We'll get into some good country. The elk are moving down from the trees."

"Coming down to eat the new grass?"

Dan nods.

"I'm looking forward to that. Bacon?" Sam sets it on a napkin to soak off the grease.

Dan nods again.

The two men sit at the kitchen table over eggs, bacon, toast, and coffee.

"So how's that art business?"

"I'm backing off somewhat." Sam gives a short account of the Leonardo saga.

Dan is somewhat familiar with Sam's work. "Sounds like a lot of big heads and grabbiness. I can see why you come out here, Sam."

"Thirsty man looking for water. It's that basic."

"So what are you gonna do? What can you change?"

"Nothing, I guess. That's the way it is."

"You find yourself coming up on a tangle of deadfall, you find another way. Same thing with a cliff wall or a box canyon or spring rush on the East Fork."

"That's dead-on."

"Now you got choices because you can see the land for what it is."

"Dan, why is it so difficult sometimes to sort things out in a place like New York?"

"Maybe because out here you're closer to the land. The land has ways that can teach a man how to live, what counts. Animals have something to say too."

"I hear you."

"I see pictures of New York. You're looking at man-built, steel-and-glass walls, covered ground. Canyons in those places probably don't teach much. But maybe that don't make sense."

"I think it does." Sam takes a sip of coffee and tastes it. He hasn't really tasted coffee in a long time.

"So are we going to be seeing more of you? Yer dad, before he died, told me he hoped you'd be out here more. He sure loved this place." Dan gazes out the window.

"That's my plan, to be out here more. I don't even know if it's safe for me to be back in New York City with the legal investigations going on left and right."

"Sure be nice to see more of you."

"Thank you, Dan. I mean it."

"I know you do or you wouldn't have said it. Ain't nothing to thank me for, though. Want to take a ride, Sam?"

Sam says nothing for a moment, looking straight at Dan with a smile. He nods. "You bet I do."

"Well, let's go then. Bring those big gray fellows. They'll give my little dog Patch a run for something."

The phone rings just as Sam reaches for his jacket hanging on the coatrack. He pauses, putting on the blue-lined Carhartt. The phone rings repeatedly as he stands by the door looking at the phone. Dan watches with patience in the open doorway. The only person he told he was coming out here was Ken so that no one could track him.

Sam decides to let the phone ring. Then the two men, followed by the big dogs, walk in the crisp May morning toward the corral.

CHAPTER THIRTY-FIVE

After six rings, Captain Jerry Higgins snatches up the phone on his cluttered desk in his office, one of the few with a door in the noisy warren of the 24th Precinct.

"Damn phone," he mutters. "Sonofabitch phone. Hel-lo, Higgins."

"Jerry, it's Donahue."

"Got something for me?"

"Yessiree, boss. Lowder death. Ricci, the irritable art dealer."

"Right. I'm listening."

"Remember that Lowder was the other art dealer who was apparently fishing off Montauk before he somehow got separated from his boat and drowned? Odd blow to the head and all that?"

"Yeah," Higgins says. "Forensics was perplexed about the wound. How, why. No clear explanation. Accidental death."

"Well, we found out Ricci owns a boat. A very large boat. Called *Espresso II* . . ."

"Appropriate for a rich Italian."

"So the harbormaster at Marsh Cove where Ricci's humongous play boat is tied up told Sergeant Petrocelli that Ricci and two other guys boarded that boat and steamed out to sea on the same day that Lowder, according to his wife, went out fishing for bluefish. Nice coincidence, huh?"

"Yeah, but not conclusive. Any more?" Higgins holds his pencil like a drumstick, taps it on his desktop.

"Yep, the same harbormaster—nice guy named Mack Malone—happened to talk to Lowder the same day, around the same time, while Lowder was gassing up his normal-size boat. Harbormaster was friendly with Lowder."

"Let's see . . ."

"Wait. Malone remembers that Lowder had no rods or lines, hooks—whatever you use out there. Lowder chatted a bit and said he was going out for a . . . 'little cruise' is what he said."

"Now it's getting interesting." Higgins stops tapping his pencil.

"So Malone's story puts Ricci and Lowder roughly at the same scene, I think."

"I think you're right. And I've got a feeling that one possibly greedy art dealer, one most valuable of all time painting, and one possibly pissed off supplier of that picture add up to a possible mess, and quite possibly a homicide. Donahue, I want you and Petrocelli to go talk to Ricci. Quiz him and bring him in if you think you've got sufficient cause."

"Glad to," Donahue says, "can't wait."

"You don't have to. Keep me informed. Good work. Pass that on to Petrocelli."

"Thanks, Chief."

Donahue and Petrocelli's plain black police car double-parks, dashboard light flashing, in front of Mark Ricci's gallery entrance. The two officers once again climb the steps and press the button. Anthea buzzes the men into the grand foyer. Her eyes widen when she sees the two policemen who paid Mark Ricci a visit five days ago.

"Good morning, gentlemen."

"Good morning to you, ma'am. Once again, I'm Lieutenant Donahue and this is Sergeant Petrocelli." Donahue smiles, trying to put Anthea at ease. "We'd like to see Mr. Ricci, please. I hope he's in."

"Yes, Mr. . . . Lieutenant Donahue. He's in his office. Shall I ring him?" Her voice catches a bit as she speaks.

"Yes, ring him and tell him we're coming up to his office. Fourth floor, was it? We'll find our way."

"Yes, fourth floor. Certainly, I'll let him know." She punches Mark's line.

Donahue and Petrocelli open the elevator cage, step into the mahogany-paneled elevator interior. Arriving at the fourth floor, the two proceed directly to the end of the hall leading to Mark Ricci's office. Ricci is not there.

Petrocelli sits in one of the elegant, gilded French chairs. Donahue picks up Ricci's phone, presses the "Reception" button.

"Yes, Mark," Anthea answers.

"Sorry, miss, it's Donahue. I would be grateful if you could locate Mr. Ricci. We're waiting in his office. Thanks."

"Right away, Officer Donahue."

Five minutes later, Ricci enters the office, straightening his tie as he approaches his desk. "Good morning, gentlemen. Sorry, I was busy in another part of the building."

"I see," says Donahue, "but you apparently answered your receptionist's call here. Am I correct?"

"Well . . . yes. Then I had something to attend to."

"What was that?" Petrocelli asks.

"I don't believe that's any of your business. I could have been in the bathroom."

"Were you?"

"What's the reason for this visit?" Ricci asks sharply.

"The purpose of this visit is to chat with you here . . . or invite you downtown for another probably longer conversation about yachts, Montauk, a trip you took some weeks ago . . . May 14 to be exact . . . two men, guests I suppose, who boarded your boat before you steamed out of the harbor. That was shortly before Philip Lowder left the harbor in his own boat on a one-way trip to his unfortunate death."

"That all means nothing to me."

"Do you remember leaving Montauk—Marsh Cove, where your boat *Espresso II* is berthed—early in the afternoon on May 14?"

"I spend a lot of time on my boat. I don't keep track of the days and times. Do you log your recreational time, Mr. Donahue?"

"Lieutenant Donahue."

"Sorry, *Lieutenant*." Ricci rolls his shoulders, twists his neck, smoothes the lapels on his impeccably tailored gray suit. His brow is moist.

"No, Mr. Ricci. I don't 'log' my recreational time, but I do remember what I do in my off time. Three weeks ago is a snap."

"Good for you, Lieutenant. You must have a wonderful memory."

"So I'll ask again, Mr. Ricci, do you remember that bright spring day? Your trip with two . . . associates, friends, whatever? The harbormaster does."

"Yes, I remember two colleagues and me. Yes, we went out fishing that day."

"Did you catch anything?" Petrocelli asks, raising his head to look straight at Ricci.

Silence. Ricci shifts in his chair, stares up at the ceiling.

"No. No. I don't think so."

"Too bad. It's all about luck isn't it?"

"Why, Mr. Ricci, didn't your captain take the boat out for you? The harbormaster, Mack Malone, said hello to you and your friends and remembers that your captain—Herb Greenough—was not with you, did not board the boat before you left. Is that correct?"

"What is this about? What does it matter that I ran the boat? It's my boat. I am quite experienced in handling that boat. What are you after?"

"Could you please answer the question? Why was your captain not aboard on May 14 when you and your . . . friends went out to sea, the same day about the same time Mr. Lowder took his boat out? Can you answer that?"

"I gave my captain the day off."

"Any special reason?"

"No, I do that sometimes."

"Okay. Was there some reason you didn't want him aboard with you and your friends?"

"No, not at all."

"Can you tell us the names of your friends, Mr. Ricci?" Donahue asks.

"This has gone far enough. Why are you here asking me these questions?"

"Mr. Ricci," Donahue says, "we're investigating Mr. Philip Lowder's untimely, and we think mysterious, death."

"Yes, I understand he fell, hit his head, and went overboard. It was tragic. He was a colleague."

"And you did business with him, including the deal of the century, the Leonardo da Vinci. We know that Mr. Ricci."

"So how can I help? What more can I tell you?" He pulls his handkerchief out of his jacket pocket and dabs his forehead.

"You've told us a good deal, sir," Petrocelli says. "Can you tell us how you know that the unfortunate Mr. Lowder hit his head?"

"It was in the papers. The *Times*, one of those papers." Ricci picks up a newspaper off his coffee table and waves it around.

"There was no mention of the head wound in any of the papers. The only source of that detail is a second report from the coroner's office, triggered by a reopening of our investigation and a new look at the forensics, Mr. Ricci, and I'm sure you haven't been in touch with the coroner. Have you?"

"No. I don't remember how I knew. Maybe I talked to his wife."

"A condolence call. Okay." Petrocelli nods earnestly, looking at Donahue.

"Mr. Ricci, we'd like to go over some of this again in depth and ask you a few more questions that might finally clear up some of the details in the case of Mr. Lowder." Donahue looks Ricci in the eye, hands clasped under his chin, elbows on the elegant arms of the eighteenth-century chair.

"Look, I'm glad to help. But I've told you what I can."

"Perhaps that's so, Mr. Ricci," says Donahue, "but we would like to continue this conversation downtown. To take your testimony so that we can close this case and move on. Would you be willing to do that? To come with us?"

"It's not convenient at this moment." Ricci clears his throat, gets up from his chair, and walks slowly to the end of his office where he stands before a 1906

Monet, *Nymphéas*, a lush painting of water lilies. There is complete silence. After a few moments, a bit more composed, he walks back to the two policemen. "I'll call my lawyer, if you don't mind."

"Good idea, Mr. Ricci. He can join us downtown while we continue our chat. Meanwhile, I'll remind you of your rights. You understand that you are not under arrest. You are not being charged," Donahue says reassuringly. He reads Ricci his rights.

"Could you please leave the room while I call my attorney, gentlemen?"

"Certainly, Mr. Ricci, we'll wait by the elevator," Petrocelli says, standing up and striding out of the office with Donahue following him. "What do you think?" Petrocelli asks as he and Donahue wait in the hallway near the elevator.

"The head wound remark was significant. I think that a lot of what we've heard is not the truth and he's stretching it. And I think there's a lot more to the story than we know at this point. A lot more."

"I'm with you on that."

"I'm that far from arrest on suspicion," Donahue says, showing a crack of space between his thumb and index finger.

Just at that moment, Ricci comes down the hall, his face a mask of alarm, his usual arrogance gone.

"Where shall I tell my attorney to meet me . . . us?"

"NYPD 24th Precinct, 349 10th Street," Petrocelli reels off.

Ricci turns back to his office. Five minutes later he comes back down the hall. The three take the elevator to the ground floor. As they exit, Anthea looks up.

"Anthea, I'm going downtown with these . . . gentlemen. I don't know when I'll be back. I'll call you if you're still here."

"I understand, Mark. I'll . . ." Her face looks puzzled.

"That's all," Mark cuts in.

The three men head for the door, Donahue, Ricci, then Petrocelli. Donahue opens the inner door, then the glassed iron-grill door.

"After you," he says to Ricci, extending his hand.

"Sort of feels that way, dammit."

CHAPTER THIRTY-SIX

The incoming tide of friends and MIs (must invites) tapers off at six-thirty. The private elevator activity serving the vast Baxter penthouse slows down, and the waiters bearing glasses of Cristal champagne concentrate on the spacious living areas where socialites who see one another several times a week are engaged in animated conversations that many have begun a night or so ago. A line trails from what was once the Baxters' "Small Library" and which is now the "Leonardo Room."

Exhibiting *The Virgin and Child with a Cat* is the sole reason for such a carefully orchestrated gathering. Those present are among the first to see the world's most expensive and currently famous painting. Polished brass stanchions from which hang gilt cloth ropes funnel people into and out of the room. The procession moves with slowness and gravity appropriate to a viewing of a holy shrine or perhaps a funeral bier in the Capitol Rotunda. There is a hush in the line of entrants and among those who exit the installation. A husky armed guard stands on either side of the door. There is no possibility of touching the lovely panel, utterly secure within its bulletproof, tamper- proof, climate-controlled transparent box. Were one to record the comments of the viewers who, after seeing the Leonardo, begin to speak several paces down the hall from the Leonardo Room, one would find that the prevailing first whispered comment is *"two hundred and fifteen million."* Sometimes repeated. *"Two hundred and fifteen million!"* A few of them are amazed that such a staggering sum exchanged hands for a relatively humble-looking painting, but most recognize the painting's worth.

Tom and Sylvie stand together in the Grand Salon near the entrance closest to the hallway leading from the Leonardo Room. They can hardly keep up with the crush of those who have just seen the Leonardo and, immediately after, are vying with one another to express their awe. Never has the city hosted a social event of equally genuine and assumed sophistication.

The Leonardo has resided in the Baxter apartment for three weeks now. Since its arrival, few have seen it. Those who have had the privilege of seeing the painting before this evening have been chosen selectively: press, major art journal editors, museum directors and curators, and a few close friends.

One of those fortunates, Sherman Bailey, the leonine, brilliant but difficult director of the New York Museum of Art, approaches Tom and Sylvie. British, expatriate, portly, impeccably dressed, Bailey is enormously respected and influential, and he has ruled the great museum for twenty-five years.

"Tom, you've met my wife, Sandra," Bailey says, gesturing to a woman in a silver silk wrap that closely matches her perfect hair.

"Yes, Sherman, several times, the last time I think at the opening of the new Photography wing."

"Of course, of course," Sherman says. "A splendid evening, this. And your exquisite new picture is, what can I say . . . earthshaking. That's it, earthshaking. There's nothing like it. Nothing."

"I hope not," Tom says. "I mean . . . I know what you mean."

"Yes. Well, did Mr. Driscoll help you find these Impressionist paintings as well as the Leonardo?" Bailey asks. "The 1875 Sisley is superb, and the Monet, it's—"

"Mr. Driscoll and I are no longer associated."

"Oh, I didn't know. Well . . ." The man peers down at his scotch and soda.

"No, it was Mark Ricci who found and offered the Leonardo, as you may have read in the press," Tom says, looking straight at him. "And, yes, Sam Driscoll was helpful in the acquisition of some of the Impressionist pictures. Including the Sisley."

Sandra Bailey and Sylvie begin chatting amiably about decorators.

"Well, whoever was advising you should be complimented. Well done," says Bailey. "Tom, I'd like to invite you for lunch sometime in the near future. Perhaps we can have a chat. We have a vacancy on the board, and a number of our board members have brought up your name as a candidate."

Tom grins. "I'm flattered. I'd be delighted to come and have lunch. At the museum?"

"Certainly. Charles Amory, our chairman, asked me to talk with you preliminarily, and I thought this was as good a time as any. I hope you don't mind."

Sylvie, overhearing is beaming. Tom feels an adrenaline rush.

"No, it would be a privilege to talk with you and Charles Amory."

"I think you two have met. You and Charles are in the same line of business, I believe."

"Uh, yes. Though I must say that several times we have been on opposite sides of a . . . business opportunity."

"Competitors, you mean?"

"Yes, that's accurate."

"No hard feelings, I hope."

"Not serious."

"Perhaps you know some of the other board members—Angus Rathbone, Frederick Wills, Gerald Lippman. All of those gentlemen are collectors."

"I believe we bid against Mr. Lippman. For a superb Redon." Tom points to it. "That one over there. He was the underbidder."

"Well, maybe Charles Amory will want to invite Mr. Lippman and a few other collectors to lunch with you and him. You can make your amends to Mr. Lippman for bidding him up and out of the Redon." Bailey winks. "Very nice to talk with you, Tom and Sylvie. Sandra and I will release you to your other guests. We'll have a look around your splendid home and its paintings."

"Enjoy yourselves," Tom says, heartily shaking Bailey's hand.

Tom and Sylvie have an instant before the next guests drift toward them.

"The board of the New York Museum of Art!" Tom whispers in Sylvie's ear. "What a coup." He steps back, beaming at his beautiful wife.

"Tom, you must have been praying to your *rarissima*, *Virgin and Child with a Cat*. Perhaps the image is a talisman."

"Talisman? What's that?"

"A charm, Tom. Something that has magical properties, perhaps good fortune."

"Yes. Yes, perhaps you're right."

At that moment, George Talbot, an art critic for *Art Times*, approaches Tom and Sylvie. Talbot is Sylvie's friend and a smart, well-informed writer and student of art history.

"Sylvie! Tom. Good evening. Thank you for inviting me . . . my God, the painting is . . . astonishing. I'm undone. Really."

"Well, I'm glad you are, George," Sylvie says. "So are we, really. The opportunity and now the reality are beyond our wildest dreams."

"I can guess that. The Leonardo is a treasure. How did you find it, or how did the painting find you?"

"It's a short story, but I'm pledged to secrecy." Sylvie winks at him to take the edge off.

"Oh, I see," Talbot says with a slight frown. "Well, that adds another veil of mystery to that puzzling iconography."

"Yes, the iconography," Tom says. "There are a number of drawings by Leonardo in museums . . ."

"The British Museum and the Uffizi," Sylvie interrupts. "Indisputably by Leonardo."

"It's unprecedented, a cat instead of John the Baptist's lamb or another traditional element. Did your curator, Sam . . . Driscoll? Did he find it for you? Did . . ."

"No, Mark Ricci had it and I bought it from him."

"Oh, I see. Is Mr. Driscoll here this evening?"

"No, George. Sam and I are no longer associated."

"Oh, that's too bad. Nice man. Intelligent."

"Yes," Tom says, glancing at Sylvie, then looking over Talbot's head as if he would like to be elsewhere.

"I must say that there will be major curiosity about this rarest find. Leonardo's known authentic paintings number fewer than twenty, even counting early collaborative works. And as you are no doubt aware, controversy continues between experts and authorities."

"Yes." Tom is clearly uncomfortable. Sylvie turns to wave at a friend. "Well, glad you could join us, George."

"One more question, Tom. Have you by chance heard any reaction from the Italians in regard to this exceptional find? The art people, museums?"

"No, nothing. Perhaps they haven't caught up to the . . . news yet."

"Oh, the news is out. I regularly cover the European press, as you might imagine. In my work I have to. Anyway, the press in Milan carried an article covering the sudden appearance of the Leonardo.

"They did?"

"Yes, and there was an editorial in the Roman press by a respected art historian, Silvio Trichetti, professor at the University of Rome and advisor to the ministry responsible for art and antiquities."

"About?"

"About the astonishing discovery of a major Leonardo and the matter of its origin. So, clearly, as I said, the word is out. Of course, one would expect that with a Leonardo."

"Yes, I suppose so," Tom says. "Well, that's all very interesting."

"Oh my, I rather thought you'd have known about this already. If you like, I'll pass along any further information that I pick up."

"Thanks, George," Tom says.

"Great evening, Tom, Sylvie," Talbot says as he heads toward the Leonardo Room where a line waits to see *Virgin and Child with a Cat*.

Tom, a bit ill at ease, moves to greet the next dazzled guest.

CHAPTER THIRTY-SEVEN

Sam sits down at a rustic wooden table by the window where he keeps his computer. The East Fork snakes along the edge of the property outside the window, and Sam takes a moment to watch it before he opens his email and scans the messages.

Ken's email reads:

Sam,

Hope I'm not disturbing you in your Wyoming retreat. I got an email this morning from Father Anselmo. He sends his best to you. The Italians feel that they have enough evidence and cause to sue for the return of the Leonardo as illegally exported property.

Of course an informal claim will be addressed to the owner of record . . . I think you will not be surprised that the Italians would like you to make public what you may have learned in Florence. What Father Anselmo told you. Anything that's relevant. I know things could get dicey. This might put you in danger. It is very likely that the claim may go to court. I don't know what sorts of agreements you and your clients have or whether you will need some sort of amnesty to be able to testify. I can look into this for you. Do you have a good lawyer?

We've talked about the vital connection with the work of art. I hope you will tap into what drew you into this field in the first place and come to terms with what it is you most deeply want to do around this. Because the Italian authorities will be sure to push you one way and Tom will be sure to push you another.

You can expect to hear from the Italians, then the legals in this country. I'm guessing that they'll be trying to reach you. I haven't given your personal email address to anyone. I see how one of the quandaries of being at the top of your game is that now you can't really outrun the game.

You've got to make up your own mind on this,
Ken

Sam pushes away from the desk, gets up from his chair, and heads out the back door toward the pasture. He shakes his head. It's stupid to go out riding with the storm clouds rolling in, but he needs to get some clarity. Twenty-five minutes later Sam and Baron approach the tree line just on the other side of the river

As he leads the young horse deep into the woods, he can feel the clamor happening back in New York, can feel Ricci and Tom tumbling over each other to figure out how to deal with the Italians. No part of him wants to go back there, and yet as he heads into the cool darkness of the pines, he knows he has to take a stand. Otherwise it will never be the same—the freedom he experiences here in the woods with his horse.

The air out there tastes sweet on the back of his tongue. He knows he should feel bitter at his career coming down around him like this, and yet he doesn't. Looking back on it all from this distance, he can see what a rare opportunity he has had to take a career all the way through to completion. The works of masters he had only dreamed of, he now knows intimately. At this new peak, he sees how he has been driven by some of the same ego push for power that drives his clients. He feels remarkably light at the thought of letting it all go. The opportunity to be driven by something else is humbling.

As he stares at an elk moving at the edge of an aspen grove far off in the distance, Sam wants to fight for the painting to go home. He wants to fight for Father Anselmo. The idea of defying Tom in that way scares him. Still, the people of Ponte Albrizzi deserve that, he thinks, and it would allow him to finally break himself free from his striving.

Sam walks into the tackroom in the barn. The hounds are ecstatic, panting with toothy smiles as he scratches their ears after a two-hour horseback ride along the East Fork. The dogs raced ahead sniffing, pausing, catching up, apparently as glad as Sam to be in open country.

After he dips the palm-sized patch of sheepskin into the squat round tin of saddle soap, he wipes the leather dressing over the skirt of the saddle. It's an unusual model, the work of a Texas maker who occasionally likes to build copies of late nineteenth-century riding gear, using specially made trees, old-time rigging, and elegant foliate scroll stamping on the skirts, fork, and stirrup leathers. The cantle rises high as does the slick fork with its perfectly proportioned horn, creating a deep seat and, in Sam's eyes, a graceful piece of sculpture. If asked, he would admit that a sensitively designed saddle ranks with some of those works of art in his other work—those he loves best.

Sam relishes this work with the saddle dressing, breathing in the aroma of the beeswax, one ingredient in the mix of emollients that preserves the deep russet color of the leather.

At the saddle rack, Sam looks down the small corral adjoining the tackroom. The horse is licking the tiny shreds of grain from the black rubber feed pan. Sam shifts attention from his work to gaze at Baron, his four-year-old, line-back dun gelding. At sixteen hands, he is big for a quarter horse. The previous spring Sam bought him from a local rancher whose wife had trained the horse in barrel racing, pole bending, and jumping, this under Eastern saddle and all of that when the bright young horse wasn't working cattle, the ranch's primary focus.

"You're quite a head turner, young Baron. *Three-ee-ep.*" Sam whistles to get the horse's attention, and the animal tied at the rail turns toward Sam expectantly, flicking his ears back and then forward again. Eye-to-eye contact.

As he finishes up with his saddle, Sam steps back to admire the deepened color of the leather. He brings the saddle to rest on his hip and carries it to its place in the tackroom. He pulls the cord for the light and leaves the darkened tack shed, dropping the wooden latch into the keeper on the old door.

"Okay, Baron, you've had your grain. Time to hit the pasture."

He takes up the lead rope and walks toward the pasture gate. Sam unsnaps the clip when Baron is through the gate. The dogs follow Sam from the corral back to the lodge.

"Come on in, dogs. I need your support."

By the fireplace, Sam drops into the old leather armchair and takes a deep breath. Even if he went into Dubois and called from the payphone, anyone wanting to know where he is— people associated with Ricci or even Tom Baxter—could easily figure it out. The locals in Dubois have known Sam for years. Sam opts for the privacy of his home.

Skype pops up on his computer screen, and he types in the familiar number.

"Mr. Baxter's office."

"Hello, Sam Driscoll. Can you put me through to Tom?"

"One moment." There's a pause, then he hears Tom pick up the call.

"What is it, Driscoll?"

"Tom, I think it's important that you know what's going on with the Italians."

"What are you talking about?"

"The Italian Heritage and Cultural Activities is filing a claim specifying that your Leonardo was exported illegally and is the rightful property of Italy and must be returned."

"Christ," Tom growls.

"I wish it were better news . . ."

"No you don't, dammit. You were against the deal from the time you returned from your harebrained boondoggle to Italy, Sam."

"Tom, I wasn't against the *deal*. I needed to get at the truth of the matter. Like any research question. Or any unresolved attribution issue."

"Look, I've got the provenance. Ricci, Philip Lowder. Bill of sale from the European owners. Clear title."

"It's shaky, Tom, as I tried to explain to you several times. Easily disputable." Again he considers bringing up the letters he uncovered at Hilda Lowder's. Something tells him not to play that card yet.

"The bill of sale came from Lowder's uncle."

"Very possibly, if not certainly, spurious."

"Right. We've been over that. Over and over it. One version against another."

"Tom, now that this is all coming to a fair legal process, I'm quite convinced that the Italians will make their case and prevail."

"Damn you, Driscoll."

"I've been your advisor for years, Tom. I've represented your interests." Sam is gripping a pencil so tightly that it is on the verge of breaking.

"I think that is less clear now than it might once have been."

"I've advised you to the best of my ability in every aspect: attribution, quality, condition, price . . ."

"Yeah, you've said that."

". . . and provenance, Tom."

"A matter of opinion, Driscoll."

"It may now be a matter of opinion. Very soon it'll be a question of proof. I'm afraid it's out of your hands, Tom."

"We'll see." Tom's voice is icy.

"Yes, we will," Sam says. Something in him has released—the reserve he once showed Tom. "I expect that the Italians will win their case and the Leonardo will return to Italy. Where it belongs."

"My lawyers never lose. They've seen me through bigger deals than this one."

"You might suggest that they start honing up on international art law and UNESCO treaties."

"Oh, now you're a legal expert as well."

The pencil in Sam's grip breaks. He takes a deep breath. "Tom, it seems probable that I will be required to testify."

"At your peril, Mr. Art Advisor."

"You fired me, Tom. I served your interests when I was your employee. Now I am a free man, on my own."

"You're right there, Driscoll."

"Simply put, Tom, I will testify to what I know, to what I've learned about the Leonardo. Just that. I will serve the truth now."

"You sound so goddamned ponderous. Jesus. You watch yourself, Sam. See what kind of legal hurt you get into when you give the bastards privileged information."

"I will answer any questions addressed to me in this inquiry."

"Driscoll, I will personally ensure that your art advisor days are over. You'll be hard-pressed to land a crappy little teaching job at some no-name abysmal community college in Newark after I'm done with you . . ."

"That's a threat, Tom. It's a good thing you can easily record conversations on Skype . . ."

"You piece of shit," Tom spits. "Enjoy your retirement, Sam."

Something bubbles up inside Sam. A harsh laugh. "Go to hell, Tom," he says, feeling a sudden lightness, like a restraint cut permanently. Tom's gone. Sam closes Skype and, a little dazed, looks out at the brilliant Wyoming day, everywhere the unforgiving sun cracking open the earth.

CHAPTER THIRTY-EIGHT

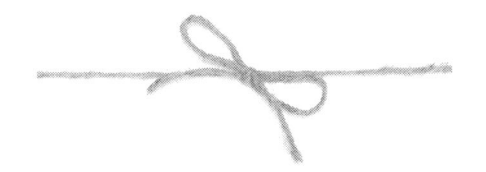

Tom Baxter sits on a couch opposite his desk. His custom blue shirt is open at the neck, his Hermès tie, knotted with a dimple, is loosened. He taps a pencil on the edge of a glass humanitarian award resting with other honors on the sofa table beside him. Taps. Shifts.

"Dammit!" He grabs the phone next to him, punches in his secretary's number. "Angela, get my Bentley," he barks.

He collects his briefcase and speeds down the hallway to the elevator. Within three minutes, his driver is at the curb. It feels like five minutes too long.

"Go to Osteria," Tom says.

The driver cuts through traffic and double-parks in front of Ricci's favorite restaurant. Tom jumps out of the car and busts through the front doors. He plows past the maitre d', aiming at Ricci's table where the dealer is sitting with his mistress. Ricci has bragged a million times about how this is *his* lunch table.

Although Ricci tries to push his mistress out of sight, they're the only ones in the back room, and she's impossibly obvious there in her white suit with her blonde hair all piled up on her head.

Ricci looks like he's having a hard time swallowing. He stands up. "Tom, something wrong? How're you doing?"

"Not well, Mark."

"What's the matter? Tired of your masterpiece? I read you had an exclusive opening. Right?" His napkin falls out of his hands, and he crosses his arms across his chest.

"Yes, Mark. We had limited invitations and limited space."

"You don't have to explain. I've *seen* the picture."

"Ricci, Sam Driscoll called me this morning. He—"

"What did your ex-curator have to say?" With his index finger, Ricci motions for his mistress to leave. She stands up abruptly and slips past Tom.

"The Italian government intends to file a claim to the Leonardo charging illegal exportation, for Christ's sake."

"Shit." Ricci sits back down, looking uncharacteristically pale. He motions for Tom to sit, but Tom just stands there over him.

"What the hell have you gotten me into besides a two-hundred-fifteen-million-dollar check made out to you?"

"Tom, I've got a load falling on my head right now."

"I don't give a damn, Mark." Tom leans in and sets his massive hands on the table in front of Ricci. "You told me Philip Lowder had clear title, from some old couple who sold the damn picture to him after the war."

"Right, Tom."

"Later, dammit, you said something about it not being quite like that, but Lowder had clear title. Then you guaranteed that *you* had legal ownership in your damn bill of sale which I'm looking at right now." Tom jerks the document out of the inside pocket of his jacket and slams it on the table.

"Just what I told you." Ricci leans away from Tom.

"So why the hell are the Italians bringing a case on the picture? What do they know that we . . . I don't?"

"I have no idea what they know!"

"Well, you'd better know and soon. You've got a hell of a lot of my money, and if this mess gets worse you're going to take the picture back and return every cent I paid you. I want to see bags of money streaming up my elevator by Monday."

"I can't do that, Tom."

"What the hell does that mean?"

"I don't have it."

"You don't have it. What the hell did you do with two hundred fifteen million dollars? Buy an Italian island and a fleet of yachts, for God's sake?" Tom's temper is shot. He shoves Ricci back against his booth. "Ricci, you may feel like you're big shit, but by the time my men get done with you, you're going to be begging to give me my money back. You'd better start thinking about finding every dollar. Hear me?" Tom's hands fall back to his sides. He adjusts his jacket.

"The Leonardo isn't going to be seized, Tom." Ricci leans in, speaking in a hushed voice. "The arts ministry doesn't know anything. You've got a copy of Lowder's original bill of sale. You know what they say, dead men tell no tales."

"It's a piece of paper, Mark."

"And you've got Lowder's uncle's bill of sale going back to . . . what . . . 1952, correct?"

"You better start praying those pieces of paper will hold up."

"If Sam's the one getting you worked up, then relax. That Boy Scout doesn't know how this world works. A small cracked snapshot of the painting the size of a playing card, that's not going to endanger this provenance."

"How do you know about the photograph? Have you seen it?"

"No, of course not. Driscoll told me about it when he was in here going on about his theories about the picture. He was picking facts out of the air."

"You'd better hope that's true."

"Tom, the word of some demented old monk is hardly going to touch you—one of the most powerful businessmen in the world. You've got a notarized bill of sale showing everything we know about ownership history of the Leonardo. There's nothing to worry about."

"If there is an action or an Italian claim, if I hear about it, you will give me my money back within forty-eight hours. It better be in bags coming up the laundry chutes. Clear?"

Ricci nods.

CHAPTER THIRTY-NINE

From his front porch, Sam watches his dogs patrol the property. One section of the sagebrush in particular has their interest. He is halfway through his cursory shuffle of the mail pile forwarded from Stonington to the Dubois P.O. Box when he comes upon a registered mail envelope. Sam holds up an official envelope marked "U.S. Federal Court, State of New York, New York City." He tears open the envelope. "You are hereby summoned . . . an arbitration hearing . . . Italian Ministry of Heritage and Cultural Activities vs. Thomas Baxter, New York . . . in regard to ownership . . . dispute in the matter of claim of illegal export of a painting . . . attributed to Leonardo da Vinci, *Virgin and Child with a Cat* . . . heed under bond . . . until proceedings are closed . . . judgment is rendered."

Shock, relief, sadness, satisfaction. Emptiness. "Finally, it's all coming down," Sam says. He stands up, arms slack at his sides, holding the summons, dropping the envelope on the porch. Inside, he gets an unopened bottle of whiskey that has sat on the shelf for years now. It was a present from his grandfather to his father on his eighteenth birthday. And when his father passed it down to him on Sam's eighteenth birthday, he told Sam not to drink it until he had moved to Wyoming for good. The freedom of Wyoming was what both Sam's father and grandfather had always craved. Sam hasn't moved to Wyoming, but he feels free in the way he imagines he would if he had made that decision. He pulls down his father's mug emblazoned with a 1940s pinup girl on one side and a US Air Force emblem on the other, below which reads "Colonel Bill Driscoll, U.S.A.F. 1944."

Because of how much he admired his father, the mug is one of his most precious possessions. Nothing, not a Monet or a Rembrandt drawing, compares. Sam cracks open the whiskey and pours a tall shot into the mug. He goes and stands out on the porch and slugs it down. As the fire reaches down his throat, he feels opened up. The whiskey is smooth. His grandfather knew a good bottle when he saw it, Sam thinks. After several more shots of whiskey, Sam is feeling better than he has in a long, long while. He careens toward his favorite leather chair by the large picture window overlooking the East Fork. He looks out to the mountainous horizon. He sinks into the soft back of the chair. Dundee drops to the floor beneath Sam's hand, settling his head on his crossed paws.

It is a little after five in the evening, and Sam sits there staring out for a long while. Though this is a momentous event for him, the mountains are completely undisturbed. He doesn't know what to do with all this new information, and so he picks up the phone next to him and dials Ken.

"Sam!"

"Ken. Lordy. I just dug a summons out of my mail."

"A summons. Wow, I'm sorry you have to go through this . . . process. And I'm sorry about the rupture with Tom. How are *you* doing, Sam?"

"I guess, bloodied but unbowed, so someone once said."

"When does the legal stuff start? Soon?"

"June 20, it says in big bold type."

"Three weeks. Time to catch up to yourself. How was Wyoming?"

"Still here. Blessed. It always is." He looks out at the aspens, new green leaves shimmering in the wind.

"I hear the Italians have a good case."

"I know they have a good case, dammit. Ever since I went to Florence, it's been clear to me, as you know, that the touted provenance doesn't stand up. I just couldn't convince Tom that the Ricci version had holes in it."

"And now Mr. Baxter is in the hot seat."

"He wouldn't listen, Ken."

"Christ. Obviously Philip Lowder knew the true story . . . was too cowardly to deal with the matter of the Italian authorities himself. So what's the situation now, Sam?"

"We shall see at the hearing, won't we?" Sam pauses.

"God, are you going to testify?"

"Yes, I've just made up my mind to."

"You'll be testifying against Tom Baxter or at least against his interest?"

"I'll be telling the truth as I know it. Just what happened."

"And in that, you'll be testifying against him."

"Yes, that's true."

"You're really going to do this?"

"No, I'm not entirely sure I am. But I think I am. I absolutely want to, Ken. This is me finally breaking loose."

"You sound drunk, my friend."

"I am a little. Celebrating if you will."

"Well, if you do come back, hire a guard to meet you at the airport. Especially if you come back drunk. You're not going to be able to live in Stonington anymore. You know that, right? Not after what Ricci has done to Lowder over the provenance."

"God, and I've heard what Tom's people have done to others too." Sam grins as he hangs up the phone and slips into his drunken joy at finally having set the course he's always wanted to take.

CHAPTER FORTY

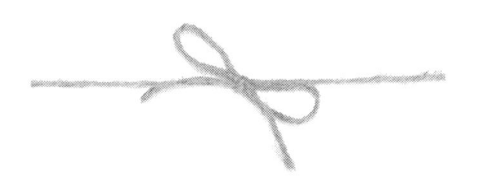

"You're here to see Mr. Ricci again, Sergeant . . . ?"

"Petrocelli, miss. Yes, we are. Could you tell him we'd like to see him, please?"

"He's with a client at the moment."

"I understand, miss. But I'm afraid it won't wait."

"I . . . I . . ."

"Call him now, please."

"Just a moment." Anthea rings Ricci's office. "Mark, the two men from the police are here to see you . . . they say . . . it won't wait." She pauses. "Yes. Just a minute. Sergeant, Mr. Ricci asks what do you want?"

"We want to show him an arrest warrant, and we want to take him downtown to book him."

"Uh, yes . . . Mark, they have an arrest warrant and—"

"Is he in his office, miss?"

"Yes, Sergeant, he's in his office."

"We're on the way up." Petrocelli holds the elevator door open for Donahue. "After you, partner."

"Mark, they're on their way up."

Petrocelli opens the elevator door and the two men head down the hall to Ricci's office.

Ricci stands in his office doorway.

"What are you goons doing, storming into my office this way? I'm in the middle of a meeting!"

The dealer turns to his client, the tall, distinguished Sir Geoffrey Helmsley. "I'm sorry. I don't know why these . . . men . . . are here." He wheels around to the policemen. "Can't you see . . . ?"

"Mark Ricci, this is a warrant for your arrest in connection with the murder of Philip Lowder." Sergeant Petrocelli reads Ricci his rights. "Do you understand?"

"Yes." Ricci can barely speak through his rage.

"Cuff him."

"Mark, what on earth?" his client stutters. "What about the Monet?"

"Screw the Monet." Ricci glowers at his captors.

"Sorry, sir, for the interruption," Petrocelli says to the astonished Sir Geoffrey. "I'm sure the Monet will wait. Let's go, Mr. Ricci."

Coming out of the elevator, the two officers pause by the huge white orchid on Anthea's desk. She stammers in shock. "Mark, I . . . what . . . ?"

"Mr. Ricci won't be coming back, uh, for a while . . . maybe never. You'd better see to things, at least for today."

"Mark?"

"Handle it, Anthea," Ricci growls.

Petrocelli opens the ornate iron door, and the three men—officers flanking a stunned Mark Ricci—make their way to the unmarked police car parked at the curb.

The officers sit with Ricci and his lawyer in an interrogation room down at the jail. "Mr. Ricci, Mark . . ."

Ricci glares at Petrocelli across the table from him.

"Let's try it again. You were on your boat . . ."

"I've told you the same damn thing about six hundred times since we started this charade."

"You're right. That's the problem. You're stuck, and your account of your little boat ride on May 14 doesn't match what we've learned from reliable and corroborating witnesses."

"That's not my problem."

"It *is* your problem. And that problem—your problem—is getting bigger."

"Yeah. How so?"

"Sergeant Petrocelli," Mark Ricci's lawyer breaks in, "we've been over and over the questions about the day and the date of Mark's boat trip. It's clear that we are in agreement on that."

"Right, Mr. Catanzaro. But we have new information that doesn't square with your client's story."

"Well, may I suggest that we convene this meeting, quit wasting Mr. Ricci's time, and you can share that information with me?"

"Nice thought. Okay. Here it is."

Ricci glances nervously at his lawyer then back at Petrocelli. His deadpan, arrogant demeanor has dipped into discomfort. He shifts in his chair, staring out the small high window of the fluorescent-lit interrogation room.

"Mr. Ricci, you've told us that you boarded your boat in the afternoon, about three o'clock, May 14. You said that you brought two passengers aboard, but you refuse to give their names."

Ricci recovers his bravado, though it's tinged with a desperation Petrocelli can almost smell. "This bullshit has nothing to do with them. Your off-the-wall ideas about a simple cruise in my boat don't mean a damn thing."

"We think there's a lot that went on before, during, and after your cruise that's critical to what is now a murder case. You know, about your deceased colleague, Mr. Philip Lowder."

"He wasn't my colleague."

"Details. He's dead, and that was awfully convenient to somebody who made a pile of money off of him."

"Not my problem."

"It *is* your problem. Here's why."

"Oh, for Christ's sake."

The lawyer picks up his manila folder and taps the bottom edge on the table. "Sergeant Petrocelli, this better be new ground. I'm ready to file a motion to set aside this . . . harassment. We've been more than cooperative with your fishing expedition. Either put something substantial on the table, or I'm going to see that my client is released."

"Too late, counselor. Mr. Ricci, on that bright day your *friends* boarded your boat, they were wearing—the two of them—dark business suits. Odd yachting attire, but then . . ."

"Who the hell cares what they were wearing?" Ricci snaps.

"Well, it surprised the harbormaster. When he agreed to be questioned three weeks later, he mentioned that he noticed the two men and described them in detail to our investigator."

"I fail to see the damning nature of the sartorial choices of Mr. Ricci's friends, Sergeant Petrocelli," the lawyer says coolly.

"Perhaps this will move you then. How about the written testimony of a fisherman who happened to be scanning with high-power binoculars equipped with a steadying device—real neat technology, like a steady cam."

"And?" The lawyer shifts back in his seat. Even his poker face can't disguise that he is inwardly cursing his client and quickly recalibrating his legal strategy. Ricci stares up at the dirty window.

"You see, he had a clear view of *Espresso II*, its name on the transom. The guy was looking for birds flying over, fish, gulping minnows, I'm told."

"How interesting," Catanzaro says. Ricci feigns inattention.

"Our witness reported seeing a much smaller boat coming up to the side of your mega yacht, Mr. Ricci. That boat matches the description, registration numbers and all, of Philip Lowder's boat. The harbormaster talked to Lowder before he went out in his boat and left the harbor, not long after *Espresso II* steamed out to sea."

"I don't see where this is going," Catanzaro says, manicured hands together, fingers supporting his chin.

"Patience, counselor. We're almost through."

Ricci looks away from the window. "Let's hope so. This is damn boring."

"The fisherman," Petrocelli continues, "well, more accurately, his binoculars—during one of his scans—witnessed one of your two guests, Mr. Ricci, whack a fourth person over the head."

"That's what he *says* he saw. His word." Catanzaro leans forward over the table, all attention.

"Not his word, gentlemen, but his image. His fancy binoculars have a camera built in. The fisherman actually never saw Lowder being attacked. But a few weeks later, when he got around to it, he uploaded the images from the binoculars—you see, he's something of a birder at the same time he's a fisherman, and he wanted to see if he'd caught any rare shorebirds digitally. Amazing what amateur enthusiasts can do for police investigations these days. Anyhow, where was I? So he uploaded some photos and found some awfully interesting ones. It took him a while to bring them in to us, I guess out of fear of your goons." Petrocelli retrieves three photographs from the folder. "Here they are." He places the photos on the table, fanning them out.

Catanzaro slowly examines each photo, handing them one at a time to a clearly frightened Mark Ricci.

"In these telephoto shots, you can clearly see, Mr. Ricci, a recognizable image of yourself, just behind the dark-suited bozos who are clubbing the unfortunate Philip Lowder . . . before in the last picture they heave the victim into the water."

Catanzaro controls his poker face. "I'll need copies of these, Sergeant Petrocelli, and a copy of the downloaded file."

"We'll see what we can do."

Ricci sags in his chair, looking now at the blank wall.

"The next step, Mr. Ricci, is indictment. And my hunch is, certain conviction for conspiracy to commit murder." Not a sound, not a movement from Ricci. "And, lastly, we know who your friends are." Petrocelli walks behind Mark Ricci. He stands at the art dealer's back, leaning on the back of his chair. "Those guys, as you no doubt know, are enforcers for Gino Mattei, whose business and pleasure is being a major player in international narcotics traffic. Won't the feds be delighted to know you are so cozy with this crime boss?"

"My client has nothing more to say at this time." Catanzaro looks tired.

"And we think we know of the connection between Mattei's money-laundering operation and your very lucrative business. God, I used to hear the phrase 'art for art's sake,' right, Mr. Ricci?"

"I think we've heard enough, Petrocelli." Catanzaro stands, looking to Ricci, sitting still as stone.

"I think you're right, Mr. Catanzaro. Let's get you back to your new quarters, Mr. Ricci."

"Screw you, you little bastard. Screw you." Mark Ricci looks smugly at Petrocelli.

"Get up, you arrogant sonofabitch, before I get one of my heavies to drag you to your comfy cell." Petrocelli sets his hand on the gun strapped to his belt.

CHAPTER FORTY-ONE

Sam is standing in the courtroom. He's already laid out most of the evidence, but now he takes the material that Hilda gave him out of his briefcase. "What she had to say is at odds with the sketchy provenance that Ricci has given us, which he attributes to Philip Lowder. Namely 'a European couple who sold the picture to Lowder in the early 1950s.'

"Hilda has a letter to Lowder's father from his uncle, who not only was in the Italian campaign during World War II in 1944, but specifically was in Ponte Albrizzi. It strongly suggests that the link between the Lowders and the origin of the painting is quite clear. Furthermore, attached to a recent photograph of the painting, she found an old Kodachrome snapshot of the Leonardo with 'Ponte Albrizzi' written in ink on the back—not in her husband's writing. The letter I just mentioned describes the church in Ponte Albrizzi. Captain Lowder mentions the church as strangely empty. No cross, no candlesticks, no picture in an elaborate frame above the altar. He adds that the Germans must have taken them. Not very likely, given the fact that the Germans were being chased north up the boot of Italy by the US forces."

Across the room, Tom is frantically taking notes and occasionally looking up and throwing scornful looks Sam's way. Sylvie's shoulders are curling in on themselves beneath a luxurious silk scarf.

Sam continues. "I would add one other piece to the puzzle. Hilda Lowder told me that Philip Lowder's uncle—the same Captain Lowder—was a trained art historian before the war and a professor of art history at Columbia. His outfit's mission was to secure important works of art as the Allies pushed north. Glen Lowder certainly would have known what he was looking at."

Tom looks at him. Sam can feel Tom daring him. He glances behind Tom too to a pair of massive, menacing-looking men in dark suits. Ricci's proxies, no doubt. Ricci himself—dressed in a suit—is handcuffed and sandwiched between two deputies at a table off to the side. Sam takes a deep breath.

"Here are the photocopies of Leonardo's journal in which he makes the connection of how this painting got from the woods to Ponte Albrizzi and also of Piero Mazza's work on the cradle, hence explaining the letters *PM* on the reverse painting."

There's a shout from the gallery. Sam scans the crowd. Tom has torn off his suit jacket and the sweat marks are visible on his shirt.

Judge Frederick Abel strikes his gavel sharply on the thick ebony block secured to the right-hand corner of his desk. Once, then, pausing in midstrike, again.

"Mr. Driscoll, thank you for your testimony. You may step down."

Sam returns to his seat next to Ken in the front row. The judge shuffles some papers and takes a drink from a glass of water. The ice clinks. The courtroom is silent as a church.

"The last three days we have heard arguments and supporting testimony in regard to the question of ownership of the painting *Virgin and Child with a Cat*, recently identified as . . . possibly, probably, certainly . . . an original painting by Leonardo da Vinci."

Tom Baxter, looking drained, slowly shakes his head. His wife, seated next to him, stares into her lap, a posture she has held since the final testimony, Sam's testimony, began a half hour ago.

Mark Ricci sits rigidly, no sign of his usual cocky energy. He glares at the judge.

"The attributions," the judge continues, "the authorship of the picture, the court will of course leave to experts. However, the identification of this painting with Leonardo da Vinci has, because of presumptions—by some—of its monetary value . . . has clearly obscured the primary question of ownership of this work of art. And, if I may say so, the presumed monetary value of the painting has precipitated acts and behavior not generally associated with works of art; I speak of deceit, fraud, and, recently, charges of . . . homicide."

Ricci mouths a "screw you" as he turns his head in disgust away from the judge toward the window.

"We must leave these matters to run their course in other jurisdictions. Our inquiry has focused, and in conclusion must remain focused, upon the questions of claim and rightful ownership."

Sam feels strangely at ease, like his whole career has been building unknowingly to this moment.

Alberto Suviero, Italy's minister of culture, turns to the lawyer who has prosecuted the Italian claim. The distinguished gray-haired attorney replies in a whisper to his client; Suviero nods. The attorney's eyes are smiling. Both men appear confident of the outcome.

"Documents produced by the Italian authorities—archival and photographic—have been presented to this hearing," the judge continues, "in addition to testimony by independent witnesses and experts who have given evidence and clarifying information regarding the appearance of this painting before and after restoration. Sam Driscoll, the former art advisor to Mr. Thomas Baxter, the presumed owner of the painting, has testified to his discovery of early documents linking this painting with a church in the Italian town of Ponte Albrizzi. Further, Mr. Driscoll's earnest search for the truth in the matter of the provenance of the picture brought to light photos and a letter clearly suggesting that the painting entered this country somewhere toward the end of 1945, stolen and smuggled by an American Army captain during the Italian campaign."

Baxter's face is frozen in an expression of repressed rage, his jaw clenched.

"Several photographs of a painting closely resembling the present picture, apparently taken before and during World War II, have been introduced by the Italian claimants, as well as written testimony from residents and clergy of the town of Ponte Albrizzi detailing an altar painting whose description closely matches the painting before us." Judge Abel's gaze moves to the painting itself, resting in an easel next to the bench. The tension in the courtroom is tangible, the attention of the packed gallery trained almost exclusively on the Madonna and Child.

"Ladies . . . gentlemen. Pursuit of the truth can be rigorous, perplexing by turns, here partially revealing the light of fact, there testing the representation of fact."

The Italians remain still, intent on the judge's summary. Tom Baxter reaches his index finger down between his collar and his sweating neck. His usually crisp, fresh appearance has dissolved into a hint of dishevelment.

Judge Abel clears his throat. "In this dispute, my finding was not difficult to reach. Abundant documentation, testimony by witnesses for both sides of the contested claim, and a capital crime which bears on this matter all have brought me to a clear and conclusive finding.

"In the matter of claim of ownership contested by the Italian Government and Thomas Baxter, recent purchaser of the painting *Virgin and Child with a Cat* attributed to Leonardo da Vinci, I find for the Italian Government and hereby render ownership and all rights, free of any requirement of remuneration or compensation, now or at any time in the future."

Minister Suviero and his attorney turn to one another and shake hands, and then engage in congratulatory backslapping, radiant smiles, and excited cries in Italian.

Across the room, Tom Baxter, visibly stunned, ignores the low-spoken words addressed to him by three lawyers, all of whom look equally grim. Sylvie stares out the window as the buzzing hearing room empties of press and spectators. She takes a handkerchief out of the Prada handbag resting on her lap. There are tears in her eyes as she turns her gaze back to the window. Her hand rests rigid in her lap clutching the small linen square as if to wring an imagined life from it.

Without a word, Tom nods to his lawyers as if to dismiss them. They rise and leave the room, filing out like the dutiful advisors they are. Tom stays seated. A perceptible sag in his usual erect and ready posture gradually overtakes his body. If every moment of Tom's past adult life had somehow been photographed, not one frame would portray such subtle shape-shifting as this moment reveals—the visible effect of unprecedented reversal. Tom has lost a contest he believed he would win, one he planned to win. His lawyers have just told him they will appeal, but he knows that appeal is hopeless. Tom has never considered the possibility of defeat, has not prepared for it. Tom has taken victory for granted, believing the Leonardo is his and will always be his. He deserves it. That's it. Why should it be otherwise? All his cleverness, his capacity to strategize, to analyze, to anticipate many steps ahead in buyouts, breakups, mergers, markets with opposing players—none of this has prepared him for this corrosive finale. Failure. He sits immobile, in silence next to his wife. Alone.

CHAPTER FORTY-TWO

"Tom! Sylvie! Haven't seen you around for a while." Woody Ellis is one of Tom's fellow squash team members at the exclusive Alliance Club. For several weeks since the Leonardo trial, Tom hasn't appeared at the club for practice, tournament play, or socializing. Neither have the Baxters been invited to parties in New York or the late-spring social season openers on Long Island. In fact, Tom and Sylvie have become somewhat housebound except for occasional dinners out, mostly business related. Both of them felt somewhat reticent about accepting Woody and Martha's bid to their "Spring Blooms Gala" at Quattro Stagione, hired for the evening by the Ellises to raise money for African Famine Relief, their favorite charity.

Sylvie is feeling depressed. Tom's nagging discomfort has been worsened by his sensitivity to the evening's Italian overtones—the heralded classic Italian cooking, mandatory pastel color dress code, Vivaldi's "Four Seasons" offered by the highly rated Bell Strings Chamber Orchestra (followed by Italian Renaissance music). Midnight promises an Italian folk dance troupe flown in from Calabria, complete with authentic costumes and old instruments.

Rich, too rich, Tom has thought to himself with rising uneasiness at the contrast of the merry program and the mission of famine relief. Now, for reasons not clear to him, he is feeling differently about all this than he once did, not only about the demanding social whirl that for so long he and Sylvie have dominated, but also about his own place among New York's glitterati, the power elite. This exclusive and hyperactive network of "ultra high-net-worth individuals" is the incessant focus of many dispatches of the closely watched Page Six in the *Post*, usually nervously awaited by the Baxters' friends.

Some days ago, Tom picked up a copy of *History and Archeology* magazine lying on the library table in his club. He read a brief article about the city of Sybaris, a Greek colony in Italy founded on the Gulf of Toronto in 720 BC. Hence the term *Sybarite*, he discovered. He read on. "By the sixth century BC the city had established its own colonites and was unrivaled in wealth, splendor and power. In the ancient world Sybaris was synonymous with opulence. Years later, an army from the city of Croton razed the city to the ground. The conquerors then diverted the course of a river to flood the ruins of the defeated city, causing a wide swath of once fertile lands to degrade into barrenness."

As he sat in the plush leather chair, alone in the club library, the magazine open in his lap, Tom was flooded with the recognition that wealth, power, splendor—opulence—were the objectives and the currencies that had driven him for so many years, day in and day out. With that perception, in those still moments by himself, Tom felt a stirring in his gut, a rising sickness, a touch of panic.

He feels that same malaise once again as he approaches the chipper, verbose Woody Ellis in this magnificent setting, this evening dedicated to address a relentless tragedy thousands of miles away. He checks himself. "Woody, my friend. It's been a while. Martha, lovely to see you. Lord, you look a . . . rainbow!"

"Tom, I hope you meant that as a compliment."

"I did, I did. Certainly!" Tom lays on the requisite air kiss.

"And you, Sylvie," Woody says, holding Sylvie gently by the shoulders, leaning back as if to focus on her face. "You get younger every time I see you. Which is not often enough."

"I wish that were the case, Woody." Sylvie musters up a less than dazzling smile.

"Well, I think so. Don't you think so, Tom?"

"Uh, absolutely, yes. Absolutely."

"What a vision for the evening," Sylvie says, surveying the elaborately decorated interior of Quattro Stagione's dining room. Great stands of flowers rest on marble tables and pedestals with cascades of hanging blossoms. A gigantic leafy arbor is set at one end of the dining room. Live boxwoods on three-foot-high redbrick planters flank the bases of the arches. This is the food station. Thirty tables, each seating eight, are arranged about the room, comfortably spaced around a circular stage in the center of the dining room. It is designed to revolve slowly. The tickets are one thousand dollars a head. Each ticket is also a lottery coupon, a chance to win one of three grand prizes: a private jet trip to South Africa that includes a ten-day stay at a famous game lodge; a two-week cruise through the Cyclades on a yacht complete with a crew, including a gourmet chef and unlimited pick of an exceptional wine cellar; two weeks in Paris, in a suite at the Hôtel de Crillon with tours of the Louvre, Musée d'Orsay, and the Guimet, guided by curatorial staff with excursions to Fontainebleau, Versailles, Giverny, also guided. The evening is a sellout, projected to raise about a million dollars if the auction, with ten lots valued upwards of fifty thousand each and a host of slightly less pricey items, sails along as the planners expect.

"Martha, you've done this brilliantly," Sylvie says, meaning it.

"Lots of help, lots of good luck. It ain't over till we carry old Peter Francis to his limo." Martha shakes her head, a smile of resignation on her face. "What would we do without Peter?"

"You're right. He loves these do's," Tom says. "And he always spends a huge bundle. Which young model is he with tonight?"

"Muffy St. Giles, age twenty-four. Benedelto d'Ai's favorite runway girl—for his leather-feather outfits."

"There's a match," Tom says, just audibly. "Well, we'll let our good hosts greet the revelers who've just arrived, Sylvie. We'll catch up with you good people." Tom forces a smile, steering his wife by her elbow, like a tiller on a sailboat. Sylvie detests this gesture. Tom has never accepted that. They make their way toward one of the bars, located at each end of the room, nodding to couples they know slightly.

Arriving at the bar, Sylvie orders her Stoli martini. Tom spies a bottle of Laphroaig on the shelf behind the bartender.

"I'll have Laphroaig in a rocks glass and some hot water on the side, thanks."

Sylvie looks thoughtfully at Tom. "Isn't that what Sam always drank? Whiskey and hot water?"

"Correct. It just seemed . . . right at this moment. Nothing to do with Sam."

"Oh . . . Are you sorry that you're not working together, all that racing around looking at pictures?" Sylvie feigns a sense of being glad those days are behind them. "All those dealer visits?"

"Hey! Hello, Craig! Good to see you." Craig Johnson, a writer friend of the Baxters, is backing off the end of the packed bar, barely managing to sandwich three glasses of champagne between extended fingers before, arms raised, he turns in place and negotiates his way to one of the small circular cocktail tables ten feet away.

"Got to call Craig," Tom mutters.

"Tom?"

"Oh, yes, Sylvie. You were asking about Sam and the dealers."

"Yes. Do you miss that? Will you miss that . . . whole . . . thing?"

"No. Yes, in a way. But no. I mean, it's been coming to me that . . . maybe we have enough pictures, enough sculpture, French furniture. In the shower this morning, I had this . . . this epiphany. What it's like to eat salted peanuts. Dry-roasted salted peanuts. Maybe I bought pictures sort of like that. Kind of got addicted . . ."

"I miss it," Sylvie says.

"Can we talk about it later?"

"Of course, Tom. Obviously this is not the place. It was just—the whiskey and Sam—it was an odd *déjà vu* moment."

"Why don't we wander a bit?"

Tom and Sylvie start to wander toward one of the circular tables. "There's Patty and Don Drombruster. Let's go say hi, want to?" Sylvie slips her arm through Tom's, clasping his arm with her other hand.

"Right, Sylvie. Okay." They approach the table where the Drombrusters are in animated conversation with another couple whose backs are to Tom and Sylvie as they approach, weaving through the now dense crowd gathered near the bar and in clusters of tables.

Don Drombruster shifts his attention from the white-haired man he's been speaking to as Tom and Sylvie approach. With a subtle but unmistakable gesture of warning he looks from his listener to Tom. Hesitantly, he waves to Tom. His partner in conversation turns around to greet the Baxters.

"Tom, Sylvie. I had hoped you'd be here. Have you met Charles Amory?"

"No, I don't believe we have."

"Charles is the museum board chairman, as I'm sure you know."

"Of course, of course."

"You're welcome to join us, we've got a few minutes before the rush to dinner. Make a little room, Patty."

"Hi, Tom. Sylvie . . . ravishing. As ever." Patty beams.

"Thank you, Patty."

"Thanks, Don," Tom says. "We've got to meet some friends by the entrance. Thanks."

"Uh, Tom." Charles Amory stands and puts a hand on Tom's shoulder. With an almost apologetic tone, he says, "I've been meaning to call you. I'm sorry to have to tell you that at the last board meeting, the board voted to limit the number of board members to twenty-one. Committee restructuring and all that."

"Really." Tom fixes Charles Amory with a cool, impassive stare.

"Yes, I know that our director, Sherman Bailey, spoke to you some weeks ago about board vacancies and your possible candidacy."

"I do remember that, yes." Tom frowns, clearly uncomfortable.

"Well, I'm really sorry that it won't work out this time."

"This time?" There is an awkward silence.

"Yes. Perhaps at some time in the future. When there is a vacancy."

Sylvie directs her attention to the large room now blustering with elegant society.

"Yes?"

"Yes. Then at that time perhaps we can talk." Charles Amory's face is bright red.

"I see what you mean, Charles," Tom says flatly. "Yes, perhaps we'll talk sometime. If we meet. In the meantime, good evening. Good evening Don, Patty, Mr. and Mrs. Amory."

Tom hauls Sylvie away from the Drombrusters and Amorys.

"Tom!" Sylvie comes to an abrupt halt halfway across the room. "What is the matter with you? That was not polite. Not polite at all." She stands directly in front of Tom in a Gaelic pose and pique.

"What do you think that was all about? That little speech by Charles Amory, board chairman?"

"He said the board was not taking new members. You heard him yourself."

"What he didn't say is 'too bad, Baxter, the Italians took your Leonardo away and you're a fool to have dealings with a lying art dealer who is on his way to trial for fraud, conspiracy to murder, and probably worse. You can't join the club, sorry.'"

"Tom. You're leaping to conclusions."

"Jumping, you mean. I wish I were, Sylvie."

Several couples drifting toward the festive dining area give the Baxters a wide berth. Tom and Sylvie catch sight of their curious looks and mild concern as they continue their exchange.

"Look, it's been a month since the Leonardo was seized."

"Keep your voice lower, Tom. Please."

"It's been a month, Sylvie. One month. Our friends don't call us. We've barely seen anyone. The few times we've been out, people we know look at us oddly. Our friends, when we see them, seem removed. Even people in my office, my own company, seem, I don't know, distant."

"Maybe you're imagining that, Tom."

"I'm imagining nothing. It's true; it's the way it is."

"You're acting upset."

"I am upset. I . . . damn upset. I'm out two hundred fifteen million. My painting has been snatched away."

"Sh-sh, Tom. Can we talk about this later? Look, there's Sandra Carson and John." Sylvie waves at the Carsons with a winning smile, then nods as the Carsons beckon to her.

"Sylvie. I think we should go home now."

"Tom, what are you talking about?" Tom looks toward the door.

"I can't do this. Let's go home."

"We can't just go home. People will think . . ."

"You know? I don't give a *damn* what people think. I think I'm leaving. *We* are leaving."

"I am not leaving."

"Suit yourself."

Sylvie turns, seemingly unmoved, and walks toward the dining tables into the milling clusters of laughing, gesturing, pleasuring supporters of famine relief. The noise level in the spacious dining room begins to rise just as the blush begins to flow and the imported band from Calabria starts up, making conversation among the two hundred and forty-nine guests more difficult. Not that anyone notices.

CHAPTER FORTY-THREE

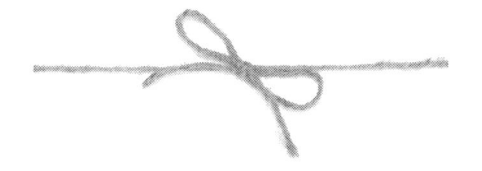

Summer is in full stride in Dubois. The heat is so dry you don't even sweat. Sam sets his cowboy boots down hard on the pavement and strolls into the post office. Now that Ricci's being prosecuted and cooperating with the feds in a prosecution of the crime boss whose money he laundered, Sam knows no one's going to be out here looking for him. No more need to hide out. His route takes him past Dan's box where he gets his mail. One of these days he'll get a box of his own, scratch his name in the tough Wyoming dirt here in Dubois.

At the front desk, he says hello to the clerk, the son of the former postmaster.

The young man lifts the little box. "What are you sending to Italy?"

The question doesn't bother Sam. He likes being out here on the fringe of three mountain ranges with more community than he ever had back in Stonington. "A belt buckle," Sam says. "It's for a friend who helped me tell the truth about a painting."

"A painting?"

"Yes, a Leonardo da Vinci."

"You got to be kidding me." The young man grins as he weighs the package.

"Of course I am." Sam winks and pays for the package. Then he turns around and steps back out into the bright of the day. As he does, a tall cowgirl of a woman ambles out behind him and then steps in front of him. He quickly glances at her figure from her worn cowboy boots all the way up to her eyes.

"You Sam Driscoll?"

"Excuse me?" Her long, wavy white hair looks like a waterfall to him.

"I heard you in there talking about a painting."

"Yes." He fixes his eyes on hers. He knows those blue eyes. They've been with him since he was a kid. And then he recognizes her, remembers the time they packed their horses into that camp on the Snake River, how her fishing line flashed out over the water in the smoothest movement he had ever seen. "Pam, I had no idea. Are you still here?"

"In for the summer. Been back every summer since 1962." She pauses.

Somehow her blue eyes are even brighter against her white hair than back when she was a brunette who dipped her hair in lemon juice to streak it blonde. "Someone told me you'd rode back into town with two dogs. No woman, I see?" she asks, looking down at his left hand with a hint of a teasing smirk.

"None," he says, full of gladness he can say that.

"You weren't lying in there about the Leonardo were you?" As she says it, she sets her hand on his arm to steer him gently out of the way of a passerby carrying a load, and he feels something he hasn't felt in a long time.

"No."

"I read about that in the *New York Times*. Read about your testimony and everything."

Right then he couldn't care less about the Leonardo. "What did you go off and do?"

"Oh, I taught. Most recently, History of the West at the University of Montana."

"What a career, Pam." He glances down at her hand there, still holding his arm. "Remember how you taught me to tie flies?"

She grins. "You were a particularly difficult student."

Standing that close to her, he can almost remember how her hair smelled. "Is that your granddaddy's truck?"

She nods.

"You kept it in good shape." He gazes in her eyes, each one the deep blue of the East Fork. "Are you in the phone book?"

"Sure am, under Pam Henderson."

"Well, I just might look you up." He doesn't know if it's the sun, but he thinks he can see her cheeks tingeing pink. As he turns to clamber back up into his truck, the dogs move around in the truck bed. He puts the window down, letting that hot dry air wipe the sweat off him, and pulls out onto the stretch of narrow highway. Sam fires up the radio, and for a minute he thinks he really has come home.

In his rearview mirror, he catches sight of Pam driving down the road behind him, her long hair rising up behind her in the wind, so white against the red canyons, and he is not sure he has ever seen a more beautiful sight. This is his own Leonardo moment. Out here on the wild Wyoming road, he feels he could create anything.

ABOUT THE AUTHOR

For more than forty years I have enjoyed the pleasure and privilege of discovering and acquiring fine paintings and works of art for institutional and private collectors.

My experience in the field includes four years of specialized graduate training and research in Art History at Harvard. This led to an appointment as an advisor to the university architects at Duke University followed by the appointment as the first Director of the Art Museum at Duke University where I also taught Art History during that period. I transitioned from Duke to accepting the position as Curator at the Museum of Fine Arts in Boston in the department of European Decorative Arts and Sculpture, where I spent ten rewarding years. Following that appointment, I served as a private art advisor and lecturer.

In writing *Provenance*, I drew abundantly from my professional life as an art historian and art advisor. I am an avid reader and I have always been open to the idea of sharing a "behind the scenes" view of the art world from an informed and educated perspective versus an overly-sensationalized one that is so often depicted in literature and the media. Making the world of art history and art collecting accessible to a broader audience has been a life-long goal. In writing *Provenance*, a story of intrigue and immersion in the realities of the art world, I hope to leave the reader both engaged by that story as well as informed about many aspects of art history—as fascinating as that subject can be. *Provenance* I hope will stimulate and, ideally, provoke in the reader a desire to pursue the fascinating history of the world of art. This book is written not only for readers particularly interested in Leonardo da Vinci and his world but also for those intrigued by endless questions and pleasures of the myriad of aspects of human nature and art.

The notion of writing this book arose out of a longstanding curiosity about art itself and the art world that profound interest has not diminished; rather that engagement expands and deepens. It is my hope that *Provenance* will inform the reader and encourage further interest in a rich and intriguing subject.

I am now retired and living in Jackson Hole, Wyoming where I am actively involved supporting the local arts organizations as well as consulting periodically with private collectors. I am also writing my second novel with the same curiosity about and fascination with works of art and human nature that generated *Provenance*. In my free time, I enjoy spending time with my grandchildren and riding my horses.

Robert C. Moeller III

CPSIA information can be obtained at www.ICGtesting.com
Printed in the USA
LVOW11s2327290615

444320LV00002B/3/P

9 781630 475376